Anneliese tried to bite and claw, humiliated by her nakedness. The skirt had fallen off. The men handled her firmly, without roughness, and immediately she sensed it wasn't going to be rape. What then, murder? The ceiling light provided only faint illumination, but enough to reveal all of the thin pointed blade in the hand of one of the men.

The one with the knife picked up the expensive skirt and quickly made strips of the cambric before her eyes. Then the other two, holding her arms behind her back, still gagging her, offered her up to the knife-wielder like a sacrificial virgin.

But there was something else, a faint odor of yesterday's perfume, and she realized that it wasn't a man who held her after all.

And then the voice said: "We won't forget you, Anneliese...."

Fawcett Popular Library Books
by John Farris:

☐ ALL HEADS TURN WHEN THE HUNT
 GOES BY   04360 $2.95

☐ THE FURY   08620 $2.95

Buy them at your local bookstore or use this handy coupon for ordering.

COLUMBIA BOOK SERVICE, CBS Publications
32275 Mally Road, P.O. Box FB, Madison Heights, MI 48071

Please send me the books I have checked above. Orders for less than 5 books
must include 75¢ for the first book and 25¢ for each additional book to cover
postage and handling. Orders for 5 books or more postage is FREE. Send check
or money order only. Allow 3–4 weeks for delivery.

Cost $_____   Name _____

Sales tax*_____   Address _____

Postage_____   City _____

Total $_____   State_____ Zip _____

*The government requires us to collect sales tax in all states except AK, DE,
 MT, NH and OR.
Prices and availability subject to change without notice.   8999

Shatter

by John Farris

FAWCETT POPULAR LIBRARY • NEW YORK

SHATTER

Published by Fawcett Popular Library, CBS Educational and
Professional Publishing, a division of CBS Inc.

ISBN: 0-445-04693-7

Printed in the United States of America

First Fawcett Popular Library printing: January 1982

10 9 8 7 6 5 4 3 2 1

In loving memory of my father-in-law,
Peter Pasante

DENEBOLA. A blue star of the second magnitude, in the tail of the constellation Leonis. According to the astrological lore of Ptolemy, Denebola prominently placed in the horoscope (rising at the time of birth, or associated with the sun or moon) brings riches and good fortune attended by many dangers, swift judgment, despair, regrets, and public disgrace.

—Adapted from Robson,
The Fixed Stars and Constellations in Astrology

Prologue

The little girl awoke in the trundle bed with a tremor of expectancy running through her body, certain that she had heard her mother calling her.

She sat up, her head coming to a level a little above the counterpane on the featherbed that took up much of the space in the small raftered room. But the bed was still impeccably made, she could see that her mother wasn't there. Nor was the new father she had been told to expect.

There were two small windows high in the gable of the bedroom, each with diamond-shaped panes that were alternately of clear and amber glass. The brightness of the moon outside was a disappointment—it wasn't morning. She lay down again, listening to the ticking of the cuckoo clock on the wall. Maybe, she thought, it was *almost* morning. She was too young to have any firm sense of time: Days were divided into light and dark, into strict mealtimes, at the modest café on the ground floor of the Pension zum Altenburg.

From across the hall she could hear her grandfather snoring heartily in the other, larger of the two bedrooms crowded under the steep roofs of the pension. She was fascinated by the sounds he was making; usually, unless she was sick, she was fast asleep by the time he went to bed, and still asleep in the early morning just before first light, when he got up. But the tickle was still in her mind, exciting her like rough wool on bare skin, she knew that she had heard the voice of her mother.

And she remembered: Not long before supper the telephone had rung. She'd been waiting, bored, in a new starchy dress with petticoats, forbidden by her grandmother even to go outdoors on the terrace to play. But there was car trouble, her mother didn't know when she would arrive. The girl tried to speak to her mother but the connection was bad; all she heard was crackling and a dim, unrecognizable voice.

She could be downstairs now, the girl thought, in the kitchen. With the new father. The girl was both curious and afraid. She wanted to sneak a look at him, to be prepared before they were introduced, just in case there was something wrong with him that would take getting used to.

Many of the men who came to holiday at the pension, which was located in a spa of no great reputation a few miles from the splendor of Baden-Baden, were missing hands or legs or eyes. The girl knew there had been a war, which had ended only a few years before she was born. Friends of her grandfather who drank in the pub spoke of this war, of defeat and lost children, in sad muted voices.

At the beginning of summer her mother had come for a few days; they drove to Stuttgart, where she saw the damage the air raids had done, the artificial mountains of rubble on which nothing grew. The girl hated Americans and said so. But her mother smiled, as if she knew a secret. At least some of them are rich, she said.

So the new father might be crippled; but, the girl thought, if her mother loved him, then he must be kind. She wasn't a bit sleepy, and she couldn't wait any longer. She got out of the little bed and put on her slippers and a pink flannel robe and left the room cautiously.

Her grandfather snored, which kept her grandmother, who was a light sleeper, awake; so sometimes she spent hours in the sulfurous bathtub at night, reading and smoking. But the bathroom door stood open to a vacant tub. The girl went downstairs, slowly at first, then with more confidence, ignoring the creaking treads, because the summer season was over and they had only one guest in the six rooms that they rented; and he was hard of hearing.

Disappointment again: The kitchen was dark and empty. So was the dining room with the stone fireplace in one corner, and the pub off the dining room, which was just large enough for half a dozen men at a time to stand at its polished bar. The girl fidgeted, wide awake, and yawned from tension. She had a premonition. If her mother hadn't arrived yet, then she was about to: Look out the window and the car would be just coming up the long hill.

The girl ran to the front of the dining room and peered down at the village of Bad Oberbeuern, at the Rhine River like a great silver fish beneath the full moon. The mysterious country of France, which she had never visited, lay beyond. Sure enough, there *was* a car, low and struggling on the grade, with headlights that looked painted on. She danced in place and then whirled and ran out onto the stone-paved terrace to wait.

The car went by with pistons knocking, and she saw nothing of its occupants in the canvas-covered cockpit. The car crossed the plank bridge over the sawmill race and disappeared around a bend of the mountain. The girl looked tearfully, blinking, away from the road. She followed the race with her eyes, upward from the treacherous log pond, in which boys had drowned, to

the needle's point midway on the dark mountain where
the race, coming together from numerous trickles and
rills, made a dramatic fall of thirty feet or more. The
race was like a turbulent, bright path cutting through
the woods and clearings—familiar and easy to follow.

She was suddenly, desperately angry with everyone:
with her grandparents, who were too busy and ha-
rassed to pay much attention to her, but mostly with
her mother, who almost never came to see her, and was
late when she promised she would come.

I don't want a new father, the girl thought. And just
let her try to find me when she gets here!

She left the terrace and set off across the hillside
that came down, thick with conifers, almost to the back
door of the pension.

Because of the moon it was easy going, or she might
have turned back after a couple of hundred feet. But
her anger was still with her, like a bad companion,
urging her on; the path was soft from rotting pine
needles and the race looked inviting just ahead.

It was shallow on the hillside, having a depth of only
about three feet except in the spring runoff season, with
a bottom of bedrock worn almost smooth by the thou-
sands of logs that had slid down it from the cutting
areas above. The sawmill was closed now, dilapidated,
but the waters of the race still fed a long deep pond at
one end of the mill and drained into a narrow chute
with concrete sides that went the rest of the way downhill to the bank of the Rhine, several hundred yards
distant.

Older children, those who could swim, climbed the
hill a short distance above the sawmill and rode the
race into the quieter pond. But even good swimmers
sometimes had accidents when they ventured too close
to the spillway, where the force of the water could suck
them into the chute and pound them unconscious

against the side walls. The girl and her friends dared only to wade in the shallows at the edge of the race and were forbidden to try to cross it, despite the temptation of small stepping stones that had washed down in storms, and broke the crystal surface during periods of low water.

Near the bank she paused, afraid to turn around and look again at the pension, knowing how small and dark it would be from this elevation. And unreachable, if she now lost heart and wanted to run for her life. The race was like a melting, bubbling mirror at her feet, streaming away into blueness, forming humps and shapes at midstream which she imagined to be sinister. Her thin chest rose and fell. She inhaled the moonlight, a pure light of enchantment. Exhaling, she created a warm space for herself enhanced by the presence of her shadow. As long as she breathed this way she felt tingling and warm, protected, immune from owls and other creatures on the wing.

Anger had turned to sorrow. She had come this far; she would go farther now, up and over the mountain, and no one would miss her. When the sun came up she would pick apples to eat. She was crying. She would find rabbits and baby animals in the woods to play with. In the morning, even if they called her, she wouldn't go home.

The uphill walk along the race kept her warm. The sky looked frostbitten with stars. It was light enough for her to see the shapes of clouds. There was a wind that shook the trees; their movements seemed flighty and perilous but she kept going, never looking back. Fortunately for her peace of mind, there were many open places, logged off, where the returning trees were not as tall as she was.

As the girl climbed she heard sounds she couldn't identify: little sharp bites of metal on rock. Sometimes the sound of the wind was too loud, and then she couldn't hear anything. Her ears were numb; her feet hurt where the needle carpet of the path had worn thin over sharp rocks.

The channel of the race deepened into a small gorge. She came to a timber bridge that crossed it.

Once she had come this far with her mother for a picnic. She knew that the dirt road would take her, in a winding descent, to the highway near the pension. The other way, she couldn't guess. But the road looked level and she was very tired, she couldn't continue to climb straight up the mountain.

At first, as she walked along the road, she had an unobstructed view to the south and west; far away there was a yellow smudge around jutting hills, the city of Strasbourg. Nearer, where the river divided the horizon in a scintillating rip like fallen lightning, she saw a tight cluster of lights that resembled a moving village. The night boat from Basel. Then the woods closed in so abruptly that even the moon was shut out.

The road began to make sharp turns. She sensed there would be no more open places, vistas of sky and river. She heard the cold splashing of a waterfall. Her own heartbeat frightened her.

Unexpectedly the girl came upon a car parked along the road. She smelled the smoke of a campfire. It promised warmth, and she was cold.

She paused beside the car, peering down into woods at a trace of firelight. The wind blew the hair away from the back of her neck, causing her to shudder to the tip of her backbone. With the wind moaning in her ears, she climbed down over boulders to soft ground and made her way hesitantly toward the fire.

It was calmer in the clearing where the fire, almost half gone to embers, burned in a pit of stones. The wind was deflected by a huge fallen tree. On stubs of the tree items of clothing had been carelessly hung: a sweater, a rust-colored skirt. There was a twisted blanket on the ground next to the fire. Through trees she saw the distant river again and the moon with red clouds, like a blood orange.

Smoke stung the girl's eyes. She drifted closer, still shuddering.

Near the blanket she walked on an unnoticed portable radio. It squealed like a wounded thing, and she ran half a dozen steps in terror before falling flat on mossy ground near the broken end of the windfall. The radio bawled unintelligibly for a few moments, then faded into silence. She got up and went back and looked at it. The plastic case was broken, revealing the sparky glow of insides.

Her mother owned a radio like this one. She had brought it with her on their picnic at the beginning of summer. She also had a skirt the color of the one hanging from the broken branch, swaying in the wind.

"*Mutter*," the girl said. She looked around and raised her voice, and called.

Unanswered, she was desperate. She began a circle of the clearing, and stopped suddenly on the far side of the windfall.

Because her mother was there, asleep in turned earth, familiar rings and bracelets exposed on her lax bare arms and hands. The girl saw a hank of hair, an uncovered ear, pale as a seashell in the tide of dirt. Her mother's face was turned down, smothering in dark dreams. A shovel was stuck at an angle in the ground nearby.

The girl's knees trembled and wouldn't support her. Her teeth chattered in a frenzy. She had seen a dog struck down in the road, motionless like this. It was death. But her mother couldn't die: She had waited in her new dress, her mother had called on the telephone, she was coming in the car as soon as it was fixed.

She reached out and touched a cool hand. Clasped it. Tugged gently. The hand fell back when she let it go, lay in the dirt without a tremor.

"Get up," the girl sobbed. She began brushing the dirt away, then scooped at it with her hands and flung it aside. As she clawed her way toward the partly hidden face, she was too shocked to find it remarkable that her mother was naked.

Behind her she heard a guttural roar, a crashing in the brush, another outcry that bristled the hairs on the back of her neck. She sprang up, turning, and saw the huge man coming at her from the dark.

If he'd been a few steps closer she would have cowered, paralyzed; but some instinct, a toughness of spirit she was too young to know much about, made her run.

She ran blindly and was whipped by branches; and the ground suddenly dropped away under her feet.

She fell a short distance and rolled over rocks, came to a stop with her nose bleeding. She was soaked in urine.

He came down the hill with great strides and hovered over her, and she saw the shape of him against the sky. She shook on the ground, having a fit. He reached down and picked her up in his arms, which were wet and cold from bathing in a stream nearby. She continued to shake and her eyes slid past his face, which she couldn't see; they stared, unfocused, at nothing.

The girl felt him moving with her, bearing her back up the hill. And that was nearly all, except that she knew it was late and that he was probably going to put her to sleep now, beside her mother.

Blood trickled into her throat, warm and oddly soothing. The tremors ceased. Her eyes closed.

One

1 For most of the day it had been raining in Frankfurt, hard enough so that the streets were awash, but the deluge slackened toward evening and the sun struck weak gold in the small round panes of the workroom windows opposite 20 Goethestrasse.

As Hans Nütterman returned to the big room, the face of the woman turning toward him seemed refracted by the sun into a luminous double image; something about her was so familiar he might have been looking at the face of a long-vanished relative in a work of ghost photography.

She wore a high-fashion corduroy leisure suit and boots. She had a burnished tan from a recent end-of-winter vacation in one of the popular sun spots, a small chin, and a catlike nose. There was a round dark beauty spot at one corner of her mouth that was fetchingly childlike, a leftover bit of chocolate from a hastily eaten cookie. But there was nothing of the child in her amber eyes. They didn't just look, they struck at you, boldly, with a penetrating light of inquiry.

Nütterman read intelligence, temperament, and perception in her glance. She would be thirty-one in August, according to her identification card. A mature and accomplished woman. She looked properly worried, but still well in control of herself. Nothing very serious had happened yet. Perhaps nothing would happen.

Hers was a face he felt he should know, and that made him uneasy. He was an inspector in the KRIPO (for *Kriminalpolizei*), state of Hesse, and he regarded his work as a calling.

"Fräulein Girda,"—he handed back her gray-covered *personalausweis* with a slight, unconscious flourish—"I feel that we've met before."

Anneliese understood immediately. "I was a model for several years. I've been on the covers of most of the magazines: *Brigitte, Petra*. But not for some time."

"Have you done television commercials?"

"I tried, but I had no talent for it. As soon as I opened my mouth on behalf of this hand cream or that dishwashing liquid, sales fell fifty percent. An advertising director once told me that I looked too smart to believe what I was saying."

She smiled; it was a brief, beguiling smile that left one charmed and hopeful of enjoying more of her good humor. She continued to regard him with absolute stillness. No obvious nerves. He'd been a policeman for twenty-five years, had survived gunshots and maniacs with razors, but she made him feel, somehow, unimpressive.

He looked at some of the sketches fastened to a corklined wall with pushpins, at empty white paper beneath a high-intensity lamp on a drawing table. There were African masks on the walls, bolts of colorful cloth flowing beneath the ceiling through Lucite rings.

"So you've given up modeling for designing?"

"Modeling never really interested me; it was a way to earn a living because at a certain age I had a look that could be sold. In a limited way, I might add. I never really caught on with the famous names in Paris or New York. Precarious work, nothing very flattering or substantial about it. I had the urge to try more, to be different. I'm not obsessed with clothes, I own very few things myself, but I love seeing my designs at parties or in the street."

"Do you own the boutique in Goethestrasse?"

"There are four of us. I had the least money to invest, but I knew the business thoroughly, and I was already selling some of my designs."

"Is the partnership amicable?"

"Of course. Friedrich and Elsa live aboard their yacht in Marbella—I never see them except on holiday. They're very young and rich and scarcely interested in business; it's all a lark to them. Our fourth partner is English, a baronet. He's an old friend."

"Platonic?"

"Definitely. He'll be eighty-eight his next birthday." An expression of mild consternation. "Which is Tuesday—I almost forgot."

Nütterman took off his steel-rimmed glasses and studied the lenses for water spots. "Why don't you tell me about the phone calls?"

Anneliese hesitated, wanting to be precise. "The first one came just eight days ago, at home, I hadn't been back from Greece for more than a few hours."

"You live alone, don't you?"

"Yes."

"The caller was a man?"

"Yes, it was."

"Recognizable accent?"

"He was Bavarian, probably from Munich. Youthful, but he sounded as if he's been away from home for most of his life."

"You don't know who he was."

"No."

"Did he call you by name?"

"Y-yes. Anneliese." She was hesitating slightly before each reply, as if she needed to concentrate to suppress a slight stutter. The inspector felt sympathetic, but also he was more at ease, doing his job now, finally on even terms with her.

"What did he say?"

"Only that—my treachery was well known, and I couldn't hope to escape."

Nütterman made a quick note in his book, waited with the pen poised for more.

"That's all," Anneliese said.

"You've no idea what he meant by that?"

"I thought it was idiotic, one of those—those calls every woman gets. I forgot about it."

"But he called again."

"It was a different man. He called here, at the work-room, about seven o'clock on Tuesday. Berliner, I'd say."

"Also a young man?"

"Just—not old. That's all I could tell."

"Was there a continuity of theme, the same type of message?"

"This one said that—unless I had a ch-ch-change of heart, and soon, I could expect no mercy."

"From him?"

"From *us*, he said."

"Suggesting that the callers are working together. And the third call?"

"Forty minutes ago." Anneliese got up suddenly, turning toward a desk with a thick glass top that was heaped with catalogues and bolts of material. There was a silver tray, a carafe, wineglasses, on one corner.

"I'd like some wine, wuh-would you care f-f-for—"

A serious spillage this time, almost as distressing to her as lifeblood. "By all means," the inspector said. She had not altogether lost her self-possession, but she was on the edge.

He studied her clinically, believing all that she had told him, yet wondering how much would go untold, and just what sort of trouble she was in. A pity she couldn't be helped, he thought.

But that was up to her.

"Have you always stuttered?" he asked kindly, accepting a glass of golden Rüdesheimer wine.

"Oh—" Anneliese shrugged defensively. "It was bad when I was a child, but gradually I got over it. Except for when I'm over-tuh-tired, or—"

"Under severe stress. So the third caller was more explicit than the others."

She took a sip of wine and afterward swallowed hard, as if it threatened to come back up.

"He s-said, 'Anneliese, you'll pay in blood for what you've done.'"

"That's when you decided to call the police."

Anneliese nodded.

"None of the callers are known to you, and none of what has been said makes the least sense. You've left nothing out?"

"No, Inspector."

"Has anyone overheard these calls?"

"Hilda—she's one of the girls who works in the shop—was here when the third man called this afternoon. She answered the phone."

"What are your feelings about these calls, Fräulein Girda? Obviously you've taken the threats seriously."

"Because—they don't t-talk. They don't try to get me to talk back to them. It's as if they have no time to waste, and nothing I say will make any d-difference."

"I see. Yes, if they're crank calls, they don't follow any pattern I'm familiar with. Aside from the calls, have you noticed anything out of the ordinary this past week?"

"What do you mean?"

"Has your apartment been entered, your car tampered with in some way—"

"I don't own a car. And if anyone's b-been in my apartment, I don't know about it."

"Have you observed anyone following you, or hanging about?"

"No."

"Do you lead an active social life, fräulein? Parties, theater—"

"I'd say so."

"Any particular young man?"

"There hasn't been lately."

"Someone in the past you may have tired of, but who isn't willing to give up so easily?"

"No. Breaking off affairs has never been a problem for me."

"Do you have a rival in your business? Someone who may be jealous of your recent successes?"

That brought a smile. "It isn't so competitive here; the German fashion industry is out of the mainstream, to say the least."

The smile faded quickly and Anneliese sat down again, as if she'd recognized a subliminal tremor of resignation and was now aware of just how unpromising her situation was.

"There's really—nothing for you to investigate, is there?"

"Well—" The inspector looked toward the windows. The sun was gone. Outside rain fell quickly again. "No criminal act has been committed, fräulein. You haven't been molested."

"Threatened, doesn't that count?"

"Unfortunately, no. Even if one or more of the callers was known to us, and in this case—"

He was staring at Anneliese when her eyes flashed around again.

"I've told you that I *don't* know them. What more do you want me to say?"

"I'm afraid it's quite a problem. You might consider changing all of your telephone numbers."

"That takes time."

"If you're worried about the possibility of being—attacked, let's say, then perhaps you could move in with a friend—"

"Can't the police protect me?"

"But that's a common misconception. We investigate crimes, or complaints where there is reason to believe a crime has been committed. But we don't provide bodyguards. We would find ourselves trying to guard half the population. Nearly everyone is afraid today, fräulein. We are all overexposed to the horrors of our irrational age. People are afraid of thieves in the house, strangers in the street, bombs in public places."

"But what am I going to do? I thought you'd help me!"

You'll pay in blood for what you've done.

She'd had little or no experience with the police, he was sure of that, but still it might be worthwhile to check with the *Bundeskriminalamt* in Wiesbaden, and possibly Interpol. She was, regrettably, more afraid, having talked to him, than she'd been when she telephoned.

Nütterman felt strongly that she was mixed up in something which she wasn't about to discuss with him. Prostitution on a posh level, and never mind that she didn't look the type. Or, perhaps, the business wasn't doing so well, and, rather than let her distant partners know, she'd foolishly borrowed money from an Italian or, God forbid, a Turk, which she couldn't pay back. He would investigate that as well: not because he had the time (he hadn't), but she was lovely and he was curious about her and he could justify a routine inquiry although there wasn't much to back it up.

Anneliese had begun to smoke. Her amber eyes were overcast by the drift of blue around her head.

"Because you take these threats seriously, there are

precautions which might give you some peace of mind. Have all your telephone calls screened; you can easily install a machine in your apartment. Try to keep your movements unpredictable, and don't have a fixed schedule of appointments. Ask a friend to call for you at home in the morning, or at work at the end of the day. If you don't wish to change your address for now, change all of your locks instead, install window guards, hire an attack dog for additional security."

She thought about it, and shuddered.

"Live like a prisoner, you mean. Or a fugitive. When I don't know why this is happening."

Your treachery is known. You can't hope to escape. It was an interesting choice of words, the inspector thought. Treachery, implying betrayal. She was at home with the rich, so perhaps she'd struck a bargain with a gang of jewel thieves, fingering likely victims. But jewel thieves almost always shunned violence. That left the narotics trade, where paranoia and sudden death were commonplace. If it *was* narcotics, and she was marked, too bad. But the breed of killers involved in international drug traffic were quick and gruesome in their dealings with transgressors. If for some reason they wanted to break her before they killed her, they wouldn't waste time with crypto-menacing phone calls.

There was still the possibility, despite his doubts, that she had told him as much as she knew.

One caller, a crank. Three callers—an unusual conspiracy, but amateurish. Yes, that was the way it sounded, despite their terseness and the ominous messages.

Nütterman glanced at his watch. "Fräulein, I seem to have all the information you can give me." She looked up, dismayed. "Try to remain as objective as possible about your callers. If they were prone to violence, chances are we would have some evidence of it by now. Perhaps all they want is the satisfaction of knowing you're terrified, unable to lead a normal life."

"But *why?*"

He jotted two telephone numbers on his pad, tore out the page and handed it to her.

"They may well give up when you're no longer taking their calls. If anything else happens, notify me at once."

"And if I'm not able to call?" she said quietly.

Expect no mercy.

Nütterman smiled reassuringly. "It's been my experience that this type of intimidation by telephone usually comes to nothing."

Anneliese stared at the telephone numbers in her hand while he retrieved his hat and mackintosh from the railing outside, where he had left them to drip on the rubber tread of the stairs.

"Goodbye, fräulein," he said from the doorway.

She still hadn't moved, but she raised her head. A long cylinder of ash from her cigarette fell to the gleaming yellow wood floor. Anneliese smiled. Nütterman was made aware of her disappointment. She'd expected, in response to her alarm, earnest young men with machine guns. *We're on the job, fräulein. No one will get close to you.* Nütterman was not tall, going gray, rather too tired for his age. She was thirty years old. Born safely after the war, in Karlsruhe. By the time she was old enough for school, reconstruction was well under way. The new German republic. Growing up in comfortable surroundings, no doubt, family intact, nourishing meals on the table every night. She had never really tasted fear. He had carried guns at fourteen in home defense of the half-demolished Third Reich, hunted rats for food in '45. So, if she'd risked her neck in some silly scheme for money, he couldn't pity her.

If it was something else, probably there was nothing he could do until she was dead. One of the limitations of his calling.

2 The inspector had been gone for several minutes before Anneliese realized she was alone and didn't want to be.

She drank another glass of Rüdesheimer too quickly to appreciate its fine qualities. There was a concert at eight, dinner afterwards, it was nearly six now, time to go home and change. But she couldn't go home, she thought. She couldn't face that emptiness, in the rain...

But this was just what they wanted, wasn't it? The inspector seemed to think so. For what that was worth—he'd been a trifle patronizing. No, that wasn't fair. It was just that he'd heard similar stories too many times before. *Nearly everyone is afraid, fräulein. We are all overexposed to the horrors of our irrational age.*

Buy bigger locks. Buy a vicious dog. Don't walk alone. Keep up your spirits. Sing in dark company.

A certain antidote for bad morale and insecurity was something new and dazzling, Dior or Saint Laurent, off the rack, borrowed just for the evening. She put on her hooded raincoat and regretfully closed the workroom (even before the phone call, it had been a day of meager inspiration and dull pages thrown in the wastebasket), went downstairs, and dashed across the narrow cobbled street, lined with good shops, that divided Goethe-strasse from the mall of Fresgasse.

Hilda was finishing up with a customer when Anneliese entered the boutique by the back door; she looked up and smiled.

Anneliese couldn't make up her mind between a silk print dress in shades of gray and green and a Dior skirt, cambric, but very fine workmanship, in a dusty-rose color she particularly liked. She was trying on the Dior in the fitting room when Hilda looked in.

"What's the occasion?" Hilda was an exceptionally tall blonde from Bremen with a wry neck and a blissful, intoxicated smile: She gave the impression that she breathed rarefied air.

"Symphony. Then dinner at Otto Kolner's."

"The banker? Is he getting serious after all this time?"

"I don't think so. I don't think I could be. Too many half-grown children for me to cope with. What am I going to wear with this?"

"I'll be right back." Hilda ducked out and soon returned with a cream-colored, lace-front *blouson* and a maroon leather belt that had several small brass buckles on it.

"The skirt needs the belt."

"Umm." Anneliese studied the full ensemble in the mirrors. "Am I dressy enough?"

"You'll want your hair up, of course. And, let's see, gold bracelets. That new designer we're buying from, the Swede who lives in Ibiza, sent us a consignment today. I'll just fetch the lot."

The bracelets were charming mythical sea creatures and tiny peasant dancers linked in golden chains. Anneliese made her selection, faced herself again, felt at peace. She would do. Music was what she craved now, to keep apprehension far away.

Then an excellent dinner, and Otto would surely ask her to stay the night. It was a possibility. He was considerate and undemanding. She halfway wanted to sleep with him. In more than a year—fourteen months?—there had been only two other men from whom she had wanted sex; neither had been very effective.

"Anneliese—the phone call this afternoon. Do you want to talk about it?"

She felt a flush of alarm and, surprisingly, embarrassment. Not so easy to explain why you were suddenly getting threatening phone calls. *You must have done something. What are you hiding?*

"I don't really know what it's all about, Hilda. There've been three calls. Threats. Accusations. I'm tired of it, and I—I called the police."

"What can they do?"

"Probably nothing," Anneliese said, and realized bitterly that she had admitted the truth to herself. *Nothing.* She would have to face up to these callers herself. It was terrifying to be the target of such harassment, but she couldn't let fear constrict her life. The stuttering had recurred today, with a vengeance, after several peaceful years. She couldn't allow herself to be manipulated into that kind of fear, the fears of childhood, of screaming fits until she fainted from lack of breath, of restraints and drugs and stuttering until she was red in the face, and of wetting the bed. She had fought that horror and won.

"Why don't you come home with me?" Hilda was saying. "You can have a long soak, then I'll do your hair for you. If you want to spend the night it's okay. Willi's in Luxembourg all this week."

"Oh, Hilda, I appreciate it, but I have to take Redeye to the veterinary. I should have done this morning. He's moping and not eating again, I think it's a hair ball."

For once Hilda wasn't smiling, and without her smile

the wry neck made her seem oddly threatening, like a wicked stepsister.

"Well—all right. Are you sure you—"

"I'll be fine."

All smiles again, fortunately. "Call me if you need me?"

"I will, don't worry. *I'm* not worried. Has the rain let up? Why don't you make a run for it, I'll set the alarm and lock up for the night."

Anneliese undressed and packed the borrowed costume and jewelry in a box. "Good night," Hilda said distantly, and the bell over the boutique door tinkled as she went out.

Night was falling, there was a murky fog in the street and a glimmer of water streaming down from the eaves as Anneliese walked through the silent boutique, turning off the track lights. She activated the alarm by transmitting a pushbutton code. Two short, four long. Anyone entering the shop by either door would have thirty seconds to alert the security guards in a building in Eschenheimer Tor by repeating the code. Otherwise a car would be routinely dispatched.

A southbound streetcar went by with a hiss and crackle as she stepped outside; synthetic lightning flared saffron-yellow in the fog that hovered within a few inches of the wet street. She could barely make out familiar neon signs a block away. Passersby with umbrellas for heads moved dimly in and out of danger as cars slashed by. Each breath she took was heavy, wet, chemical on the tongue.

Anneliese had missed her westbound streetcar to Opernplatz, where she regularly changed for a stop that was only two minutes from her apartment at 90 Oberlindau. The U line underground from the city's center also would get her home, but she had farther to walk at either end.

She felt lonely standing there, and nervous because she couldn't see well. It could start to rain again at any moment. The underground was drier. There was a car at the curb across the street, its flashers going, and she thought briefly of how nice it would be to hire a taxi. But this car wasn't a taxi, it was a gray and expensive Citröen—and anyway it would cost her nearly five dollars to go from Goethestrasse to Oberlindau.

Too much. After a couple of slow years she was now earning a little better than twenty-six thousand dollars annually as her share of the proceeds from the boutique, a comfortable sum but no fortune in one of the costliest cities in the world. Also she'd enjoyed ten days' vacation and paid for two business trips to the U.S. during the last nine months, a severe strain on her budget.

Anneliese turned and began walking toward Hauptwache, feeling ruefully virtuous and wondering what she would do with all the money if somehow her designs caught on in the States.

Two doors down they were changing the display in the window of a rival boutique, called Orbit, which catered to younger and less-affluent Frankfurt women. They played loud rock music all day. The personnel were androgynous, with close-cropped heads of orange and purple and erotic eye makeup. The styles offered were as ephemeral as mayflies.

There was a single bronzed-glass window that bulged toward the sidewalk like a huge, insectival eye. Anneliese had passed the window a thousand times and was often impressed or amused by the flair and inventiveness of their decorator. Outer-space themes. Grotesqueries—a mannequin draped over the sill of a rhinestone-spangled guillotine.

Tonight she was attracted by a revolving yellow light suspended in the depths of the window. She stopped for a longer look. A shock wave expanded in her chest, numbing her tongue, turning her knees to mush.

A slim white unadorned hand seemed to reach out of the strange window, as if it were groping for her. The bodiless arm was buried in debris. Glass eyes, perched surrealistically on the limb of a miniature dead tree, studied her reaction. Anneliese glimpsed her own morbid, haunted face with each quick-changing round of the eight-sided yellow light.

Shock turned to nausea. In revulsion and horror she ran down the street, stumbled, knocked against a man, dropped the package containing the expensive borrowed clothes. She fumbled in the wet for it, momentarily blind, her brow sopping cold.

For a few whirling, disastrous moments she knew she must go back, smash the eerie, telltale glass, fasten her small hands around the offered wrist, and fight with all of her strength to free the body from the awesome drag of the grave.

It wasn't too late, it wasn't!

Brush the stubborn dirt from the thick lashes and the eyes would open, the clogged mouth would smile again.

Oh darling I was having such a good nap

Cars, horns, a mangle of traffic. She'd wandered witlessly into the middle of Rathenauplatz, had nearly been struck in the heavy fog. Everything came to a suspenseful halt; she turned slowly in hood and slicker, all lit up, then fled to shadows. The streets ground back to life.

Behind Anneliese a gray Citröen CX 2400 sedan emerged from Goethestrasse. She stood sobbing on a corner. The big car idled within view, just waiting.

3 On that Friday in April, forty-five hundred miles from the dreary emerging spring along the Main River, Savannah was already in full bloom and having its first heat wave of the year. For three days temperatures had been in the nineties, with humidity to match. The 120 members of the McHenry High School band ("The Dixie Dazzlers"), wearing only short-sleeved white shirts and khaki skirts or trousers, were dripping wet by the time they had marched the six blocks from their campus to the main parking lot of the hospital complex.

They broke ranks for free soft drinks provided by the Ladies' Aid Society, then reassembled listlessly on the scorching bleachers that had been set up for them below the flag-draped speakers' pavilion. Behind them workmen were still installing windows in the new six-story wing of the hospital. The pavilion was partly shaded by a canopy, but the bleachers were not. The kids grumbled obscenely about this oversight, then struck up a concert version of a rock number from a recent film hit. A red-haired sophomore clarinetist passed out reaching for a high note and was carried off to the emergency room of Riordan Memorial to recuperate.

All of the cameramen from the local TV stations dutifully recorded this happening on film. Then they turned their attention to the small motorcade, which had come into view up the street. Four policemen on motorcycles, red lights flashing but no sirens, then six cars, stately as limousines but not quite so ostentatious: new, top-of-the-line Buicks and Oldsmobiles.

In the third chauffeur-driven car of the motorcade, Neddie Riordan McNair looked at the heat-sizzle above the surface of the asphalt parking lot, then settled back next to her daughter-in-law. It was wonderfully cool in the car, and she'd already made up her mind she wasn't going to budge, no matter what.

She cleared her throat and revived a theme that had been on her mind since well before the luncheon.

"Reba, I don't know what you've got against the entire Savannah educational system."

Reba smiled, but her nails were into the heel of her right hand again, an old reflex to slow down her tongue. Lately she'd been drawing blood.

"Some of our schools are very good. But the fact is, none of them can keep up with Sharon."

"I don't pretend to know everything," Neddie replied, with a henlike lift and aggressive jut of the head that served to deny the spoken humility, "but could it be Sharon's just been pushed too hard and too fast? She's barely ten years old."

Don't I know it. At six Sharon had taught herself to play chess, and had not lost a tournament she'd entered since then. Her reading skills were college level, her I.Q. was in the one-fifties. At seven she had begun to create her own books, sometimes writing and illustrating one a day. Remarkably imaginative and perceptive stories, each with a beginning, a middle, and an end. Now, curious about the moons of Jupiter, God only knew why, she was building her own telescope with just a little help from her father.

"Kids set their own pace. But she badly needs the intellectual stimulation she'd get from other gifted children her age."

"Gifted," Neddie said, as if it were a vulgarism. "She's just got too many smart bumps, and that's wrong for a girl. Spoils her for a man, if you know what I

mean. I'll tell you what I was doing when I was Sharon's age. Collecting dolls. I had the finest collection of porcelain dolls—well, you've seen my dolls, Reba."

Oh, Lord. Reba looked at the lead cars, loaded with politicians who were undoubtedly draining off the last of the drinks they'd brought from lunch, before stepping out into the fiery midday sun. And it astonished her to realize how badly she wanted a drink too, had wanted one almost from breakfast. Most of all she yearned to be up front where the conversation must be scatological, scandalous, and very funny—good seamy political gossip. She just wasn't good with women, never had been. She was cut out to be one of the boys, but doomed by marriage and circumstance to the endless Junior League scuffle, with too many other bored women her age.

"And sending her away to school—I just can't *conceive* of how you could do that to the child, it'd break her heart to be packed off like an orphan."

Reba had to smile at the absurdity of Neddie's complaint.

"She'll be in Atlanta, staying with my cousin Ralph. All the kids have known each other since they were yea high, and they get along just fine. Also the school's only four days a week, so Sharon'll be home with us the other three days."

"All that driving back and forth to Atlanta? David's got enough to keep him busy."

"I'd do most of the driving. I wouldn't mind." An understatement. It would be a release: fast, fast driving in the turbocharged Porsche on her way to get Sharon, the top down, rock pounding on the radio.

The motorcade had come to a stop near the speakers' pavilion. Neddie sighed.

"Reba, honey? I don't know: I just don't know if I'm feeling so good right now."

"Do you want me to get Frank?"

"Would you? I'd surely appreciate that."

As Reba started to get out of the car—and it was like opening an oven door—Neddie suddenly put a hand on her arm. Reba turned and faced her reflection in the jet-black left lens of the glasses Neddie wore. To conceal a glass eye she never quite felt comfortable with.

"You'd tell me if there was something wrong between you and David. You wouldn't let me be the last to know, would you, Reba?"

Now, where had that come from? She felt uneasy in the old woman's grasp.

"Everything's fine with us. Why would you think anything's wrong?"

"I don't know for sure. But I think lately there's been tension between the two of you, something that maybe it takes an outsider to see."

"Oh—well—David spent an awful lot of time practicing for the Masters', and then there's been all that labor trouble at the mill. You said yourself, he's got so much to keep him busy. He's tense, and that makes me tense, I suppose. It'll pass."

The clutch of Neddie's hand turned into a fumbling pat meant to be soothing.

"Yes," she said vaguely. "Well, fine, then. I hope you don't think I'm sticking my nose in where it's not welcome. I've never been like that, Reba. But David's happiness—and yours—means so much to me."

"Of course, Mother Riordan," Reba said with a dead-level smile, and she went off to speak to her father-in-law.

Frank McNair stood half a head taller than the other men around him, and although he was nearly sixty years old, there wasn't a hint of a stoop yet. He had a full head of black hair just beginning to show needles of silver-white, and the powerful, high-waisted body of his youth—not heavy, but with the prominent long bones, thick sinews, and wide shoulders of a mountain man. He always seemed to have strength to spare, wells of reserve energy, even when he was taking a breather from the demanding sports he loved.

But lately Reba had begun to worry about Frank, and she wondered if others saw the subtle changes in him. And, if they did, when something would be said about it.

All the men were enthusiastic golfers, and they were still talking about David's letdown in the final round of the Masters' golf tournament, completed the past Sunday in Augusta. An amateur, David had been well up on the leaders' board for the first three rounds, but Sunday on the back nine his wheels fell off, as the pros put it. He'd bogeyed or double-bogeyed six of the nine holes and finished with an unimpressive 79.

Byrum Hollins said, "I think he could have got it together on thirteen. But when they added ten yards they placed the pin where you can't depend on that good tail wind any more."

"Used to be a piece of cake even with a four-iron," Lee Darbee said.

"Hell, now you could just barely scuff it up there with a four-iron, no matter how close you get with your wood." Byrum mopped his steaming brow. He was a fair and golden-haired man so beamish he'd been stuck with the lifelong nickname of Sweets. "Frank, it's goddam hot, how come we didn't decide to do this in the cool of the evening?"

"You're on the hospital committee, Sweets," Frank reminded him.

He turned and reached out to shake hands with Burton Bowdrie, the senior senator from Georgia. Over Bowdrie's head he spotted Reba. She was aware, again, of the pensive slackness of his face just before he smiled. His eyes were unreadable behind the dark sunglasses he'd been wearing lately, even indoors. Mild conjunctivitis, he'd complained. A little slow to clear up.

"Frank?" Reba said, and they all looked at her. With admiration and, in the case of a couple of well-known lechers in the crowd, covetous appraisal. Not that she'd ever want one of them, but it improved her morale to know she was holding up pretty good even in this heat.

"Yes, honey?" Frank said. "You all know Reba, don't you? David's wife?"

Reba smiled quickly at a couple of strange faces, then said to Frank, "Neddie thinks she'd just as soon stay in the car, if that's all right with you."

"Neddie's the smart one today," Bowdrie said, fanning himself with his hat. He'd been in the Senate for thirty-four years. He looked like an aging jockey, with a slight hunch and twist to his torso as if from too many bone-jarring falls. He had a bantam's virulent temper, astute eyes, a crooked, sharp-toothed smile. He looked as if he earned a living doing hole-and-corner things. Selling two-dollar neckties. Running a curbside shell game. Five minutes with Bowdrie made a believer of any man. His voice was a marvel: full, honeyed, commanding. When God finally addressed the multitude on the Day of Judgment, he was going to sound just like Burton Bowdrie, the Great Persuader.

"Of course it's all right," Frank said. He glanced at Mark Sams, whose father's law firm devoted itself almost exclusively to the business interests of Riordan and McNair. "How long's the program, Mark?"

"There's the invocation, then some introductory remarks by the senator, then your turn, and we're done—"

"Done to a crisp," Bowdrie said, fanning away, and everybody laughed.

"Why don't we get started?" Frank said. "I'll be back in a minute."

He took Reba by the arm, a courtly gesture she'd always much admired, and walked with her to the chocolate-brown Oldsmobile where Neddie was waiting.

"Is she sick?"

"No, no. Just frazzled. But she thinks she's letting you down if she doesn't get up there and sit right beside you through the whole thing."

"Good Lord," Frank said softly. "She could have watched it on television tonight, for all I care."

A back window of the Oldsmobile glided down. Frank looked in on Neddie and smiled. She was sitting erect, making an effort for him, but to Reba she looked wispy and pallid. One of those women who go on and on despite formidable illnesses and critical operations. As always, she seemed more like Frank's mother than his wife, although there was only eleven years' difference in their ages. Women get old but men get distinguished. But even in photos Reba had seen, taken shortly after Neddie and Frank were married, Neddie had still seemed old for her years—or, perhaps, just rigorously old-fashioned.

"I'm being more trouble than I'm worth," Neddie announced, showing a full inch of her upper teeth in a hot grimace of asperity.

"Neddie, this heat took us all by surprise. Reba'll stay with you."

"I sure will."

"Don't forget to take off those dark glasses so we can see what you look like, Frank."

Frank opened the door to give his wife a peck on the cheek, then walked quickly away, toward the pavilion. Despite the heat wave, they were drawing a crowd— the band, the TV cameras, and there wasn't that much to do in Savannah at any time of the year. There were interns and nurses from the functioning wing of the hospital, attendance mandatory, and flocks of youngsters on bicycles on their way home from school.

"I don't know why he doesn't visit the eye doctor and get rid of those dark glasses. They don't become him at all."

"Neddie, would you like a cold soda?"

Jasper, the family chauffeur and handyman, turned in the front seat.

"Something to drink, Miss Neddie? I'll get it for you."

"No, no," Neddie said impatiently. "Let *Reba* do it. I don't like for you to leave the car when the motor's running."

Reba smiled, mostly to herself, conceding Neddie's genius for subtly but unmistakably reaffirming her place in the family hierarchy. She walked across the softened asphalt feeling dull and flatfooted and wet around the throat. If someone would kindly turn on the big lawn sprinkler, she wouldn't be embarrassed to run barefoot through it.

She was halfway to the shade at the edge of the parking lot where the Ladies' Aid had set up their ice-filled washtubs when the band struck up the national anthem. Reba kept going anyway. Everyone—except David—had assembled on the speakers' platform. Frank was looking through his note cards, shaking his head slightly, irritably, raising a hand to his face as if the sun was bothering him despite the dark glasses.

Reba helped herself to a diet Dr. Pepper for Neddie, sinking to midarm in the shocking ice water. When she looked up she was pleased to see David, getting out of the car he'd parked behind a piece of yellow construction equipment. The Reverend Riley T. Enlaw of the Second Presbyterian Church had begun the invocation; he would be succeeded by a rabbi and then a monsignor for religious parity. David, the knot of his tie relaxed,

Palm Beach jacket over a muscular forearm, glanced at Reba and drifted toward the shade. Reba popped a lump of ice into one cheek and sucked on it, then leaned against the trunk of a tree. She sized him up as if for the first time, thinking how good it was to feel, after eleven years of marriage, a tidy surge of sexual antic- ipation, the desire to preen and rub, prickling and sen- suous, against his hard body.

"Hi."

"Hi," he said. He kissed her. "Cold lips."

"Warm heart."

He was nowhere near as tall as his father, but more appealingly made. Not a wrong bone or ungainly angle anywhere. He was a comfortable six feet and she never had to stretch to reach his mouth. David, like his father, spent hours each day working hard at games—swim- ming, squash, golf. He had the natural athlete's ability to be always in the right place at the right time and make it look easy. Twice a week he also worked out on a complicated chrome monster in a gym, weight ther- apy for the knee and shoulder injured in a bad auto- mobile accident four years ago. There was a scar on his forehead from the same accident, like an oval drop of wax on the deep tan.

Today his gray eyes seemed to be withdrawing into his head and there were brackets around his mouth, too deeply scored for a man just past thirty.

"How're the negotiations going?" she asked.

"We put the new wage-price concession on the table and they bit. I think we'll have a contract before the day's over."

"You look bored."

"Just tired. But I'm learning a lot from Fedderman, he's a hell of a negotiator." David fished in a tub and popped the top from a can of 7-Up, in no hurry to take his place on the platform.

"Big day," he said, and yawned.

"David, there's a lot of talk about you, I heard them at lunch."

He smiled edgily. "I know. Quite a few people lost their heads after the second round and started betting on me. They have no idea what it's like, the pressures on an amateur in a major tournament—"

"I don't mean golf, David. Politics. The First District seat in Congress. I think Burton's made up his mind to declare for you."

Instantly all signs of fatigue vanished; David was alert, vibrant, his competitive engine turning over smoothly. He no longer looked as if he wanted to be someplace else. He *was* bored, she thought, not a new thought; but then, tremulously, she wondered, *With me too?*

"Dad's been working on Burt. But I didn't think he'd bring off an endorsement."

"That's important, isn't it?"

"I'd win the primary. Then if I didn't do something really dumb before November—"

"Trying to talk yourself out of it?" she said teasingly.

He was looking at his father. "No way. It's what we've always wanted." He drained the 7-Up can and crushed it. "But better than I hoped for." He put his arm around Reba, not quite an afterthought, and she was comforted, vague doubts swept away by his excitement and anticipation. "Congress. Jesus. Think of it."

"Quite a change for us." They'd been to Washington several times, and she loved it: all the canny, huckstering people dwarfed by their own monuments. "Burt says getting into politics is like getting religion. The night you win a big election, you're born again."

David was silent, and she realized he didn't want to talk too much about his candidacy. Not until he was sure of Bowdrie's endorsement, the assent of other important Democrats whose help he would need to win the primary. Superstition, not lack of confidence. At Augusta he'd attempted the impossible, competing against the world's best golfers, and finished in a tie for eighth place. He felt badly only because money had been lost on him. "Someday I'm going to win it," he had said calmly, walking off the last green. Nobody could doubt him.

Reba rested against David's shoulder until the invocation was concluded. She knew how good they looked together, two dark heads, eyes of a similar lightness. She'd always been a stringbean, but she knew how to dress; the ballet lessons her mother had insisted on for so many years had developed instinctive grace, a light flowing step. She had kept up the dancing but stayed away from competitive sports, from David's arena.

Tension, Neddie? Yes, because she couldn't fill all the idle hours with advanced degrees and child-rearing and David had always hated the paper mill and the rest of the family business, he'd marked time all of his adult life awaiting signs and portents, the proper casting of the bones that would sanctify his entry into politics. So there'd been a little too much partying and drinking this past year. Not typical of David, though she'd recognized in herself her daddy's all-consuming passion to reach the bottom of every bottle as quickly as possible. There had been a couple of bad mornings when she couldn't remember the night before. Tension, and you might as well add some flinty, pointless arguments about Sharon and her future. *But Neddie, it's never gone badly with us in bed, which is probably something you don't know too much about—*

David looked curiously at her, as if she'd been trembling against him. The high-school band had forged ahead with another musical interlude. Frank had his eye on them, and he wasn't smiling. Reba remembered her promise to stay with Neddie.

"I'd better go; your mother's waiting for me in the car."

David nodded. There was a big circulating fan on the pavilion, but it didn't appear to be cooling anyone. Because none of the other men were without their jackets, David reluctantly put his on and straightened his tie.

A couple of shapely nurses gave him a big hello; David smiled in passing but not as if he could remember who they were. Weekenders at the Okatee Yacht Club, Reba thought, pure gold in their torchy bikinis, and she scratched a sometime itch: Would he, did he, just because they were available? Thank God he wasn't one of your lawn-party studs, men swank as Latins in their tight, sharp, show-off clothes, always questing after the frolicsome poppies who filled the roster at every affair. When you laid that kind of trash with regularity, it bred carelessness and then gossip, which she surely would have heard. Nor did he fool around with any of the sexual malcontents in their set, the young matrons who made it plain that they didn't get enough at home. That was shitting on your own doorstep.

Maybe on a business trip to New York or Frankfurt—but in that case she'd never know, the one security she needed most. Like his father, David had an old-fashioned respect for people, no matter who they were, and that included women. He had always paid more than casual attention to matters of honor. A fine instinct for the fitness of things. Do something well, or don't do it at all.

If he's ever going to fall for another woman, Reba thought on her way back to the car, it'll be with someone who has more beauty, brains, and class than me.

Since there are only a few of those around—Liv Ull-
mann, for example—the odds are good he won't run
into one of them. Sorry, Liv. But you're probably a little
too old for David anyway.

"David's here," Reba said unnecessarily as she got
into the back seat of the car with Neddie, but she felt
as if she needed an excuse for dawdling.

"He was born ten days late," Neddie said, "and he's
been trying to make up for lost time ever since." She
had said it often, but Reba smiled anyway and opened
the can of diet Dr. Pepper for Neddie. David had taken
a seat beside his father and was talking to him. Frank
nodded and gave David's knee a squeeze.

Thank God they were finally getting around to the
speakers. Burton Bowdrie was introduced, and he approached the microphone with all cameras focused on
him. Reba lowered the window an inch so they could
hear.

"...not my intention today to enumerate the many
outstanding philanthropies bestowed on the city of Savannah by four generations of the Riordan family. It
was my privilege to enjoy a close and enduring relationship with D. C. Riordan. He was deeply concerned
about the welfare of all our citizens, black and white
alike. And his fondest wish was to see the best-equipped
hospital in the state of Georgia standing right here."

D. C. Riordan had died only a few months after Reba
and David, both juniors at Athens, had started to date;
she had only fragmented memories of a pale old man
with weak arteries and angry eyes, steeped in bile to
his breastbone and a constant aggravation to Frank,
whom he obviously despised for the long-ago crime of
marrying his spinster daughter. Teatime in the parlor
of the house on Bull Street had been like a scene from
The Barretts of Wimpole Street.

"D. C. passed on before he could complete his great

work. But fortunately there was a man who had the vision, the ambition, the high-minded ideals, and the tenacity of purpose to finish what D. C. started. His son-in-law, and my esteemed friend, Frank E. McNair!"

Neddie's head was laid straight back against the velour seat cushion, and she sipped her Dr. Pepper as if oblivious of the ceremony outside.

"Do you know I almost died having David? Of course we probably shouldn't have tried, at my age—I was forty-one then—but Frank wanted a son so badly, and fortunately he turned out to be a healthy, strong baby. I wasn't right for two years—well, I haven't been right since, to tell the honest truth. But you know that doesn't make any difference, David was worth any amount of suffering."

Reba, having heard this before, said nothing, but then Neddie didn't require answering. She was content with her memories of sacrificial childbearing.

As she watched Frank approach the microphone, Reba thought, How would you explain him to someone who's never met him? She loved David but she wasn't embarrassed to say that she'd always had a crush on his father. First of all there was his size, but he had a gentle, sure-footed way of moving—David claimed he could walk through a flock of pigeons on the street without alarming them. And he was peaceful to be with, a concerned listener, a reassuring presence.

It was difficult to exaggerate when you talked about his strength. If you had any kind of fight on your hands, you would look first for Frank McNair. Reba had been with him on Factors' Walk, sundown two years ago, when a few of the hairy-chested motorcycle creeps who infested the area had buzzed them—once, twice, three times, coming closer with each thunderous pass, sewing them up in loops, giving them no way to retreat. Her impressions of what happened next were incomplete, because of the incomprehensible speed and savagery with which the fifty-seven-year-old man had acted.

Frank sent one of the big snarling Harley-Davidsons flying with a sidelong kick, then snatched a biker from his seat as he roared by. He then proceeded to shake the boy until his eyes were bloodshot and his front teeth chipped half away; the jagged remains made pulp of the biker's lips. The others, Reba assumed, just vanished. Because the street was suddenly deathly silent, except for the choked, panicked cries for help from the boy. And Frank had scared her, really scared her, because ferocity had dulled to a chalk-faced maniacal intensity, she had been sure he would suddenly fling the boy head-first against a tree or curb, killing him . . .

The applause for Frank dwindled; he took a last look at the note cards in his hand and spoke.

"There is no one of us who is so self-sufficient, or enterprising, that he cannot profit from the hard-won wisdom and inspiration of a great man."

"Doesn't he speak well, now," Neddie said dreamily. "Why, when I first met him, all his breeding was in his mouth, you might say. He worked, and he *worked*, to lose that awful mountain twang."

Had Frank married Neddie just to improve his lot in life? Reba had heard all the stale gossip at the old-timers' exclusive rendezvous, the Edinburgh Club. But she couldn't believe that a man with Frank's integrity would have endured a loveless marriage and twenty years' unrelenting hostility from D. C. Riordan for the sake of a success that surely would have been his anyway. Besides, it was obvious, every day, how deeply Frank cared for Neddie.

"Some found him cold," Frank said. "Stern, unyielding—perhaps unfair in his expectations."

You don't say. Even David cheerfully admitted that his grandfather had been impossible, and that he'd once dreamed of emptying a load of birdshot into the seat of the old man's pants. Reba glanced at Neddie, who had a faint smile on her face and a dribble of Dr. Pepper on her chin. It looked vile and amusing at the same time. Reba looked at Frank again. There was a jerky blur of light across his chest, as if someone nearby was trying to signal with a mirror.

"But no matter how difficult the situation, no matter what problems he was faced with, D. C. would say, 'I can do more.'"

He hesitated, perhaps distracted by the light. David had called a policeman over and was pointing. Reba looked around. There was a group of small boys on bicycles near the back of the crowd, and one of the boys was idly twisting his handlebars. The mounted round mirror caught the sun at a certain angle, hurled it blindingly.

"He saw no reason for any of us to be less demanding of ourselves."

"Poppa," Neddie said, "God rest, I hope you're listening."

The light struck Frank full in the face and hovered at the level of his eyes. It seemed to penetrate his dark glasses like a bolt of lightning. Reba, apprehensive, sucked in her breath. Frank looked momentarily paralyzed; then he began to shudder. The note cards tumbled from his hand and were widely scattered by the next turning of the fan.

David hurried to help his father. The reflected sunlight danced away, reappeared on the brassy lip of a tuba below.

Frank stooped to retrieve his cards. He seemed bewildered, even disoriented. Reba groaned softly. Frank's hands trembled as David sought to steady him. Frank seemed, for a sickening few moments, incurably old.

Neddie's good eye was closed. She hadn't looked at

her husband and she didn't now, but she nodded soft encouragement.

"Go on, Frank," Neddie said. "Go on with what you were saying."

4 The house of Otto Kolner in Frankfurt faced a park on a narrow, quiet street near the thoroughfare of Kennedy Allee. From the large second-floor living room of the house, a glass window-wall perfectly framed the new, thirty-eight-story tower of Kolner's bank, which was located across the river in Theaterplatz.

Supper following the concert was served buffet style. Otto's social secretary had achieved a stimulating brew of guests, including a newspaper publisher, a cancer specialist who was the most recent winner of the prestigious Goethe Prize, an absurdist playwright, a radical lawyer, a titled movie producer from Hong Kong, and a statesman from an African nation Anneliese couldn't remember having heard of before.

"German children are spoiled," said the publisher, whose paper Anneliese didn't care for: it was even farther to the right than the Springer press. He had a head like an aging buffalo, too large for his lightweight body, and he carried it badly, a result of shrapnel-damaged muscles he had suffered during an air raid in '44. He was also a little drunk and a little clumsy, having already stepped on her foot while maneuvering her into a corner. "Including my own children," he continued. "They have so little knowledge of what we've accomplished since the war. They don't seem to care about the enormous amount of work that went into the rebuilding of the republic. They've always been prosperous, why should they care?"

Ordinarily Anneliese would have changed the subject, or made an excuse and just left him standing there, but he was a shade too petulant and overweening.

"Ideas matter more than money when you're young."

"Our students are too easily confused by the wrong ideas, don't you agree?"

"Confused, perhaps...but they know right from wrong. They have nothing but contempt for Nazism, and for the cynical attitudes that have permitted Nazis to remain in government all these years. But what troubles them most is the weakness of a purely materialistic philosophy—work, earn, consume, and we'll all stay strong and rich. If we subscribe to such a philosophy of *Konsumterror,* then we're too easily controlled."

"Are you a Marxist, fräulein?" the buffalo said with a cold smile.

"No, I've never been a Marxist. But at the university I was politically active; I joined the German Socialist Students' Union, the usual things."

He sighed, insufferably. "A rich breeding ground for young radicals. And radical sympathizers."

"Nonconformists. And if we had a common theme, it was antifascism."

He was obviously annoyed by women who had any political sensitivity. "A paper tiger. Fascism can no longer exist in today's Germany."

"There are other forms of intimidation, no? Today we have no effective opposition to the Christian Democrats. Thirteen percent of the jobs available in the Federal Republic are civil service jobs—and too many young people have entries in the Central State Protection files, perhaps for nothing more than harmlessly taking part in demonstrations. Their entries will some day prevent them from getting government jobs. Civil-rights lawyers are everywhere on trial, on vague charges—'conspiracy,' 'defaming the state.' Such charges are frightening. What do they mean?"

"Those who have no respect for our system of justice must have their freedom restricted. Terrorist sympathizers will not be tolerated."

"The voice of the authoritarian state," Anneliese said, getting a little red in the face. She felt a hand at her elbow.

"Anneliese," Otto said, guiding her smoothly away, "come and pay some attention to me. Another glass of champagne?"

Anneliese shook her head. When she was clear of the publisher she took a deep breath.

"Thanks, Otto. I'm afraid I was antagonistic."

"Unwittingly—I overheard your remark about Nazis. Between you and me, there is some speculation that Herr Epps as a young man served with Himmler."

"Oh, dear. I *am* sorry, Otto."

"Think nothing of it. But try to understand how difficult it was to resist them, in my day. If it wasn't for the fact that my father was half Jewish, a *Mischling,* I might have become an SS member myself." He turned and looked at the silvery rounded tower of his bank, raised his glass, and drank deeply. "Instead, I had to settle for denouncing the family of a friend of my father's, also a *Mischling.* I believe all but one of them died at Bergen-Belsen."

"Oh, Otto."

"That's dreary of me. I apologize. I was only trying to point out that the less perfectly we understand ourselves, the more impassioned we become about the deadly and irrational things of life: love, politics, money."

Champagne came around on a tray: Anneliese was served carelessly and nearly half a glass splashed on her *blouson*. Otto eviscerated the shaky maid with a glance, then offered a clean handkerchief to Anneliese.

"It shouldn't stain," she said, "but perhaps I ought to wash it out."

"Go up to my suite," Otto suggested. "I'm afraid one of the young ladies was ill in the powder room, and it hasn't been put right yet."

Anneliese left the living room, pausing as she did so to let one of the dogs go by. There were four of them, two-hundred-pound tawny mastiffs, and they circulated freely wherever Otto was at home, in Germany or in São Paulo. In addition to the dogs there were armed guards in the house, although at a party you couldn't easily distinguish them from his guests, and two more guards monitored closed-circuit TV in what had been a butler's pantry downstairs. Otto had been forced to live this way since the murder of his close friend Dr. Jürgen Ponto, head of the Dresdner Bank, in his Frankfurt home.

One of the assassins of Dr. Ponto was his goddaughter, a member of the radical terrorist group known as the Red Army Faction. Anneliese had been slightly acquainted with Susanne Albrecht—she was a steady customer at the boutique until she decided that she'd had enough of "gorging myself on champagne and caviar," and took up a Kalashnikov submachine gun instead. She committed the crime holding red roses in one hand, as if she were making a bizarre kind of debut.

Otto's suite was on the third floor, behind double walnut doors. Anneliese had never been inside, and she paused to study the portrait over the mantel in the paneled sitting room: his late wife, young children at her feet. Though she didn't covet Otto and was not overwhelmed by maternal feelings, the serenity of this group portrait gave her strange qualms; she felt as if she had trespassed too casually and was a disturbing influence on a charmed place informed by sorrow.

The bedroom was almost spartan: a low bed without a headboard, a brown leather chair, a big modern suspension lamp for reading. The bath was more elaborate, and cheerful, a room about twenty feet long by twelve feet wide. Baskets of tropical plants, each with its own sun-spot; thick orange towels, a barber's chair, a folding table for massage, a step-down onyx tub, enclosed shower, sauna, toilet compartment. There was a control board on which Otto could dial any lighting mood, midday blaze to nocturnal blue.

Anneliese was using the toilet when they came in. Two or three men. She had only a startled glimpse before all lights but one went out and she was snatched up with her pantyhose below her knees. A gloved hand sealed her mouth before she could scream. They were wearing black stocking masks.

She tried to bite and tried to claw, humiliated by her nakedness. Her legs were neatly bound together by the mobbed pantyhose. The skirt had fallen off. They handled her firmly, without roughness, and immediately she sensed it wasn't going to be rape. What then, murder? Only the ceiling light in the shower had been left on; it provided faint illumination through the opaque glass. But there was enough light to reveal all of the thin pointed blade in the hand of one of the men. Her insides felt like cold rusted machinery. Her neck, which had been twisted as she struggled, ached. She felt an involuntary dribble of urine.

Three of them for sure. The third man, the one with the knife, had picked up the expensive borrowed skirt. His knife was like a razor. Quickly he made strips of the cambric before her eyes. Then the other two, holding her arms behind her back, still gagging her, offered her up to the knife wielder like a sacrificial virgin.

He was careful as he slashed the *blouson* to rags, not drawing even a drop of blood. But by then Anneliese had stopped struggling. Her head was dizzy with horror, her vision blurring.

They jammed one of the cotton gloves in her mouth, dropped her on the pile carpet. For a few moments the one with the knife held her head up by the hair. Anneliese's face was inches from the flat, stocking-black face. She could see the glint of eyes, the mashed-down nose. Her hands and feet were cold. She had the highly stressed, roller-coaster feeling that comes just before fainting.

But there was something else, a faint odor of yesterday's perfume, and she realized that it wasn't a man who held her after all.

"We won't forget you, Anneliese."

Words in a windy tunnel. She was released. She didn't feel the soft drub of her head hitting the carpet again.

5 Reba was hot and sticky and irritable.

Especially irritable, and a little unsteady on her feet. Not for the first time in her life, but it was definitely the first time she'd ever been this bombed a full hour before sundown. You couldn't count her wedding day, when they'd had to revive her with an ice-cold bath before sending her packing on her honeymoon. That had been nerves more than champagne.

Her eyes smarted and her head felt stuffed, from the frozen daiquiris and from the chemical fog that had been laid down before the start of the garden party to keep biting flies and mosquitoes and see-nots away. See-nots were the worst. They were tiny black stinging insects that thrived in the low-down heat and humidity of subtropical Savannah, and they had never been as bad as they were this spring. You could temporarily discourage them—some of them—but it was nearly impossible to kill the bastards, no matter what you sprayed them with. They'd be back...but hopefully not before she had another drink.

Neddie was probably watching closely from her rocking chair on the round porch that overlooked the garden, keeping track of Reba's trips to the bar, but Reba was past caring. Just behind Neddie, in the library of the landmark home on Governor's Square, a good part of David's future—and her own—was being decided by eight or ten men, who had been talking for more than an hour now. Not only hadn't Reba been invited to the meeting, she'd been snubbed when she hinted that she wanted to join them.

For the most part she blamed Burton Bowdrie, whose nineteenth-century attitudes toward women were well known—she could just kill the little squirt—but David was not to be so easily forgiven either. He could have come up with something brave like "Where I go Reba goes," but Burton had given him the fisheye and a hurry-up wag of his cocky cigar, so all David said was—mumbled would be more like it—*"I'll fill you in later, honey."*

What were they doing in their smoke-filled room, putting together a shady deal? Did someone have to be paid off in order for David to run? The First District incumbent had died of a heart attack at the age of seventy-one just a few days before he was to open his campaign for reelection; his wife was an amiable idiot who couldn't hope to retain his seat, the race was wide open, and probably David didn't even *need* Burton Bowdrie. But he was powerful, and it was a bad idea to get on the wrong side of him.

"Another daiquiri, Miss Reba?" Barnaby said with a big smile. He catered most of the important parties in town, and knew everyone's drinking habits by heart.

Make it a double, Reba wanted to say, but she knew she would start feeling very guilty along about the time somebody had to drag her feet-first out of one of Neddie's prized azalea bushes.

"No, Barnaby—just club soda and a squeeze of lime this time."

Barnaby's smile didn't change that much, but she sensed his approval, and Reba wondered if she was beginning to show up badly. She fussed self-consciously with her hair and smiled back at him, demonstrating her lucid, sober gaze. But her heart festered.

Don't I rate any consideration? Listen, David, wives like me don't come along every day. You know something? I'll be in there working too, your beautiful shoulders and lazy gray eyes won't bring home all the votes. I'm first-rate, bud. Star quality, and you better appreciate me.

"Mom?"

Reba took her club soda from Barnaby and turned. "Hi, darlin'."

"You look funny," Sharon said. "Don't you feel good?"

"It's the heat." God bless all the children, who never seemed to show more than a faint dew of perspiration even in the hottest weather. Oysters were roasting on a charcoal grill nearby, chickens turned on a spit while their distant cousins, two of Frank's ultramarine-and-topaz peacocks, cakewalked royally through the poisoned air at the rear of the walled garden. The combined odors—greasy smoke, pesticides—were giving Reba a bad stomach. She took her daughter by the arm and walked them away from the bar.

Sharon was wearing a long pale-green skirt and a knit halter. Ten and a half, and the top of her head was already a little above Reba's shoulder—the one thing she hoped was that the girl wouldn't grow too tall. But her figure was good, fuller than Reba's, she would round nicely into shape where her mother was either skimpy or narrow.

"What're you up to?"

"I was talking to Jimmy Wiggins. Aren't you having a good time?"

"Well, I guess so, yes. But it's a funny thing—the good times don't always seem to be happening when they're happening."

Sharon glanced at her, not taking all of that in. She had a pretty, deadpan face, and her eyes had turned out like Grandpa Frank's, black as buttons. Frank's father had been half Cherokee, and the strength of the Indian genes persisted. She was a grave, mannerly, self-absorbed child. Sometimes Reba wished for a little more frivolity. Sharon liked sports, fortunately, but only those in which she could excel alone—swimming, riding. She got along with other children her age, but on her own terms. When she played with them she seemed to lack spontaneity, she played a little too correctly, as if her mind were at a distance solving equations, mulling the origins of the universe.

Reba often lamented that her daughter had enjoyed a very brief childhood—somewhere between the ages of two-and-a-half and three. Since then she had been nearly all business. If Sharon had had brothers and sisters around, their influence might have softened some of her single-minded intensity. But additions to the family would have meant adoption, and even the fair-minded Frank was opposed to that.

"Mom, when will I get my period?"

"Oh—in about two years. We discussed that. Why?"

"Jimmy says that I can't have a baby until I've had my period first. Is that true?"

"That's what you-all were talking about? Well—no, it isn't true. I don't think. I'd have to ask Dr. Shields."

"Jimmy can make his penis hard, but he can't get anything to come out yet."

"Sharon—"

"What's wrong?"

"I think you'd better leave the sex education to Mom, not Jimmy Wiggins."

"We were just talking."

"I hope that's all."

"What are you so mad about?"

"Nothing to do with you."

"Could I get something to eat?"

"No, it isn't ready yet, they'll let us know."

"All the other kids are eating."

"Snacking. You know how I feel about snacking this close to supper."

"Oh, Reba!"

"Grandma's calling you."

"Yes, I heard her." Reba sighed. "Stick around, baby, they'll be serving soon."

Sharon's mouth twisted. She had a way of looking at you, flat and unchildlike, that denied all access.

"Do you have to call me that?"

Reba shrugged helplessly. "But you're the only one I've got. No more chicks in the nest."

"Mother."

"Sorry, I know I promised, I'll do better." She gave Sharon a kiss. Sharon held still for two seconds, then gracefully broke free and ran for the gate.

"I'll just be across the street at Emily's you won't have to call me I'll be back in fifteen minutes honest."

Reba turned and trudged up the steps to the porch. Neddie was saying to one of her lady friends, "So I told her she wasn't going to serve me breakfast with those nasty-looking little braids dangling all over her head, I forget what the nigras call them, corn rows or something like that; I said, 'Well, if you can't come to work in my house with a decent hairdo, then you can't work for me at *all*.' Oh, Reba—is something the matter? Your eyes are just slits."

"I must have an allergy."

"I don't believe you've met my friend Sally Wingate Locker, from Lexington, Kentucky? I guess you *have* heard of the Winlock stables."

Reba faced a genteel white-haired lady with a virulently sunburnt face and smiled numbly.

"I don't think so. How do you do, Mrs. Locker?"

"Reba is David's wife. Sally just sold a two-year-old race horse for more than a million dollars."

Reba licked her lips, which were dry and flaky. She felt a lovesick tugging in her breast. She wanted to see her husband badly; she wanted, in fact, to be held by him, and the hell with what anybody else wanted right now.

"Really? I don't know anything about racing, what makes a horse worth that kind of money?"

"He's faster than whistling piss," said Sally Wingate Locker.

Reba started for the library doors.

"Don't rush off," Neddie said.

"I haven't seen my husband for a while."

"I don't think the men are ready to be *bothered* yet, Reba."

Something in her tone stopped Reba. Looking at her mother-in-law, she saw only the blackout glass, behind which unkindness and malevolence seemed to dwell like goblins in a city on the dark side of the moon.

"Aren't they?" she said in a tight furious voice. "Well, if you'll all excuse me, I'll just go to the bathroom then."

She chose another of the French doors that lined the covered porch and let herself into the dining room. She fled to the stairs, got halfway to the top of the four-story house, before she started to bawl. On the third floor, which mercifully was deserted, she entered the nearest bedroom (it happened to be Frank's), and sealed herself inside to finish her gut-wrenching cry.

After ten minutes, or fifteen, she sat up exhausted on the blue velour bedspread with the late level sun in her eyes.

Self-pity had made her drunker than daiquiris, and the hangover was a pip. Her left eyelid was twitching. Her lower lip was sore and bulbous; she had chewed it. Her hair—combs out of place, dangle of chaplet—was like a half-constructed birds' nest. She heard voices, the faint music of a harp, a peacock's cry. Life was not fulfilling too many of her expectations, but it was time to lift her chin and try again.

She slid off the high bed and wandered around, one shoe missing. She kicked away the other shoe in a girlish tantrum that provided no satisfaction, and leaned on the deep windowsill; shimmied glass afforded a full view of Governor's Square, old and expensive houses all around, most of them certified museum pieces. In the lambent Savannah dusk, all that was missing from the great old days were carriages and gaslight. Hot-pink dogwoods blazed, the sun glanced piercingly off the bronze vane of a rooftop, the breath of night was sultry, fanned by the faint wings of departing pigeons.

It was bearable now. In the morning, of course, they would wake up to dew-beclouded lawns and the brute miasma from the paper mill.

She was standing in front of a tall mirror and trying, with the fake tortoiseshell combs, to repin her hair the way José had done it, when the bedroom door opened and Frank came in.

The suddenness of it, in the shadowed room, startled her. She turned, hair in her eyes, and tried to smile, tried to wave away like a magician her embarrassment at being there.

"Frank, I'm sorry, didn't think you mind if I—"

He didn't seem to hear her. He headed for the bathroom. In one hand he was holding a ten-pound plastic bag of ice cubes. The bag had broken and ice was spilling on the carpet. He hadn't noticed or he didn't care.

He wasn't wearing his dark glasses. He'd had them on so much of the time lately it was strange to see him without them. When she drifted over in front of him, bewildered, not knowing what else to say, he paused and looked at her. The look was crazed. His eyes appeared to be alight from the inside, as if by a sear in the brain. He made a sound in his throat that was guttural, full of spit. He put out a hand as if to gently ease her aside, but an erratic surge of nervous strength caused the hand to jump powerfully and strike her on the shoulder.

Reba hit a chair before she stopped spinning. The bathroom door creaked shut behind Frank.

Oh my God, she thought, more thoroughly frightened than she'd ever been in her life, *get David.*

Reba was halfway to the door before it occurred to her: *No, he doesn't want that. Whatever's wrong, he doesn't want them to see him this way.*

She turned around and went to the bathroom door. Listened. She heard ice rattling into the washbasin. Frank was groaning. She knocked. Ice cubes seemed to be falling everywhere, there was a great chattery splash of them, then a charged silence.

"Frank? Let me in please?"

He wouldn't answer. Reba swallowed hard and turned the knob, opened the door a crack.

Silvery light in the big blind window. Frank big and dark against that light, standing with his legs spraddled, his face down and head half-buried in the mound of ice cubes he'd made in the basin. He was clutching the top of his head with both hands. Beneath the ice he sucked in great drafts of arctic breath.

Reba stood trembling in the doorway, for almost a minute unable to say a word, to catch her own breath. All the bad dreams were coming true today.

"Frank. Frank, what's wrong?"

He slowly lifted his head from the nest of ice. His eyes were wet.

"Get out of here, Reba, goddam it!"

But he had no balance and he was wobbly. He sat down hard on the tile floor, banging the high tub with an awkward elbow. Reba seized a towel and kneeled beside him. The crazed look was going from his eyes. His breathing, though still ratchety, was becoming more deliberate. He took the towel with trembling hands, used it.

"Are you sick?"

"No," he said. "Not what you're thinking."

"What, then? Do you want me to call Mitch—"

Frank was a long time answering. Then he said with a sigh, "Reba, I've seen all the doctors I need to see."

"I'll get some painkiller—"

He looked up then, draping the towel around his neck. Finally he was calm, his big hands relaxed.

"Did I hurt you?"

"What? Oh, no." She shrugged the shoulder to prove it to him.

"I didn't mean to be so rough. You were in my way."

"You looked—as if you hurt so bad—"

"It isn't pain. Not like any kind of pain I'm used to. It's just lights flashing on and off in my head, driving me crazy. Ice helps. It's the only thing that does." He covered his face for a few moments, thinking. "Better now," he murmured.

"But what's *wrong*, Frank?"

He looked at her again, a sweet and defenseless man, and she wanted to hug him but didn't dare—there was still a tiny trickle of fear down her spine, what if the monstrous thing suddenly happened again? He could crush her without meaning to.

"What's wrong can't be fixed. Take my word for that. Then—I suppose we better have a talk."

She rubbed her head in agitation, then reached out and touched his forehead with her fingertips. He smiled, grudgingly, at her perception. Reba was horrified.

"Oh. Oh, no! In the *brain?*"

"Where they can't get at it. They said, well, cobalt, *maybe*. I said—no. Shut the door, honey, this is not a good time for somebody to walk in on us."

Stunned, she obeyed him without thinking. Frank raised himself slowly to a seat on the edge of the tub.

Reba began picking up ice cubes, just to have something to do.

"Nobody knows yet?"

"Not yet."

She hadn't thought she could cry any more, but her eyes were burning from salt.

"We can't lose you—Dad. We just *can't*."

Frank looked steadfastly at her, drained by ordeal. But he had stopped trembling.

"Well, you're going to, and you have to be tough-minded about it."

"David—lives for you. In everything he does, everything he's tried to be."

"David still has a long way to go. Up to you to see that he gets there. All up to you, Reba. Now listen, I've got to depend on you to keep this to yourself until I figure out how to tell David, and Neddie."

Oh, no, Reba thought. *Please don't do that to me! Because if David finds out that I knew and didn't tell him, he'll never forgive me.*

"Reba," Frank said, fixing her with an eye that looked slightly dangerous again, "it's my responsibility to tell them. You understand that, don't you? Let me do it my own way, in my own time."

Reba kept rubbing her head, and the tears kept coming.

"All right," she said at last, choking on her promise. "All right, Dad. Whatever you say."

6   Midday on the Main. Anneliese awoke in an unfamiliar bed hearing birdsong just beyond the half-lowered steel shutters of the windows; the light that came in was even and tempered by new green leaves, not the streaky rawness of sun, she was on the garden side of Otto Kolner's house. And in his daughter's bedroom. Anneliese dimly tried to recall the girl's name. She was the oldest, with her mother's wide cheeky face and lucent brow; now she had it: Brigitta, away at school near Zurich.

Someone was using a sizzling hose on cement below, probably to clean up after all the rain. There was a hothouse aroma of flowers in the bedroom. It was too early in the season for the garden to be in bloom. Anneliese raised up and looked at starlike spring flowers, perhaps a thousand of them in vast bowls, each flower perfect in shape and primary color but forming in the mass distant nebulae, constellations in flight around the room. She wished for her sketchbook and thought of clean, newly screened prints.

She had slept in a striped flannel nightshirt, also Brigitta's, but discovered upon rising that there were clothes for her, unfamiliar, unmistakably new, and the correct sizes. Underthings, French corduroy jeans, an epaulet shirt, walking shoes, an exquisite Hermès jacket in thin vanilla suede, soft as the underside of her tongue.

More of Otto's thoughtfulness, which she emphatically didn't deserve.

There was a note. He'd gone, early this Saturday morning, to his horse farm in the Neckar Valley to await delivery of a brace of Polish-bred Arabian stallions, and would she care to join him for the weekend? A car and driver were at her disposal.

Worth thinking about, but first she had to go to the bathroom.

Anneliese wasn't prepared for the knot of fear, like a swollen tonsil in her throat, as soon as she thought of being alone in there. Defenseless again. They had entered this guarded house so easily, and found her, and left her symbolically mutilated, unconscious on the floor. She turned and went immediately to the bedroom door and locked it, leaned against the wall until a whirling spell of coldness and a violent heart subsided.

She couldn't be sure just how long she'd lain on Otto's bathroom floor, but probably no more than five minutes had passed until she was conscious again, and so nauseated that she barely made it, crawling, back to the toilet before throwing up her dinner. They'd removed the brown cotton glove from her mouth before leaving, so, except for her ripped clothing and incipient bruises, there was no sign they had been there.

A maximum of ten minutes, then, before she had the strength and the wits to go to the telephone on the wall by the barber's chair and summon help, and by then she was too late. There was a noticeable absence of commotion in the house below—no mastiffs barking, alarms ringing, sirens in the street. They'd already escaped, unnoticed. Anneliese wrapped a towel around herself and sat down in the barber's chair to weep helplessly.

The intruders were gone, and no one was going to believe a word of what she had to tell them. Not the police, not Otto himself, though he had known her for a year and liked her very much, possibly even loved her. But Otto had surrounded himself with the best security available—even an armed raid on his home was likely to fail—why, then, should three men (a hazy recollection—could it have been two men and a woman?) risk being shot to death in order to penetrate the house, seek out Anneliese, remove two articles of reasonably expensive clothing, and shred them? Or had that been the point of it all? She didn't know, couldn't remember what had been said to her, if anything, her head ached and she couldn't stand this *fear* any more.

Were you raped, fräulein? the inspector would ask, and she remembered with a distasteful shiver his skepticism earlier.

No.

Was anything of value taken from you?

No.

They made no attempt to forcibly remove you from this house?

No, no, no!

Hopeless. They would look at her with polite, frozen smiles, as if she were a neurotic, a crazy person.

Couldn't she easily have done the damage herself, with Otto's conspicuous straight razor? A fit of childish pique. Nütterman's skepticism reinforced. You see, first it was phone calls, now this! Help me, won't you? Do something!

But we're very busy, fräulein. With real criminals, not phantoms. Perhaps a good therapist would be of more benefit to you under the circumstances.

Nothing. She could do nothing, say nothing, without making herself look a fool—bad enough with her clothes in tatters—how was she going to explain that to Otto?

In the end Anneliese took a five-milligram tranquilizer from a bottle she found in the medicine cabinet, gathered up the ruined shirt and blouse, stuffed them deep into a laundry bag, and summoned Otto, who had begun to miss her, to the telephone. Making an extreme effort to be casual, aware of the mailed fist of a stutter in her throat, she improvised a story.

"Otto, I'm afraid I've just m-made things worse trying to get the champagne out, and there's something on the skirt too, a spot of grease. I just *can't* wear these things again tonight! This is presumptuous of me, but your daughter and I are about the same size—"

Otto, as she hoped, was gracious and understanding. A maid arrived shortly with a selection from Brigitta's wardrobe. Anneliese put together an outfit agreeable to her taste, then made her way downstairs to the free-wheeling party, smiling fixedly, her brain becalmed in marshmallow, idly turning over timetables, thinking of a far country where she'd never been and might be inspired: India, perhaps, although Indian designs were reaching the market this year in a tidal wave, but in India she could just wander around relieved from the threat of—safe until she—

No. For that had to be the real point of their behavior

tonight, to demonstrate to Anneliese that she was available to them any time, in any place of their choosing. Regardless of dogs, guards, guns, remote hideaways, inevitably they would come, with new and deadlier mischief. Never telling her why. She could die not knowing.

The outer surge of the party caught and sucked her painlessly toward the hot bright center; along the way she took on a couple of drinks and adopted a wide-eyed listening attitude to manage increasingly unintelligible conversations while she nursed a secret weeping, hugging herself tightly inside. A mastiff brushed by her, half out of focus as she glanced down, dreamdog prowling the boneyards of civilization. His rugged, stony head, the bite of a vault door slamming on your wrist—would *she* have the nerve to try to sneak by him?

Doom again; the hooded heads of the intruders surprising her, either they had peerless confidence, or—the thought was a tiny chilling spark leaping from the bog of her perceptions—they had inside help.

Make it simpler still. They *were* inside, had been all along. They'd come to the party too. She thought of the careless, apprehensive maid who was not so indirectly the cause of it all, of fifty strangers, any of whom might have been watching her all evening, waiting for the moment she would be most alone.

"You're not feeling well," Otto said, coming to her rescue for the second time.

She smiled a meaningless, teary smile, and could not explain.

"I'll have Schluetter drive you home."

"Otto. Could I stay?"

So, as the party came to an end and the house was cleared of suspicious faces, Otto put Anneliese to bed in Brigitta's room. He had the grace not to put himself to bed with her. At her request a dog was posted outside the door. Her capacity for surprise and intrigue exhausted, too humbled to feel any more fear, she had piled on the covers and fallen fast asleep....

As she showered and brushed her teeth and wondered if her churning stomach was due to apprehension or hunger, Anneliese realized she owed Otto more than she could repay. But still she ruled out a weekend at his farm. It would be more than a diversion, it would be an act of outright avoidance, and she couldn't afford not to resume her normal life at once.

They had her, she admitted it (showing her gritted teeth to herself in the mirror). Whatever they wanted they could bring about in their own good time. While she walked on the street, worked at her designs, washed dishes in the kitchen. They could torment her...but they wouldn't break her spirit. She would live, somehow, without jumping at each ring of the telephone. They seemed to have progressed beyond that sort of thing anyway. No good trying to anticipate a future move, it would only drive her completely round the bend, flinching at shadows and the accidental bump on the street. She was worth more than that. She had *value*, which they could never steal or extort.

Downstairs she picked at a light lunch in the kitchen while she glanced at newspapers: *Bild-Zeitung, Allgemeine*. Her losing streak at Toto-Lotto was intact after nearly six years. The right-wing press was still featuring old news, the assassination of two Tribunal terrorists almost a month ago. There was speculation that a round of gang warfare was in prospect between rival radical groups—the Tribunal, the RAF. One guess was as good as another, and *Bild-Zeitung* was using theirs to justify a call for harsher government methods in dealing with all terrorists.

Anneliese put the newspaper aside with a grimace

of annoyance and wrote a letter to Otto, thanking him for his kindness and gifts.

It was about sixty degrees outside, with hazy sunshine, trees mildly in leaf, pools of rainwater, leftover winter chill in the stones of a wall and the space of a sunless alley. She had refused the offer of a car, but as she walked toward Kennedy Allee and the heavy traffic northbound to the center of the city, she felt almost feeble with doubts about her ability to survive the rest of the day.

She might have been coming out of hospital after a long convalescence with her senses curiously distorted, no longer in stride with the city in which she had lived for most of her adult life. She couldn't accurately judge the speed of oncoming cars, and was afraid to step into the street. Children playing in the park nearby seemed threatening to each other. An old man cleaning windows gave her a sidelong look in which she interpreted a complex secret life: diabolism.

Time ticked frantically by her and she felt caught out of bounds, searching for credentials that would justify her presence to the unseen people who owned these houses, this street, the entire city—and now her own life.

Anneliese realized then just how thoroughly she'd been victimized by her callers, by their audacious act of terror the night before. She'd anticipated being nervous, afraid—but she was unprepared for this kind of hallucinatory displacement.

She fought it and gained a few moments' useful perspective. Her eyes seemed to focus more sharply. She took a deep breath.

She was a victim, and she despaired. But she kept walking. There was simply nothing else to do.

7 On Sunday morning, just before nine o'clock, the blue-water motor sailer *Denebola* left the Okatee Yacht Club near Savannah for three days of cruising the coastal islands of southern Georgia.

She was Swedish-built, of mahogany and teak, fifty-two feet overall and with a large superstructure, but the topsides were well arranged: It was no hardship for a two-man crew to handle the full spread of canvas on a ketch rig and sail comfortably as far east as Bermuda, or south to the Lesser Antilles. Three years ago, shortly after taking delivery, Frank and David had talked excitedly of a much longer cruise, across the Caribbean to the Panama Canal, then north perhaps as far as San Francisco. *Denebola* had been well fitted for long offshore voyages by the man who had commissioned the yacht, then enjoyed her for only a few months before the failure of his brokerage business in the big Wall Street shakeout of '74. Frank had installed a Loran-C direction finder to go with the automatic pilot, emergency position-indicating radio beacon, VHF and short-wave radios, four compasses, and a radar reflector attached to the flag halyard.

The stockbroker had named her *Denebola,* for reasons unknown to them. But there was feminine grace as well as strength in the name, and it flowed well off the tongue: Den-eb-o-la. So, after discarding a dozen other possibilities as being either too poetic or too commonplace, they had accepted the original name.

Nothing had come of their desire for a dream cruise, six months or more, a long sun-baked time of renewal, for deep turquoise dives and frenzied billfish, sudden tempests, moldering ports of call, strange alluring women to admire, arguments of an intensity that only men who care deeply about each other dare to have.

But the *Denebola* had rarely been out of the water, even in winter, for the three years they had owned her. What was rare was for the two of them to have time together any more. It had been eight, no, ten months since their last short cruise alone, without obligatory guests: family, friends, business associates. And David felt happier, freer than he had in a long time.

Before the long serious conversations, there was work to do, and he was already totally involved as his father steered them down the Wilmington River channel past Skidaway Island. The wind was holding steady on the solid blue Atlantic. Light to moderate running conditions. They crossed a tricky northwest meander off Wassaw Island, then went to a spinnaker and autopilot for a brisk southerly run before the wind. They fell to the topside chores: scraping, mending, lubricating.

A burning subtropical morning, gusts of high cold spray, the spanking red-and-yellow sail. Music from a husky SX-650 Pioneer receiver in the main saloon amidships. Frank fumbled a chrome socket wrench over the side and turned for a long look at David, as if he hoped his son hadn't noticed. His lips were tight with exasperation, eyes unreadable behind the extra-dark lenses of his sunglasses.

"Let's have some coffee," David said, smiling.

"Iced," Frank said.

When David returned with two tall tumblers, his father was sprawled on the long foredeck of the cockpit under the Bimini awning, his back against one of the raised Lexan hatches. He took a glass from David, gave his golf cap a half turn to the right, and pressed the cold glass against the side of his head.

"Slowing down," he said, with an odd, baffled smile. It wasn't noon yet.

"Tired?" It was unthinkable and, a moment later, shocking. His father had never looked this way. Yesterday, bent over cruelly, fumbling after the spilled note cards, a savage shudder running uncontrollably through his body. Now the lost wrench, as if his mind had wandered, his hands had gone numb. And this: something ponderous and invisible sitting on him, and he was trying to be casual about his inability to catch his breath, to spring up refreshed.

"Dad, maybe you need a checkup."

"Had one."

"And?"

"I'm good as gold."

Little by little, as he sipped his coffee, Frank got back his strength and some of his good spirits.

David said, "I don't like the way the engine revved when I started it. We may have picked up something back at the marina that fouled the propeller."

"I'll dive with you to help you check it out. I need to look at the keel anyway—she's overdue for bottom work."

"Well—maybe you shouldn't. I mean, I can handle it, if you just want to take life easy for an hour or so."

Frank politely considered the offer, though his expression was tense.

"No. No, I need the work. Some hard labor, that'll put me right. I just haven't had enough activity lately." He turned the bill of his cap back to shade his already well-protected eyes, looked up with a skewed grin for his son. David earnestly sought those eyes, failed to find them.

"Never will see the day I drag ass behind you, Davey."

"No, sir, I don't expect that'll happen."

Frank shifted his long legs and sat up, and something in his movements recalled in David a nearly forgotten timidity: His father had been the Biggest Man In The World. It had been a long breathtaking lift to meet his father eye to eye. He could still feel that quirky sensation in the pit of his stomach as he dangled in Frank's grip; hands that covered all of his ribs, fingers that met across his shoulder blades, thumbs big as a dog's paws, heavy but gentle against the frail chest bones. There had always been a giant in David's house, in his life. Thank God he was still there.

About three in the afternoon they anchored in a broad channel between Sapelo and a smaller, no-name island and went overboard in scuba gear in fifteen feet of sunlit water to cut yards of frayed hemp from around the propeller shaft. Frank held up his end, as he had promised, and seemed invigorated when they were topside once again.

They changed into denim shorts and ragged shirts, took the loaded dinghy ashore in a mild chop that hadn't been there an hour ago. The sandy, greenish water of the channel was turning dishwater gray. By then it was obvious that the wind was backing all the way around to the southeast. There was going to be rain later, probably some heavy weather along with it.

Frank liked to do the cooking when he didn't have to do it in the galley of the boat, where he had a bare inch of headroom and not much space for his elbows. He liked his fish grilled over a driftwood fire, potatoes baked in foil in beds of hot ash. He liked Mount Gay rum straight from the bottle, and he could drink a lot of it on outings such as these. He liked a good cigar, and he liked to smoke it while blasting clay targets to bits with a made-to-measure Franchi trap gun that cost seven thousand dollars. Today his shooting eye was off enough to annoy him, and he seemed to be drained, too quickly, by the complex demands of trap shooting.

The sky darkened and the sun glinted fiercely in and out of mounting clouds. A rising wind blew sparks from the fire Frank had built; David finished packing away the guns and took a long look at the *Denebola* riding in the channel, at an anchor chain taut against a north-west current that seemed to be running at better than one knot.

"I'm not all that satisfied with the bite of the leeward anchor," he said.

"Change it, then. And Davey—break out another bottle of rum."

David glanced at him and grinned.

"I'm having a damn good time today," his father said, "but I think I can improve on it."

David carried the gun cases to the dinghy. Frank took off his dark glasses to clean some of the salt from them with a handkerchief. He glanced up just as the sun was breaking, like molten gold from a tipped beaker, through clouds and scrub pine to the west. His constricted pupils flared at the touch, his brain was partly consumed by an equalizing, awesome brightness. He fell and lay hunched and kicking like a powerful animal ruined by gunshots.

David looked back and saw him.

From that angle Frank looked as if he were making love to an unseen woman, and at the peak of his orgasm. Suffering with ecstasy. For several seconds David was in the grip of a horrid lethargy, a reluctance to intrude. It seemed so private and devastating. Then he ran.

8 In the dark of the Atlantic, sheet lightning pursued the *Denebola*. There was a strengthening wind, and the following sea was getting sloppy. During the last ten minutes waves had begun to break, tentatively, over the bow. Rain was in the air, but the squall hadn't hit. The two men had hoisted a storm jib earlier, and at his father's request David set the autopilot.

Then, emotionally stalled, he stayed topside staring blankly at the binnacle compass in the cockpit, listening to his father just below him singing along with Wilma Lee and Stony Cooper in a bawling, brush-arbor baritone. They were the popular sacred songs of his Appalachian youth. That Old Testament religion of blood and rue. Evangelists, possessed by the simple villainy of their faith, whipping the heathen home to Jesus in humid tents. Frank had allowed himself to be married in the Church, but thereafter he refused the Catholicism of Neddie and the Old Man, which hadn't made his lot in life any easier.

Weepy mandolins and a dobrol, steels to humble the howling wind. "Walking My Lord up Calvary Hill." "Thirty Pieces of Silver."

> ...Thirty shekels of shame
> Was the price paid for Jesusss—
> On the cross he was slain.

Confronting a fate as broad and black and pitiless as the sea itself, David thought: What if. What if.

There's always something that can be done. Just think of it, then, and by God, do it fast!

Let me give you some idea, David. Suppose you have a glass ball, a little smaller than a golfball. Think about swinging a fungo bat as hard as you can, and blasting that glass ball into a million pieces, some so small you can't see them with the naked eye. That's what happened inside my head. And each of those bitty pieces could get to be golfball-size too, if I had brains enough to hold them all, or lived long enough.

Which I won't.

I won't, David. But I'm not in pain, may never be, and that's a blessing.

"Hey, Davey! You fall overboard, or what?"

Shuddering, his face and hair misted wet, he slid back the companionway hatch and went down the steep ladder steps to face his father's erratic, unaffordable good cheer.

Only the lights over the breakfast bar were on. Frank turned down the volume of the stereo receiver when David appeared. He had helped himself to another bottle of rum from the liquor cabinet. The boat was rolling, jarring just enough so that they had to use the overhead rails to steady themselves. Frank was barefoot on the shag carpet to give himself a little more headroom. His face was flushed from prolonged rum, but nothing—drink, fatigue, despair—had ever clouded the acute obsidian of his hooded eyes. The persistence of his gaze would surely endure, beneath pressed-down lids, forever.

The thought frightened David, and he felt a growing numbed spot at the level of his breastbone. He sat down in one of the padded swivel chairs in front of the bar.

"Do you want something to drink?" Frank asked him. "Beer? There's Three Horses on ice."

"Not right now. We're making about six and a half

knots—we should raise Savannah a little past midnight. Dad, we could make better time with the diesel."

Frank shook his head. "Nothing's there I'm in a hurry to get back to. Stay under sail, Davey. I need the time to talk to you. Sorry our fun got cut short. I wasn't going to let you in on my—problem—so quick, but maybe it's the only way."

"Dad, we can't just give up! We'll go anywhere—Germany, Switzerland: Maybe they can't operate, but there must be something, a drug they're experimenting with, that'll dissolve the tumor."

For a few moments his father was grim, unfriendly, as if he resented the intrusion of even the faintest hope.

"Sorry, David. When it comes to brain tumors, they haven't had much luck with Laetrile. If it had been a smaller mass they might have been able to poison the damn thing with conventional chemotherapy, and I would have come out of treatment looking like the mummy's ghost. But it's too late, the tumor grew like a son of a bitch, and now it's busting loose."

He timed the rolling of the boat and poured a couple of fingers of rum into a glass, which he handed to David. He had a sharp odor about him, of sunburn and boozy sweat.

"Looks like you're going soft on me. Drink that, it'll help."

David stared at the glass in his hand. He disliked rum. The best of it tasted like burnt sugar to him, and the hangovers were horrendous.

"How long?" he asked.

"Bill Peck thought maybe three or four months. But I'm going downhill faster than he anticipated. The only thing that really bothers me is I don't know just how I'm going to die. I don't want to get really repulsive—the staggers, the shits, no way to communicate any more. But I guess there's not much I can do about it."

"I can't just let you die," David said. The fear was now so great it seemed fraudulent, conceived in a dream. His father, deep in drink, had never looked so fit and resilient. David persisted: "I have to *do* something."

"I got you out here to say three things. Well, you know about the big C. The second thing is, I want you to go ahead and run for Congress. And win. I'm counting on that. It's a good way to use your life. You've got energy, ambition, and a sound conscience, thank God. I never met a man whose morals were improved by politics, but I think you'll be one of the rare exceptions, or I wouldn't urge you to go ahead with it."

"I can't. Not without you there."

"Listen to Burt and you'll do okay." David glanced up. "I know, I know, he drinks too much and he's benefited from a shabby deal or two. But Burt is dedicated, and he's won the power and influence to make some important decisions for the good of this country. Learn from Burt, and don't be too impatient to play by your own rules up there."

The boat creaked; loose cutlery rattled in a galley drawer. Frank poured another generous shot of rum for himself and said with a sweet, pleading smile, "Now let's just try to relax and think about the good times, David. Think about the good times for a while."

"You're going to get drunk."

"No I won't. Time's too precious to waste that way. God, would you believe, I feel so—*joyous* right now. I'm not lying to you. I'm going down the rapids in a birch canoe, falling out of an airplane without a parachute, and I'm not so damned afraid. I'm afraid for you, that's all."

"I can take care of myself," David said, trying to smile and at the same time conceal the razor edge of his pain.

Frank slumped on the wraparound sofa opposite the nav station; his long legs extended halfway across the saloon. His eyelids lowered as if he were contemplating sleep, but the rolling of the boat lurched him out of it.

"Remember the time we were at the old place up in Carolina, D. C.'s hunting lodge in the Smokies? You were nine, ten years old. I forget. Anyway it was along about sunset and I don't know what made me walk outside to the porch, maybe you'd been quiet for too long. There you were riding that old balloon-tire bike on a rail six inches wide, playing circus—and the drop off that porch must have been a good three hundred feet down the side of the mountain. One of the few times in my life my hair stood on end. Boy, you could take some wild chances. But even when I had to punish you I admired your courage."

"Do you know what I wanted for my twelfth birthday? A hot-air balloon."

Frank laughed. A little of the rum slopped from the glass David was holding. He drank the rest of it without thinking, his eyes bright, responding eagerly to the sound of his father's laughter, needing to keep it going.

"Damn it, I still want one! I want to sail across the country in a balloon."

"I'll go with you. I've always thought if you could get up high enough, and travel fast enough, you could stay ahead of the dark."

The sharp swerve back to the reality of the moment dulled David's enthusiasm; Frank gestured, trying to get their moods airborne again.

"I told you, I'm not all that afraid of dying, David. What I meant was, morning's always been my best time. Out early, just walking, with a dog or a gun."

"Remember old Sparky?"

"Oh, hell yes, the most gun-shy dog that ever lived."

"I think Sparky would've run away from a loud cow-fart."

Frank laughed again, but it was perfunctory. He shifted his weight on the sofa and banged an elbow against the mahogany bulkhead as he mistimed the motion of the boat.

"I guess there's three things in this life I never had much use for: a weak-hearted dog, a timid child, and a man who couldn't face up to his responsibilities."

"Let me have the rum, Dad?"

"Sure."

David poured three ounces, passed the bottle back to Frank, who was slouched down with his bare feet braced, just riding out the weather, eyes on David, trace of a loving smile on his face.

"How old were you that year I went off to dwell among the Krauts?"

"Oh—seven, I think."

"You probably don't remember too much about it."

"Yes I do. Mother was sick a lot, and I missed you. I used to cry at night."

"Well, it should have been a three-month job, then it stretched to six months, and then I made it last ten when they didn't really need me any more—the mill was in good shape."

"Why'd you stay?"

"Because there was a woman," Frank said.

David drank more of the rum, the warmth spreading like sunlight to annul a brief shadow of regret. He'd always wondered if his father had taken other women to bed, but it would have been unnatural if he hadn't, given his vitality and enduring sex appeal. So, way back when, he'd had a German mistress—

"Like nobody I've known before, or since," Frank said, as if justification was in order.

"Oh, I see."

"It happens."

"Sure. Then it was—pretty serious with you."

"Yes. I knew nothing could come of it. But I couldn't break away. Even though I realized—she would ruin me, or I would ruin myself."

Lurch; tilt; roar and slam of heavy water across the bow. On the stereo Wilma Lee and Stony sang dimly of Jesus. Frank's eyes were heavy-lidded again. But his eyes were fixed too nakedly on David, who was reminded of chilly mountain nights, campfires, the ghost stories his father loved to tell. The young, solemn faces around the fire pit and his father's seriousness, his will to make them believe in the strange gruesome tales from Poe and Lovecraft.

David wished the conversation hadn't taken this turn; he wished to give back the dignity his father somehow had lost. But he was curious too.

"Did Mother know?"

"She must have sensed that I was involved with a woman. But she trusted me to do the honorable thing and not betray her—or the family."

"Dad, it's perfectly normal for a man to get a little bit lonely and—"

"Her name was Pauline," Frank said.

Time to go, David thought. He didn't want her to have a name. His head was a little fuzzy from the rum, and the shadows of the wilderness had come too close; there were stirrings in the fire pit that troubled him, he had no stomach for the ending of this story. It was time to check the compass, make sure the autopilot was working properly. Because the *Denebola* seemed headed, not for the familiar harbor of Savannah, but a lonely and uncharted reach.

"Pauline Girda." His father's eyes opened a little more at the sound of her name; in the set of his mouth there was suspense, and deep bitterness. "She was determined to have me. She would have destroyed my marriage. Pauline wasn't reasonable at all. I would have paid her something. Taken care of her. But she wouldn't listen."

Steep roll of the ship; her recovery seemed a little too cumbersome and slow to David, and there was a hell of a lot of rain on the Lexan hatches overhead. He had fallen toward Frank; his hand was on his father's knee.

David looked up with a shrug and a smile.

"Sounds like a mess. How did you get out of it?"

His father's hard black eyes, wide open now, daring the children to sit still for phantoms and ogres, for one more dreadful revelation.

"I killed her," Frank said.

9 "I murdered her, David. I strangled her. Broke her neck. I only remember bits and pieces after that. I must have been in deep shock."

"Dad—now listen, Dad—"

"I tried to bury her, but I just couldn't finish the job. Then I—"

"For God's sake, don't you know what you're saying?"

"Yes, I know what I'm saying. I dragged her out of the grave and through the woods to a sawmill race that flows into the Rhine. Then I threw her into the water. She went all the way down." He looked at his hands, as if they were exhibits at a trial he was privately conducting, years after the fact. Then he began to cry.

The *Denebola* plunged, trembled, settled groaningly

on her wide beam, was lifted homeward again by the
force of many fathoms and the staunch sea wind. In the
saloon the lamps had toned to mere afterglow, a bearable level of illumination for his father, so secretly rav-
aged, a victim of the goodness of light. David sat
amazed, observing him; for the first time he saw him
as impaired beyond hope.

"Bullshit," David said. "It's the tumor. It must be.
Don't you understand, what you said just now was—
pure bullshit, it never happened."

His father continued to cry, from an emotion that
wasn't clearly imprinted on his face: He seemed neither
relieved nor sad, nor particularly penitent. It wasn't
unmanly of him, but David was shocked. At the same
time he felt an impulse to rude laughter, as if a ribbon
of mirth was being jerked through his body. Suppress-
ing it brought on a spate of hiccups. It was so fucking
absurd, and so terrifying—vision of Death as a low-
comedy figure with a cardboard scythe.

"Maybe," David said, "maybe you knew some woman
in Germany twenty-five years ago, but the rest of it—
Jesus. I'm sorry, I'm so sorry. I can't stand seeing you
like this. I want to help, but I just don't know what to
do."

He poured more rum for himself. His father sat
hunched forward with elbows on his knees, hands
folded at his mouth, blinking, pressing out more tears.

"Pauline," he said, "threatened my *life*, David. She
didn't care. She didn't understand that I had no background, that I had to work damned hard to win my
place in the Riordan family. You're still a young man.
Thank God you've never had to fight a war. So you
don't know yet what you'll do when there's enough
fear."

"Do we have to talk any more about this?"

"I haven't told you everything yet."

"But I don't want to hear any more! You're *sick*, Dad; and I just—don't believe it."

"You have to believe me. I thought, well, I've got a few months, there'll be time, I can handle it myself. But I know now I don't have time. When I go down again I might not be able to get back up."

The leap and fall of the *Denebola* sent them both sprawling helplessly; David had a quick look at the oscilloscope of the Loran-C, and at the compass. Then he went to help his father right himself.

"It's ridiculous. You couldn't kill anybody, you don't even like to hunt."

Frank dried his eyes with a pocket handkerchief. "I didn't think I could kill her, either. I remember thinking, *I've got to let go now, she'll die*. But I couldn't stop."

"You ought to go back to the stateroom and lie down."

"I'm not tired, I'm not *drunk,* and I haven't been confused or crazed by this thing in my head. In the war I killed Germans with honor, sometimes hand-to-hand. I killed in a passion, and I killed out of fear. Ten years later, in another kind of rapture, I killed Pauline Girda. Maybe if she'd been something else, a French or an English woman, I couldn't have done it. Maybe that night I was just killing another German who had threatened me. I've always wondered how it could've been so easy, and why it was—so essential that she die."

"You couldn't have lived with yourself this long. The guilt would have used you up."

Frank nodded, slowly. "I've suffered. I've had a soul-sickness for twenty-five years. Not entirely because of Pauline. The really horrible thing was, she had a child. A little girl named Anneliese. She couldn't have been more than six years old at the time. She saw it."

David found that he still had some capacity for astonishment.

"What do you mean? Don't you see how crazy—if this little girl saw you...do anything to her mother, you wouldn't be here. They'd have thrown the goddam key away!"

He had spoken gently at first; then anger made him shout and jump up and slash the air with one hand, as if he were invisibly under attack by hornets. The ship rolled particularly hard at that moment, and David, despite his instinctive sense of balance, was slammed backwards painfully against a hanging locker, spilling most of his rum. He drank the rest and reached, possessively, for the bottle.

"No; all she saw was Pauline lying half-buried in the grave I tried to make. I was—wandering around, I think, out of my head, and I heard the girl crying for her mother. I must have scared Anneliese, coming up behind her. It was dark. She ran and fell down a hill and hurt herself, not too badly, but she was unconscious for a while. That's when I threw the body into the river."

David slumped down dispiritedly with the bottle of rum between his thighs, finding that he had to breathe through his mouth to pacify his queasiness. He had never been seasick in his life, but he was just holding on now, aching to be home.

"The girl would have told the police everything she saw."

"She did."

Finally David had to laugh, but it was highly stressed laughter, manic.

"She would have told them about *you,* I mean."

"Anneliese Girda didn't know about me. She never saw me. And I didn't know she existed until I saw her on her hands and knees beside—"

"For God's sake, you said you were screwing her mother, then you had to know—"

"Pauline worked as a designer for a toy manufacturer in Frankfurt. He was an old man, impotent, but extremely jealous of Pauline. We had to be very careful. She traveled a lot on business, so we met in other cities—Hamburg, Berlin. Anneliese lived with her grandparents, who owned a small pension in Bad Oberbeuern, at the edge of the *Schwarzwald*. I don't think Pauline saw much of her."

There was no way he would shut up, David realized. He felt feverish, restless, but drugged by his father's persistence. He saw that it was of no use to try to point out the gaps and flaws in the story that was endlessly unfolding; his father would only work harder embroidering detail elsewhere in order to divert him. It was also pointless to try to resist with silence. Better to have it all said and over with, then maybe they would both have peace for a little while.

David opened the bottle of rum and drank from the bottle.

"That's where you say it happened? What were you doing in the Black Forest?"

"Pauline rented a car, and we drove down from Frankfurt. We had engine trouble along the way, so it was late when we arrived. Instead of going directly to the pension, Pauline drove halfway up the mountain and we parked in a secluded spot that overlooked the river. I built a fire, we spread blankets, we made love..."

"In the woods?"

Frank smiled, briefly, a flash of his old hearty good humor that made David feel unsure of himself.

"You know the Krauts; they like it better behind a bush than they do in bed." He was sober again, hands clasped, staring at David. "Then Pauline told me she was pregnant."

"God," David said, and looked down, as if resenting the fact he had been made to respond. He outlasted a shiver, which was taken up by the larger jarring of the boat in the trough of a wave.

"She made her demands. I had to divorce Neddie, move to Germany, marry her. She was in a rage. She'd never talked to me that way before. No one had. It made me sick inside. I stopped her."

The bluntness, the inhumanity of the claim, dismayed David.

"It doesn't happen that way. You can't just kill somebody and walk away and never get caught."

"It happens. Sometimes in place of stealth there's dumb luck. I committed a crime of passion. Then I did everything wrong. I didn't try to cover my tracks. I don't even know what happened to the shovel. Maybe I threw that in the river too. I drove the rented car north, abandoned it in the first city I came to, caught a train back to Frankfurt. I just sat in my apartment for two days, waiting for the police. I would have confessed to the first person who showed up at my door. If I had gone outside I would have blurted it in a bar, gone down on my knees on a street corner. That's how bad off I was."

"Why didn't you?"

"I had a phone call from Savannah. I talked to you, David. You wanted to know when I was coming home. You missed me so much, you said. Didn't I love you any more? That woke me up. I hung up the phone and dressed and walked out of the nightmare. Twelve hours later I was home."

Rum was insatiably demanding rum; that was dangerous, he couldn't handle it like his father could, but on the other hand drinking rum had narrowed the limits in which he was required to function. David felt giddy and bereft, remembering the child he'd been, now recalling as well the tearful phone call which had fetched his father home so many years ago. That much, at least, was true.

"It was that easy. You just—walked out of the nightmare."

"But it's always been right behind me, Davey. Even in broad daylight. I can't begin to tell you what the dark was like, for so many years."

"Nothing ever happened? Nobody found out?"

"One of our German representatives was in Savannah a few months later; he had a newspaper with him, and there was a summary of the—the Pauline Girda case."

David looked up sharply. His head felt as if it were about to sail off his shoulders; he had to hold it still by anchoring one hand in his hair. His father seemingly had stepped into a trap he couldn't get out of. But David was worried. Maybe he hadn't.

"I just glanced through the account, I was afraid to show too much interest. Pauline's body washed up on the French side of the river, and that complicated matters for the police. They didn't have much else to go on. I told you, we were careful about our affair. Are you sick, David?"

"You're *making* me sick. Where's—the goddam newspaper now?"

"I didn't keep it."

"You didn't keep it. But I could find—a copy of that newspaper if I looked."

"Save yourself the trouble, David."

"You got away with murder, and you never told anybody?"

"No."

"Why in the name of God did you have to tell me?"

David said with a fierce grin, willing to share any joke, no matter how obscure.

"Because of Anneliese Girda."

David winced and went back to the bottle.

"What about her?"

"I have to know—that she's all right. That she has a life, a good life."

"What difference does it make now?"

"It's the only way I can have any peace before I die. But I know I don't have the time to...David, for the last ten years I've been putting money in a safe-deposit box at the Bank of Atlanta. Almost two hundred thousand dollars."

"Two hundred—" The weight and reasonableness of money in the bank, a possibility that the facts of distant murder were preserved in newspapers' morgues, destroyed more of David's resistance. It was almost as if he could see faces now, imagine the displaced bones of a broken neck. His heart thrashed like a live fish in the hand. "Oh, no," he said dully.

"It's for Anneliese," Frank said. "But I was always afraid to go back to Germany. There's no statute of limitations on murder."

"Safe-deposit box? Where's the key?"

"In my desk at home. Right-hand drawer. The box is in Anneliese's name. You have a power of attorney from the bank, so you can open the box no matter what happens to me. I want you to see that Anneliese gets the money."

"I suppose—that means you know where she is."

"No. My brother will help you find her. You can trust Joby Ben. Tell him everything, David. It doesn't matter now. Just find the girl for me."

David had another drink. It had no taste, only a mild afterfire. He realized he'd had too much, that it all needed to come back up, and quickly, or he'd be useless the rest of the night. He got to his feet, swaying, lifting his knees high, doing a tricky balancing act on the sole of the cabin.

"Careful, David—"

Little bits of time were getting lost. The next thing he knew his face was inches from his father's. His stomach burned.

"Swear to me it's true, you killed her, swear that!"

There was no flinching, no anxiety to be forgiven in the set, brave eyes. The giant had fallen, but he was unbroken.

"Accept it, David. Accept what a man can do. And try to do better."

"Then I hope you suffered! I hope you hurt like you've hurt me."

A flicker of pain in his father's eyes, attribution of the necessary wound.

"You poor son of a bitch. You miserable bastard. I love you. Goddam you! Father. Father. *Daddy!* God."

Frank put his arms around David and held him. He had turned his face away. David began to sob.

10 Wind and fierce weather awakened him; he was shaken in the bunk of the aft stateroom, one leg hanging off, hands clawing for purchase on the taut red-and-yellow blanket. The lights were low, like radium held in dense glass. His mouth was parched, as if he had been drinking seawater. He felt hollow behind the eyes, where nervy, flitting dreams still played against the hard whiteness of skull.

David sat up and nearly swooned as he braced himself against the continual plunge and roll of the ship. The head door was swinging, banging. Where had they come from, and where were they going? Worse, how long had he lain there, passed out cold? He remembered the storm jib, the autopilot, and was gripped by a shudder of distrust.

Perhaps his father had gone topside and had taken over at the helm. He needed to retch, and staggered into the head, but not much came up. His head ached, but it was solid, clean pain, he didn't feel poisoned. Then he had got rid of the rum in time, although he couldn't remember throwing up.

What he remembered, starkly, was the bad news, a life coming apart before his eyes, revealing dry rot where once a marvel had stood. His eyes were fuming, he banged his helpless head on a cabinet above the little sink before he could back out of the compartment.

Being alone, in near-darkness below, with the ship seeming to run blindly in seas that felt monstrous, scared him. But as his head stopped spinning he became aware of the reassuring throb of the Volvo diesel. He felt better. His father had gone to power, he could cope, he hadn't had another attack. It was sudden light that brought on the convulsions, light passed on brilliantly by the plagued brain in surges hot enough to blast nerve fibers to skeins of ash. He would be in his element now: rain, wind, and dark.

David went forward, stopping at the electrical panel to turn on more lights below.

A couple of circuits were weak; lights flickered. He looked into the forward stateroom and knocked on the door of the head, but his father wasn't inside. He put on an Ensolite jacket over his racing suit and checked the heading at the nav station. The autopilot was still engaged. They were off course for Tybee Light on a new heading, which would put them well to the east of Savannah Beach in another hour and eventually bring them to the North Carolina coast in the vicinity of Cape Fear.

He made the course correction, to a port tack, opened the companionway hatch, and went halfway up into the dark and an easing rain.

They were running sixty degrees to the wind on some steep, fast swells. The pedestal-mounted wheel of the *Denebola* turned independently of any guiding hand, as it should have done. But the cockpit was empty.

David scrambled out and shut the hatch, screaming for his father. He couldn't see anything, fore or aft, but as he listened for Frank's voice he could hear a flutter in the jib, as if a seam or two had given way.

David tumbled below again and flipped on the spreader lights. He was already shaking with the knowledge of how futile it was.

Topside, the floodlights, mounted on the main and mizzen spreaders, illuminated every inch of teak deck from the bowsprit to the stern pulpit: the stainless-steel hardware, the sheets and rigging, the ropes and safety lines. All the hatches were dogged down.

The lights also showed him some awesome waves.

The automatic bilge pump started as the cockpit flooded to his ankles. He had to grab the wheel to keep from being thrown to starboard out of the cockpit. He looked around again, frantically.

David noticed the taut Dacron safety line then, running from a midships cleat over the top of the safety rail and into the water.

He started out of the cockpit, but the tilt and plunge of the ship reminded him that he would be overboard in a matter of moments if he wasn't careful. He unloaded a safety harness from a cockpit storage compartment and clipped line to it, inched his way forward to the mast and secured the line to a ringbolt there. Then he scrambled for the safety line in the water, and began to pull, bracing his feet against a hatch, his back to the mast.

He got nowhere; the deep weight at the other end of the line would not yield.

The *Denebola* rode steadily down a dark, hanging wave. David was inundated, fought his way up off the deck reaching for more of the suddenly slack line. This time he gained a few feet, and suddenly it was coming, coming up out of the dark and wind at him.

David groaned and pulled harder, the skin of his wet hands wearing, blood bursting beneath his nails.

A new wave bounced David's head off the mast, filling it with sparklers. He sat up choked, hacking on salt. In the outer edge of the light cast by the spreader floods, water and light combined to form a billowy, translucent green sphere. David saw a glum hand floating, rising well into the sphere; the flop-over of weighted arm; then the lift and upward roll of a shoulder, like a shrug, and the emerging head, matted black head nearly upright and turning to David with the full, smooth, sated roll of the body, the bleached and eerie face catching, leaflike, to green, as if it were some kind of versatile fire that burned out there.

Then another swell turned him loosely back like a big dog on a leash, lifted Frank McNair higher, held him in bubbling suspension for an instant before the irresistible gravity of the deep sent him cascading down toward the frantic, hauling hands of his son.

11 At a quarter past one in the morning, the Okatee Yacht Club was unnaturally alight; a small hellish storm of red lights was caught between the overarching trees at the entrance and the cypress-board sides of the two cottages that contained clubhouse and restaurant. Below the cottages an ambulance had been driven past the long boat sheds to the corner of the concrete pier, near the harbormaster's office.

Reba parked where she wouldn't be in the way, walked quickly through wind and a scatter of rain past official cars—Thunderbolt police, Chatham County sheriff, Coast Guard—and down wooden steps to the pier where the *Denebola* and a Coast Guard cutter were moored end to end. She recognized Lee Darbee and Byrum Hollins sharing an umbrella beside the ambulance. She and David lived only five minutes from the yacht club, but apparently everyone else had been notified, summoned before she had.

"Sweets?" Reba had been only half awake and not nervous during the quick drive, but now she began to shiver. They looked at her. "Where's David?"

Darbee gestured toward the *Denebola*.

Reba drifted automatically toward the midships gangplank, but Byrum said, "Maybe you better wait with us another minute or two. Shouldn't be long."

The look on Reba's face urged him into an explanation of sorts. "No, no, he's perfectly all right. Captain Niles of the Coast Guard is talking to him. Bill and Mark Sams are with him too."

"Lawyers? Does David need a lawyer?"

"No, you see, it's a routine investigation. Coast Guard has to be called in whenever there's a fatality at sea."

"Why don't you take the umbrella?" Darbee said. "Rain just won't let up."

"Have some of this hot coffee," Byrum said. "Haven't touched it yet. You like it black, don't you, Reba?"

Reba nodded and took the styrofoam cup from him. She looked vaguely at the waiting ambulance.

"Where's Frank?" she asked Byrum.

"Mitch is looking at him now, you know there has to be a certificate, but they'll be bringing the—uh—they'll bring him topside any time now."

Reba tasted the coffee, and it burned the tip of her tongue.

"Does anybody know what happened?"

"They were beating their way home using a storm jib," Darbee said. "Frank went topside to look around, and David said he probably dozed off for ten, fifteen minutes; when he woke up Frank hadn't come back. A little later he heard a thumping noise against the hull, and when he investigated, well, Frank was overboard, tied up in the safety line. The way it looks, the jib was coming apart and Frank may have had some idea about letting it blow free of the ship and switching to power. He should have called David, of course. Maybe he tried to release the foreguy and the lazy guy tightened under his waist and heaved him overboard. For some reason Frank wasn't wearing a vest. David had a hell of a time getting him aboard. He still can't open the fingers of his right hand."

Reba felt the beginning of facial neuralgia in one cheek, and stroked it.

"Doesn't sound to me—like he's all right."

Some men in slickers had come topside to the cockpit

of the *Denebola*. They were handling, with difficulty, the body of Frank McNair, which was wrapped in something rainproof. It was slippery aboard and the boat was rocking. They fumbled the body getting it to the pier. Reba wanted to go and help, they were showing him so little *consideration*. She began to cry in the rain.

Darbee and Sweets went instead to assist the other men. With five pairs of hands the task was made simpler, the body seemed light and insubstantial as they placed it on a stretcher and wheeled the stretcher a little way to the ambulance.

As the body went in, Reba could make out the shape of Frank's head in the canvas shroud, and she thought of the defiled brain cooled at last in a cataclysmic sea; wistfully she imagined him smiling. Her neuralgia was out of control, the vision of one eye blurred. The attendants had shut the doors. David appeared on deck and he stood there unsteadily with the ambulance lights on his face, watching, his eyes slowly shrinking into the dark as they drove his father away.

Then he shook hands, using his left hand, with two Coast Guard officers, and jumped ashore. He landed, a little off balance, near Reba, and she put the umbrella down and reached out to steady him.

"There wasn't anything I could do," he said.

"I know."

She tried to hold him more tightly, to get a better grip, and David groped back at her; it was awkward, they were both in slickers and had no firm sense of each other's bodies.

"Who's with mother?"

"Everybody. Helen Sams, the Beauregards, Monsignor Carnes."

"Let's go," David said.

He walked ahead of her, paused for a few words with their friends gathered at the foot of the stairs. Reba understood that they would take care of the *Denebola*. David lunged up the steps three at a time. He was standing by their car, a red Porsche, taking off his rain slicker, when Reba caught up.

He took one look at her distressed face and squinched clouded eye and said, a touch impatiently, "You can't drive. I'll drive."

"All right." She was glad to be spared the effort. The pain had penetrated all the way to the roots of her tongue, it was crawling along the scalp. Even her hair hurt. David was always good in an emergency, she thought passively. Nobody could ever imagine what he'd suffered for the past couple of hours. She was stricken with sympathy, powerless to talk about it. Death didn't unnerve her nearly so much as blood, or a broken bone. A broken heart.

They were both fast drivers, but tonight, getting to Neddie's, he thoroughly frightened her on the wet roads. He drove as if his father's death had given him the freedom to extend the limits of allowable risk, as if he were, briefly, not to be touched by Fate. Reba gulped two Percodans from her purse, knowing they would make her groggy, but it was either that or total incompetence, and the remainder of the night would be long.

"Sharon all right?"

"Yes. Peg Mackey came over to stay until we get home."

Despite the speed he maintained even near the center of town, David was driving mostly with his left hand. The right one looked bruised and fat as it sat clumsily on the wheel; the fingers were frozen inward in a spasm, the nails jet-black from underlying rupture, as if all of his heavy grief had been forced there by the heart, swelling the hand to the bursting point.

"David, your hand—"

"Nothing to worry about. Mitch could have given me a shot of Luminol. But it probably would have knocked me out, and I don't have the time right now."

She probed carefully, hoping to relieve some of the pressure.

"David, what happened to him?"

"I honestly—don't know. An accident."

"Yes. But they said he wasn't wearing a vest. That wasn't like Frank."

"No, it wasn't. We all make mistakes."

"Watch where you're going. *Please*."

"Sorry." David downshifted, made a wide skating turn into Bull Street; the lights of the big house on the east of Governor's Square appeared through the dense, pale, dripping trees.

"God," David said in a hushed voice, "doesn't it look sad? All lit up and waiting for him."

He mugged to get his face under control; glanced at her with a sweet, unexpected smile that nearly moved them both to tears. Despite her dizziness and dampened neuralgia, Reba was thrilled, touched in a poignant, sexual way. She wanted him to know, and put a hand on his rigid right forearm as he parked the car, hitting the curb awkwardly with a front tire.

David's face had reset, he had raised his guard, there was too much iron in his gray, furious eyes. Reba wondered if Frank had told him about the tumor. If so, he shouldn't seem this way, so angry and dismayed, there was something wrong that only David knew.

What if—the possibility had been at the edge of her mind for some time—Frank had killed himself to spare them all the pitiful spectacle of his decline and death? How would she feel?—Despairing, but not angry. Relieved that he wouldn't have to suffer. Death by drowning was supposed to be almost as easy as dying in your sleep. A few moments of suffocation, and it was over.

Perhaps David didn't see it that way. He had once limped through two miles of wilderness with a broken shoulder and a knee no man should have been able to stand on, dragging the other, unconscious victim of a Jeep accident. He'd saved them both through sheer determination. He would have wanted to fight for his father's life, too—he had nearly ruined his hands to bring Frank aboard the boat, too late.

All right, that was the source of his anger. And it was going to take time, she would just have to understand and help him.

Jasper let them in. Red-eyed, inarticulate in his grief, the old houseman shook David's better hand until David winced. Reba kissed the Negro's seamed cheek and led him gently aside.

Neddie had come halfway down the winding stair on the arm of Monsignor Carnes. She had her Bible and rosary in one hand. She looked pleasantly distracted, like the guest of honor at a middle-of-the-night surprise party.

David hugged his mother.

"You're not to blame yourself," she said in a clear loud voice.

"I don't."

"I know it isn't the thing to do any more, but we'll wake him in the parlor. Not that I have anything against Tucker and Harcum's, but all the men in this family were waked in the parlor. I want his friends to see him, one last time, in the house where he lived."

"All right, Mother."

David walked her down the stairs to Reba. There were other men and women waiting in the front room. Neddie smiled and touched Reba's cheek with an outstretched hand that almost missed. Reba saw that her single, metallic eye was wild with vacancy.

"I never thought I'd outlive Frank," she said. "I'm not prepared. I don't know how I'm going to do it."

"Mother Riordan, you still have so much to live for."

"Thank you," Neddie said graciously. Still smiling, she relinquished David and passed into the front room.

David leaned against the doorjamb and looked soberly at his clawed hand. He tried to flex it.

"See if there's coffee?" he asked Reba.

"I could fix you something to eat."

"Yeah, I think so. A sandwich. I threw everything up, seems like hours ago. It was rough out there."

He glanced suddenly and apprehensively at the stairs, as if he'd heard a peremptory voice.

"I'll be upstairs. Dad's room."

"Okay." Reba went into the kitchen. As always after taking Percodan, she felt about nine feet tall and one inch wide. Someone had already made a big pot of coffee. She found ham and cheese in the refrigerator, a fresh loaf of bread baked only hours ago by Neddie's cook, Louellen. The bread was still warm. She made a sandwich, poured coffee, carried everything up to Frank's bedroom.

David wasn't there. He had turned on the desk lamp, and the right-hand drawer of the desk hung open. She put the tray down and looked in the bathroom. No David.

Reba met Jasper on the stairs as she was going down.

"Is David in the front room?"

"No, ma'am, he gone to Atlanta."

"*Atlanta?* What? You mean, right now?"

"He left about a minute ago. In a big hurry."

"For God's sake, he's in no condition to drive to Atlanta by himself tonight!"

She ran past Jasper to the foyer, went outside on the stone porch. The lights of Governor's Square were dimmed by a cataract of rain. The Porsche was gone. She couldn't believe it.

Reba whirled to find Jasper in the doorway. Her panic jarred them both.

"Why?"

"He just said I was to tell you and Miss Neddie—"

"God damn it," Reba said, wiping the rain out of her eyes, "he'll kill himself!"

But that wasn't it. She was most afraid of the impulse, not the possible consequences. David was good at the wheel and not a wild man, he would come home again. Still, she felt saddened, excluded, not useful. She had known too much, was half prepared for Frank's death and the large task of seeing David through. He was gone now, but she would wait. It was what she had to offer: all of herself.

Reba went back inside before she could be drenched to the skin.

12   Dr. Bill Peck was a frail man with the languid gestures and sore eyes of an old priest offering the five A.M. mass in an empty church. He wore a faded Tartan plaid robe over his pajamas. There was a closed-up chill of air conditioning in the den of his home in one of Atlanta's elegant neighborhoods, a staleness of cigars. He collected letters of men of medicine—Lister, Pasteur, Fleming, Cushing—and some of them were displayed in the den, along with their photographs. While David drank strong coffee and contemplated the unremarkable surfaces of genius, the neurosurgeon pulled a slide projector and screen from his closet and set them up.

"Simplest way to explain what was happening to your father is to give you my introductory lecture on the human brain, the one I give when they call me up from the high school." He mounted several slides on the automatic projector and dimmed the overhead lights in the den. "I wish I had Frank's angiogram here, you could see for yourself exactly what the tumor was like. But I can point out to you where it was located, what areas were involved."

The screen lit up with a full-color schematic drawing. The power of the Kodak lamp also seemed to ignite in Peck a lifelong ardor for his subject.

"You have to see it the way I do, David, to appreciate what a fantastic piece of work it is. The brain's not just a static mass, it lives and pulsates with each beat of the heart. That much we can see. But what we don't see are the electrochemical interactions, the passages of sodium ions, the minute, mysterious transfers of energy that give us life, memory, intelligence, ability."

Click. Click. More views of the brain, from different angles, appeared on the luminous screen.

"There are ten billion neurons. And we know as little about them as we know about the planets of Andromeda."

David looked both interested and confounded; he looked, angular in a Barcalounger, tense as plate glass.

"Dad said he wasn't in pain. Was he lying?"

"No. The brain has no sensory nerves. Doesn't need them, it's well protected."

"But it can't protect itself against tumors. Why was it so hopeless, why couldn't you operate?"

Peck stood to one side of the screen, and put his finger on the thalamus.

"This is where the CAT located the tumor—the computerized axial tomography scanner. It's a machine that takes dozens of X-ray pictures from all angles. The angiogram confirmed my worst feelings about the tumor—that it was a malignant glioblastoma, involved with a major blood vessel, and beginning to spread into adjacent areas, interfering with the flow of cerebrospinal fluid within the brain."

David's cup rattled against the saucer; he cleared his throat, plaintively.

"You couldn't get it out?"

"David, think of a bowl of Jell-O. Suppose you make it with a stone the size of an apricot suspended deep in the gelatin. Afterward you decided to dig in with a spoon to get at the pit. By the time you've finished, that nice firm bowl of Jell-O is a churned-up mess. Churn the brain that way, the patient can't survive."

"Flashing lights bothered him. Gave him the shakes, he couldn't control himself."

"In the human embryo, eyes form in the midbrain region at about seven weeks of age. So the midbrain is the center of vision. A little bit down the stem we come to the medulla, which controls breathing. Here, above the midbrain, in this deep fissure, is a motor strip controlling the activity of the left and the right sides of the body. The tumor wasn't symmetrical, they never are—it was reaching into a lot of sensitive areas and bound to cause seizures, which we couldn't regulate either, even with Dilantin."

David studied the image on the screen and thought of the tumor as a third, lidless eye that had matured inward until it became powerful, staring the brain into fits and nightmares. In the nimbus of fatigue around his head, hallucinations jiggled.

"How long do you think he had the tumor?"

Peck shut off the slide projector and dialed the lights up again. He poured coffee for himself.

"It could have been there for most of his life. I don't know where it came from, or when, or why it suddenly decided to grow."

"What could the tumor do to him? Change his personality?"

Peck rubbed his eyes. "Are you talking about a psychological disorder?"

"Yes."

"I'd say there was a possibility that a thalamic tumor could cause a subtle personality change. The prefrontal lobes generally govern how we behave and what we believe, although there are other regions—the hypothalamus, the amygdala—which, if infarcted, can change the way we react to stimuli. A normally timid man can easily become enraged."

"Could Dad make up a...a wild story, with no basis in fact, and believe, absolutely believe it happened?"

"Hmm. Before he told you this story, how did he appear to you? Confused about where he was, and what was happening to him? Was he behaving irrationally? Did he make incoherent statements or show a loss of memory?"

"No."

"You don't want to tell me the story, but I can see that it's upset you. Was it a long story, with a lot of convincing detail? It was. And you questioned him about the details? Was he logically consistent, or did he contradict himself?"

David shook his head. "He said things—I can check out. If I want to."

"I'd be inclined to rule out an organically derived psychosis. But—when a man learns he has inoperable cancer, the news can be devastating emotionally."

"What do you mean?"

"I'm out of my depth here, but I'm sure a psychiatrist would confirm that Frank—or anyone else under extreme stress—could exhibit a fixed delusional pattern without impairing his ability to function in the world."

David's right hand, less swollen now, the mottled fingers relaxed part way open, lay palm up on the gleaming nut-brown Naugahyde of the Barcalounger. The chair creaked a little beneath his slowly settling weight. His mind seemed jammed at the point of an irreversible conviction.

"But Frank took the news well," Peck continued. "I've known him for half my life. He wasn't a man to go to pieces, no matter what ordeal he might be facing. I don't think I need to tell you, David, I'm sorry as hell. I had a lot of respect for your father."

David found his voice, which was cracked. "We all did." He looked at the neurosurgeon with the glarey-eyed passion of a soul half-dead for sleep. "I'd better be going," he muttered.

"Back to Savannah?"

"No. I have some business at the bank downtown, soon as they open." He looked at his Rolex watch, becoming frustrated. "I can't make out the time," he said bitterly.

"Quarter to six." Peck yawned. "Jennifer's slumber-party friends are strewn all over the place upstairs, even in the hall. But you're welcome to the couch there, David. I could stand another hour in the sack myself, before rounds."

13 They were trout fishing in the Sangre de Cristos at seven thousand feet, in a meadow surrounded by glowing aspen and the peaks of mountains snowbound to the timberline. The color of the sky was a scalding, high-country blue, not filtered through layers of moisture and dust particles. In shaded coves along the stream that had begun to flow heavily with meltwater, snow banks were hanging on, crusty and with razor edges, in places still deep as a man's thigh.

David and his father fished thirty yards apart, absorbed, solitary, in their high-gallused waders and slouch hats looking like odd birds of prey. They fished a landscape of smooth brown stones bright as eyes, trembling with vision beneath the clear water. The river came down to them in a peal of light that shriveled the senses, and dwindled in a vein of quietness deeper than the sky.

David's line backlashed into a windfall and he worked quickly, guiltily to free it, before his father could turn and notice his predicament. As he tugged at the line, he became intricately tangled up in it. Meanwhile his father had caught and netted a gorgeous rainbow. He walked upstream to show David, smiling, his face fixed in the crude emulsified ridges and shadows of an underexposed snapshot. The rose-dappled trout flivvered in his upraised hand. The water was higher now, flooding over the tops of his waders, filling them. David, struggling to free himself, tore the fine black line to shreds. His father reached out to give him the fish. It slipped from both their hands. His head was sidelong in the current now, and the water roared like a falls into his open mouth. It looked as big and dark as a cavern. The fish swam inside, a last moody gleam of silver. Panicky, flailing, David swam after the fish, knowing they were both about to be swallowed.

14   At a quarter past ten David was in the main office of the Bank of Atlanta. He was unknown there, the family firm did business with another local bank. His power of attorney was accepted without question. In the safe-deposit vault he removed the big steel box. It seemed as heavy as a well-filled garbage can. He lugged it into the cubicle reserved for him and closed the door.

The money was all his father had said it would be: layer upon layer, thin stacks of used bills. There were two sheets of an accounting which Frank had kept, with a variety of pens, the last entry just three weeks ago.

Old deep secret money, hundreds and fifties and twenties, ten years' worth of formalized penance, disturbed now by David's hand and releasing slow gases in the neutral vault air, a baneful stench that brought a cold sweat to his face. Here was buying power for a more livable hereafter. A treasure trove obscene in its smugness. The shrewd discipline of a man of means.

Other men would lick their lips; David itched to burn it. For the money proved nothing except the fact that an obsession had existed along with a pearly growth that might have been dormant in his father's head for most of his adult life.

It had been a useful, well-ordered, profitable, and enjoyed life, largely without pain or distraction except perhaps for the subdued fantasy that preceded an explosive maturity for the seed-tumor. The fantasy was murder, and the accumulated money held no authority for David: It was false testimony.

He should have felt better for this judgment, but in fact he was trembling in the too-chill brightness of the little room, as if by uncovering the money he had breathed contamination, a teething virus that gripped him in the bones.

Did you kill yourself? David thought. *I don't blame you. But how could you leave me like this? I don't know what to believe.*

His father had planned meticulously the ending of his life. A body lost at sea poses serious legal problems, so he had arranged to be drowned but recoverable, in such a way that there could be no onus on the family. No one but David would ever have to know why. Frank McNair had plunged into the sea not as a riddled, deranged man, but assured, through trust in his son, of his ultimate redemption.

His confession had been no less meticulous, David had to concede that. An incredible story, but well-made. David, having assumed an ornament of fantasy, turned this ornament around and around in his mind, looking for tarnish, for an eggshell fragility he could pulverize. Instead, he was mesmerized by a certain hard brilliance, an inner glint of psychological verity. *In the war I killed Germans with honor. In a passion. Out of fear. Ten years later, in another kind of rapture...*

If it was true, if his father had committed murder, then there was someone else who knew the story exactly as he had told it. She would know what only the two of them could ever know, because she had been there.

David looked again at the name on the card, the nominal owner of the safe-deposit box.

Anneliese Girda.

He put the box back in the vault and went home.

15 On a sullen April afternoon, Joby Ben McNair walked the six blocks from the De Soto Hilton on East Liberty Street to Governors' Square. He didn't own a presentable mourning suit, so he'd changed into dress greens on arrival, after a tedious trip by Starlifter from Main/Rhine airport to the Military Air Command terminal in Charleston, South Carolina, and a shuttle flight down the coast to Hunter AFB.

It was his third visit. The last had occurred about twelve years ago, following the wedding of David and Reba in Reba's home town, Columbus. He and Frank had taken a two-day float trip down the black Ogeechee, drinking white rum and eating cold Chinese food, fishing for striped bass in the watery front yards of romantic old plantation houses. Joby Ben was coming up on full colonel then, and Frank pretty much had what he wanted from life too: The Old Man was finally in his grave and Frank was running things, although he hadn't yet changed the name from Riordan and Company to Riordan/McNair, as if he superstitiously feared some sort of withering blast from the direction of D. C.'s resting place amid the old brick tombs and graybeard yews of Colonial Park Cemetery.

No matter, the company was flourishing and Frank had just shelled out almost nine million dollars for the old Henry Ford place, eighty thousand wilderness acres in two counties, part of which they were traveling through on the lugubrious current of the Ogeechee. Much of the land was used to grow pulpwood trees to feed the big Savannah mill that smelled so evilly on the northeast wind.

Riordan and Company turned out a hell of a lot of toilet paper in that mill, enough in a year to blot up a fair-sized Georgia swamp. Joby Ben couldn't resist joking about the tissue-weight foundation of the family fortune, because he knew for a fact that Frank was ten years old and able to read the outhouse catalogues cover to cover before he realized there *was* such a thing as toilet paper. Now that he was irrevocably rich, Frank didn't like to be reminded of the sore old days; not that he had pretensions, Joby Ben decided, but because his upraising had been so bitter, his struggle to escape mean origins so frustrating, it made his blood thick and angry to think about those times.

Joby Ben turned into Bull Street, passing an elegant hodgepodge of Greek Revival porches, Victorian gingerbread, wrought-iron gates, and tiered verandahs; a cat slumbered in a cave of warm ivy, one orange paw extended stealthily onto the sidewalk. Windless dogwood petals drifted down into the glare of his JAG brass, as if dislodged by the weight of his footsteps. A pedestaled man in knickers and a cocked hat peered greenly at him through the split trunk of a tree. Spanish moss was scanty, almost missing from the oaks and gums along the many neat squares. It was an air-breathing plant, phasing into memory as a result of automobile pollution.

For Joby Ben, adolescence had been simpler; in the beginning he lacked Frank's grit craving for the finer things of life. But the war, which he had fought from Sicily to Berlin, had opened his eyes. Europe was a scorched mess but still fascinating, and he coped well with the military mind and hankered to give orders himself after battlefield promotions to master sergeant. He was barely twenty-one on V-E day, faced with the choice of re-upping or going back to the rough, mostly illegal ways of earning a decent living open to him in the mountains of north Georgia.

Frank suggested another alternative, and bullied him into taking advantage of his G.I. Bill. In his moodier, younger days, Frank had whipped him often and painfully, and Joby Ben was still in awe of his brother's great strength and glowering will. College was the quickest way out of the low life, and, having provided for his own future by marrying Neddie Riordan, Frank was now ambitious for his little brother.

Hitting the books hard after so much indifferent schooling was refined torture, but Joby Ben compensated by having an easy time with the coeds, who were swept under in waves by his casual advances. He already knew that good looks won the skirmishes in life, but charm took the battles. Joby Ben was a good drinking buddy. There was a touch of the country philosopher about him. He was observant and funny about his fellow human beings. He was cocky but not vain; he had nothing to be vain about. Except for a close similarity of frame, Joby Ben didn't resemble Frank. He had quite a case of the uglies: his mother's square, squashed-down face, beetling testy brows, a nose so small you couldn't find it the first time you looked, lips that were too meaty and seemed to be turning inside out when he smiled his chock-full, toothy smile. The Germans had been responsible for a deeply pocked cheekbone, a shot-away earlobe.

Those were the deficits, but there was something

meltingly, tenderly winsome about Joby Ben. He had a fair childish complexion that pinked sentimentally at times, and humidly lashed, bright-blue eyes as lovely as a woman's. They seemed to be in the wrong face, as if someone changing a billboard had only partially pasted the tough, cigarette-selling mug over the dreamy *eau de cologne* girl. His gaze implied a poetic soul, a vast imagination that didn't in fact exist. Joby Ben had a pragmatic, hard-shell legal mind, and he had done very well in his career as an Army lawyer.

Reaching Governor's Square, he reacted to the overflow of limousines glinting blackly around the stone hub of the Riordan house with a mixture of distaste and dread.

Negro drivers marked time in twos and threes, falling into aimless pecking orders, shedding the light of their pale shirts beneath the shade trees; in their presence, their springtime languor, the attitude of crossed arms and the angle of a napping head, he found something intoxicating: Here was vintage Old South, time imprisoned peacefully, a rich and elegant heritage preserved, velvet nights murmurous with the approval of ghosts. There was money in Savannah, but it flexed its muscle largely in defense of the past. The young strove to be cynical, but they existed in a weir of echoes, and the lotus was all around.

Frank's roots had taken here, but Joby Ben, after only an hour in town, felt a need to stir himself, walk too fast, hone an edge of recklessness, drink like a fool, do anything, to resist the climate and the agreeable somnolence.

He wasn't well known to his in-laws and didn't feel he belonged, even at his own brother's wake; perhaps that was why he'd chosen to dress officially, for the recognition and automatic status his rank conferred. Savannah had Hunter and it had Fort Stewart—a lot of local people owed their living to the military. It showed in the way the Negroes, particularly the younger ones, straightened as he went past them and mounted one side of the double stone steps to the porch of the house.

A tall black boy in a black suit let him in, and he stood bewildered for several moments in the haze of the long foyer that went back to a circular staircase and thronged parlor and dining room. A bit of reflecting brass shot at him through the crowd; it was brass on the massive bier that occupied the parlor.

Seeing the coffin gave him a mild fright, and he felt reluctant to meet anyone's eyes: Frank was the indestructible one, it was Joby Ben who had the touch of diabetes and the swelling in the prostate that sure as hell was going to mean trouble someday and the minor heart attack the medics didn't know about and which he seldom acknowledged even to himself. He could find no logic to this order of recall. He smelled food and wished he hadn't.

"Joby Ben?"

He turned, grimacing, toward Reba, for a couple of seconds not recognizing her as she lowered her head to squeeze past a stout colonnade of couples blocking the wide entrance to the front room. He had last seen her three years ago when she and David and their little girl—Sharon?—had stopped in Frankfurt on their way to the summer music festival in Salzburg. He'd always liked Reba, for no better reason other than that she shook hands well and always looked him in the eye, as if she were teasingly aware he was hiding affection for her.

As soon as she touched him, brushed his cheek with her lips, he sensed in Reba a timidity like his own, so he put an arm around her.

"Reba, you're still the prettiest girl any of us ever married."

"I was afraid you couldn't get here," Reba said.

"We've been trying a hell of a long-winded case, they won't miss me a coupla days."

"Don't know why you won't stay out the house with us."

"I don't want to be any bother, the hotel's comfortable. How's Neddie?"

"Holding up real good; she's been an example to all of us."

"David?"

"He'll make it. You know he'll never love anybody like he loved his father."

She said it as if he needed defending, as if Frank's strong presence had somehow made her marriage to David more secure.

"Don't you go gettin' way down, Reba; you got too much to offer to be anybody's second-best." He had seen Neddie, looking ancient in widow's weeds. She was seated in the front room, her back to the parlor in which Frank was being waked; there was a young plump priest beside her on the horsehair sofa. "Well, I'll just pay my respects to Neddie. Then I could use a stiff one, honey, no lie."

"Bourbon?"

"Old Grand-Dad, straight up."

But he never got close to Neddie. Not that he really wanted to. As Reba left, Neddie turned her head and looked directly at Joby Ben. In one significant glance she acknowledged him, put him in his place, and dismissed him forever.

After a while he went back to the parlor and looked at the body.

The shades were half drawn, the light in the parlor was soft, the made-up face mute and heroic on glowing silk. Joby Ben was feeling a little more confident. Even with his liabilities, he knew he could survive another twenty years. Just had to watch the diet and get regular, moderate exercise.

David found his uncle standing beside the coffin. He had brought the Old Grand-Dad with him. David looked bruised, desperate around the eyes; he was grim and stilted from nerves.

"All I can think of to say is that it's a damn shame. He had some good years left."

"There's a lot I need to talk to you about," David said, his voice harsh from strain.

"Any time, boy."

"Maybe tonight. I don't know, I may have to stay with Mother—can I call you, even if it's late?"

"I'm available," Joby Ben said, squeezing David's shoulder.

It was a gentle touch, well-meant, but it seemed to bring David almost to tears. He trembled and excused himself.

Looking after him, Joby Ben took a slow sip of bourbon, thinking, *He's a good boy. Frank taught him a few things. He can handle himself.*

But something had been gutting David, even as he stood talking to Joby Ben. Something that hurt far worse than the loss of his father.

Joby Ben looked in the coffin again, chafing with admiration.

So long, Frank. You had a terrific life. You made them respect you in Savannah. You were worth a goddam fortune. You had a son to love, and it's no good getting to be our age without a son. You had luck when you needed it. You incredible son of a bitch, you got away with *murder*.

Unless you talked too much before you died.

16 Neddie liked her garden best when it was lit the old-time way, by torches, which Jasper wrapped with cheesecloth and soaked in kerosene and set out for her in iron brackets along the walls; she liked the mellow spring evenings when her azaleas were in full bloom and stiff breezes kept the bugs away from their part of town. She needed, tonight, to prowl around, fuss with her pots and plantings, try to collect her thoughts and take a deep breath from time to time. Peering up at all the family faces, grave with condolence, sometimes reaching in vain for a name *(I haven't been too well for the longest time, Neddie, I expect that's why you didn't know me right off),* had been arduous for her, and, although she had wanted them there, they were in the end too many, they flickered like candles before her dimming eyes, consuming all the air around her head, drawing the breath of life from the house in which she needed to survive.

Now there was earth at her feet, smoke in her eyes, grit beneath her nails: *that* was living.

"This branch—" she said, poking her cane into a crimson cloud bank that was deformed by a single brown and crinkly bough, "some kind of burrowing beetle's got at it. And the one over there"—she pointed this time—"which your father and I brought all the way from the Okefenokee and planted when you were just a toddler, it'll be ruined if we don't spray soon. Frank was going to stop by the garden center today.

I suppose Jasper can do it next week, but spring is slipping by so fast this year."

She was diverted by the screech of a peacock as it flew clumsily but with a passion from its trellis perch to its mate at the rear of the garden; she drew closer to David, leaning a little more heavily on his right arm.

"Those peacocks. I never have liked them. They never amused me the way they did Frank. He could sit for hours and watch them strut their gaudy stuff. Maybe I'll get rid of them and have a cat again." She smiled. "Maybe I'll have the cat first, and see what happens."

"Mother, I think you ought to move in with us."

"Oh, no, David, you know Reba and I don't get on that well. And this is my home. I've always lived here. That house of yours, you'll have to forgive me, it's like the lobby of every Ramada Inn I've ever laid eyes on. But that's a matter of taste, I suppose. I just don't feel any sense of *privacy* with all those glass walls."

Neddie turned and gave him a long look and pursed her lips, as if it had occurred to her that his suggestion might in fact be an ultimatum, prompted by concern that she couldn't look after herself any more. She dug her fingers into his forearm, a show of strength.

"Now you know I'm perfectly fine here with Jasper and Louellen to run the house. I'll be content for you to stop by every day. I've got plenty to keep me busy. The memorial for Frank at the college. Plenty to do."

"Well, it has to be lonely for you. It'll be hard, Mother. You and Dad were never apart very often."

"His business, and his little fishing trips. That's about all."

"Didn't he go to Germany once? For almost a year?"

"That's right. When Papa bought that German paper company. Frank did a good job. I think Papa really began to accept Frank after that."

"I was too little to remember when he came back. Had he changed much?"

Neddie paused to set a lawn sprinkler at a different angle with the tip of her cane.

"I don't understand the question."

"Did you notice anything different about him?"

"No."

David pushed aside an overhanging branch of a fig tree; there was a quick starfall of moisture in the orange air.

"What I mean is—"

"I guess he did pine for a while," Neddie said reflectively. "For his little German sweetheart. But he got over it."

"His what?" David had stumbled, just a little, on the uneven bricks of the path. Neddie looked quickly at him.

"The girl he was courting over there. You had better take a pill tonight, try to get some sleep, David. You don't look good."

"I'll be all right. How did you know about that girl?"

Neddie sighed. "Oh, David, it's all ancient history, and I'm feeling kind of tired now."

"We'll go in. But I want you to—Mother, I need to know—did he ever tell you about her?"

His anxiety made her rigid. "Of course not! Frank had dignity. He would never have brought up any kind of sordid business no matter how much he needed my *forgiveness.*" Neddie cleared her throat, as if the memory of his peccadillo had instead inspired words of bitter condemnation. "But I'd hear him some nights carrying on in his sleep, grinding his teeth—" She looked suddenly at a high lace window of the house, perhaps expecting to see herself there, a listening shadow trying to comprehend the unstable passions of men. She withdrew, hunching a little; her face turned grim. "Calling her *name*—" Neddie started, amazed by the freshness of this outrage, and didn't say anything else for a while. Then she gestured, to clear the air.

"David, now, I hope what I'm saying doesn't serve to tarnish your father's image in your eyes. Frank was a young and vigorous man, and I never was in the best of health after I had you. Not to mention the big difference in our ages. All I really cared about was that he treat me with love and respect."

She closed the subject with a jab of her cane at a black spider in her path; it curled up into itself, as if reabsorbing the essence of its spilled life.

"Do you know her name?" David asked, spellbound.

"David, I don't understand your morbid interest in some trifling little—" Neddie wavered and shot him a look that was unmotherly, a jet of acid, as if she held all men accountable for her late husband's appetites. "Oh, all right, I *ought* to remember her name, he'd cry for her in his sleep like a whimpering dog. Pauline! Pauline! And I'd have to lie there and listen. There were times, I suppose, when it was almost enough to...make me jealous. Isn't that funny?"

Instead of laughing, she panted, undone by her own fervor; she turned a poor color.

David helped her into the house, where she refused to let him call the doctor. All she wanted, Neddie insisted, was to go to sleep. Louellen sat with her while David waited downstairs in the kitchen until he was sure his mother would be all right.

He and Jasper played dominoes and listened to some old records by Blind Lemon Jefferson, and David drank a great deal. Twice he excused himself and went to the dark parlor where his father was; he came back the last time haggard with grief and almost unable to contain his wildness. He drank more and finally left for home at twelve-thirty in the morning, in such a state that Jasper was worried he'd never make it.

17 Reba was awakened by Sharon climbing into the bed with her.

There was a lamp on in one corner of the bedroom. She had left the floor-to-ceiling windows open earlier, before falling asleep with a copy of the new Taylor Caldwell in her hand. A breeze that smelled of backwater came through the fiberglass screens.

"Where's Daddy?" Sharon asked, sitting crosslegged in her flimsy nightgown. She had a dried milk-mouth from an earlier trip to the kitchen.

"I don't know; what time is it?" Reba looked at the clock beside the bed. Twenty past one. Her left arm was waking more slowly than the rest of her, it felt prickling and numb.

"I heard him drive in a little while ago," Sharon said. "There's a light on in the clubhouse."

The clubhouse was a low stone-and-pecky-cypress building at the foot of the sloping back lawn, by the river and a small-boat dock. Reba and David did most of their heavy entertaining in the clubhouse.

She raised up in bed and looked toward the river; there was a ladder of light from a jalousied window lying across the green-willow tree.

"That's where he is, then. I guess he wants to be alone right now."

"Could I sleep with you?"

"Sure you can! Just curl up right here."

"Will Daddy move me when he comes to bed?"

"He'll move you."

Sharon picked up a glass from the night table and sniffed it.

"That was just a little something to help me sleep better, baby."

"Everybody's drinking too much," Sharon said.

"I can handle my likker, kid," Reba said, and she flopped down cross-eyed. Sharon giggled.

Reba was reaching out to pull her close when a shotgun went off in the clubhouse.

Reba sat up, momentarily filled with disbelief; Sharon was openmouthed, she looked confused. Reba slipped off the bed and started for the windows, then stopped, her hands raised: It was as if the slow odorous exhalation from the river turned into a freezing wind, a howl that blanched her; she turned back and ran from the bedroom, barefoot, all but naked in her pearly nightgown. There was stark terror in her face.

Everybody's drinking too much.

She ran with the sound of the gun booming in her head, like thunder in a barrel, repeating itself as she approached the clubhouse. She remembered David as he had looked following the wake: exhausted, bereft, beaten.

"Mother!" Sharon screamed, as if she'd fallen on the outside stairs and hurt herself, but Reba winced and kept going, she was almost skimming across the big lawn. A seared window vomited glass at her and she cowered on the flagstones surrounding the clubhouse, then groped at the door and threw herself inside, too panicked to scream.

It was different from what she had imagined; in some ways, worse.

David stood near the center of the room. He looked like a ghost in all the gunsmoke. He had lowered his slide-action shotgun. About half of the paneled wall on the river side of the clubhouse was demolished. Framed photographs of David and his father in chummy attitudes hung tattered. Of boy and man nothing was left, nothing. A muscle throbbed in his jaw. But as the smoke thinned she could see that he wasn't bleeding anywhere.

They stared at each other. His eyes looked terrible, they looked gored.

Sharon came into the clubhouse and bumped against her mother's elbow. She hung back, half behind Reba, tears in her eyes. Reba was aware that her feet hurt. She glanced down at torn and bleeding toes. Her teeth began to chatter from shock and anger. She glared at David.

"My *God*. What next?"

"Sorry," he said. "I don't know why I did it." The shotgun slipped from his fingers and clattered on the floor; Reba flinched. "I don't know why," he said again, with a slight sigh.

She limped across the room, not caring what else might be broken underfoot, and put her arm around him. He was paralyzed, slippery from sweat. She heard dogs barking, neighbors calling. Sharon sobbed.

"Come on," Reba said to her husband. "Come on, David. With me. Come now. Sweetheart. It's all right. Just come."

After a minute or two of patient coaxing, David allowed himself to be led from the clubhouse.

18 The woman tried two gates to the courtyard and garden before finding one that let her in, on corroded, screeching hinges. There was no moon, but a corner streetlight burned her into the serpentine brick path before she stepped into the heavy shadow of the four-story house. As if disturbed by her quick movements, a ginkgo tree made a noise of Swiss bells, and beneath its hard shiny leaves a peacock stirred, unfolding arabesque eyes in natty shades of blue.

She had no experience with peacocks and wondered if they were timid, or if they attacked like watchdogs. This one settled down again in a whisper of fine feathers, and she turned her attention to the house, alert for any sign of life. It was after two in the morning. She'd had the street to herself, walking from the hotel. No lights were showing in the windows. She felt safe enough, if a way in could be found.

Directly ahead of her, on the second-story level, was a semicircular porch backed by tall windows or French doors with white curtains. The woman walked up the steps as if she owned the place. She had the height to go with her poise, and in her best black dress and a black mantilla she looked like a Spanish dancer.

The first door she tried opened easily. She went inside.

A library; bookcases with glass doors. The globe of the streetlight was like a small moon just outside, and she was aware of her rippling reflection as she passed through the library to the foyer of the house.

In front of her was a big room spooky with mirrors and ancestral portraits; down the hall there was a staircase and two more doorways. One of them had to be for the parlor.

There was less light on the north side of the house, and the woman's eyes were slow to adjust to the predominant brownishness of the parlor, the outsized mound of a casket that was the only furnishing. Costly flowers stewed in their own fragrance. She saw a removed, neat, disembodied face lit by an uncertain source, as if he'd had a hard waxing before being set like a jewel into the stuffed plump box.

There was something about the prominence of his head, the way he was displayed, that rooted her; it was as if, flooded by tribute, he enjoyed a half-life still, in darkness a shade or two beyond the night which the living experienced, and could survive, as if he were aware of her, with a watchfulness more chilling than vision.

The woman felt agitated rather than afraid. She hated the wretchedness of this kind of show, as if he'd been a prize in his lifetime and was still too precious to part with. Didn't anyone know better?

Only a look, she'd promised herself, but displeasure was overheating her face, causing the worm of a big vein in her forehead to throb.

She approached the casket and stared down at him, a touch of childhood fantasy in this moment. But she felt a stinging disappointment too: Imagining him dead had been so much more satisfying.

She reached out and touched the striped silk tie they were going to bury him in; pushed harder with stiffened fingers against the chest bones. As if to be acknowledged. Her lower lip protruded meanly. Her head was boiling now, there was a furious blush on her cheeks. She made a fist and struck his chest. Then again. And again, harder, grunting from the effort. She used both fists, pounding away in a frenzy of abuse.

The parlor lights, mounted in chiseled glass all around the walls, struck back at her. She stood amazed in the sudden glare, off balance, her chest heaving.

"What do you think you're doing?" Neddie cried out in anguish.

The woman looked around, instinctively pulling the mantilla across her face to hide it.

Neddie, standing in her nightclothes in the doorway with one hand still on the light switch, brandished the cane she held in her other hand. Her emaciated face was lime white, shot through with livid patches of veins. There seemed to be a perfectly round, black hole where one eye should be.

The woman had no fear of anyone alive, but she was superstitious about witches and the evil eye. This one looked capable of a shooting magic, the power to deaden limbs and wither tongues. She ran, escaping through another doorway into the living room.

"Jasper! *Help!* Call the police!"

In half a dozen strides the woman was across the foyer and at the library doors.

Neddie was still calling loudly for help, but her old voice was muffled by shock and by the thick walls of the house. She could scarcely be heard out in the garden. The woman risked a quick look before slipping through the gate to the street, saw an indistinct black face at a lower window. She went directly across the deserted street, which had a dividing strip planted with palmetto, and into an alley. She walked fast, but without worry. She didn't look back again.

She was at the De Soto Hilton within five minutes, and went in by way of the basement garage, avoiding the lobby.

In the elevator she unpinned her mantilla, folded it,

put it into a pocket of her dress. She recombed her hair. Her face was damp from exertion. She wondered now what kind of furor she had left behind, but what difference did it make? The only problem was, the old lady might have caused herself a heart attack. So, that would make two of them they'd have to bury.

She let herself into the room as quietly as she could. But he wasn't sleeping. He was sitting in the dark smoking, a drink in one hand; she heard ice rattle in the glass as he swallowed.

"Just where the hell have you been?" Joby Ben said crossly.

She smiled slightly, unzipping her dress, and decided she might as well tell him. He was going to hear about it anyway.

19 Frank McNair was buried on Tuesday afternoon in the old cemetery a few blocks from his home. Neddie, recovering from the scare she had received the night before, was able to attend, but she was so heavily tranquilized she could barely hold her head up. Only the immediate family and close friends of Frank's were there. Afterward David went to his office for two hours of business meetings that couldn't be postponed. When he was finished, a little before six o'clock, he drove straight to the yacht club in the Porsche.

Joby Ben was waiting for him aboard the *Denebola*. He stood in the bow with his hands on the starboard railing, leaning over the river. Sunset was bringing in the tide, a glittering surge across the mud flats and exposed roots of mangrove trees on the far shore.

He turned his head when David joined him. It had been hot all day, and the temperature remained close to ninety degrees. David took off the coat of his dark blue suit and loosened his tie.

Joby Ben said, keeping his voice low because of the way sound carried on the water, "I don't know much about boats. How did he do it so it looked all right?"

"When you're working a boat in rough weather you have to use a safety line. You can attach one end to your flotation vest, or a harness that gives you the freedom to move around the decks. You have as much line as you want, depending on the size of the boat and what you need to do topside. Dad was using his harness and an extra-long line. He attached it to one of the midship cleats. We had a torn jib, and it appeared he was trying to do something about it and got swept overboard. When the doctor looked him over, he found a gash on his head near the hairline. As if the ship had rolled and toppled him against the mast or a handrail. If he was dazed or semiconscious, which is a reasonable assumption, he would have been overboard in a hurry. The first big wave. So he was in the water, and it looked as if he was trying to fight his way back, trailing at the end of that twenty-foot line, and got wrapped up in it. Fortunately; otherwise he might have been chopped to pieces by the propeller. But he must have calculated that too. He didn't want to make it any harder for me than necessary."

"Jesus. Why'd he turn the engine on?"

"To keep me out of trouble. He changed course slightly, taking *Denebola* east of Savannah but inside the shipping lanes. It would have been open water until I finally woke up." David shook his head wearily. "He didn't miss a thing. Made himself look a little careless, but not foolhardy."

"Who else knows about the brain tumor? Can you trust the doctor and his staff?"

"Nobody's going to volunteer information. The insurance company won't check too closely if the marine safety officer was satisfied. What have you found out?"

"Haven't had much time to work on it," Joby Ben complained. "You sprang this on me kind of sudden, and we're five hours behind Frankfurt here."

"How long does it take to check newspaper files?"

"Already done. One of my SJAs got back to me a little while ago."

David stared at a passing Bertram; there was a big curly dog standing in the bow pulpit, barking his head off. "It's all true, isn't it?"

"The facts of the Pauline Girda case," Joby Ben said carefully, "match up with what Frank described to you. Her neck was broken; her little girl discovered her in an open grave; later her body turned up in the river a little downstream from the French village of Selz. But anybody can read a newspaper; her murder might have made an impression that stayed with him all these years."

"Does that explain the safety-deposit box? He rented it ten years ago. He put the money away a little at a time—"

"Hell, Davey, who knows how long he was a sick man? Nobody, not even the brain specialist, can say that tumor wasn't giving him hallucinations, or delusions, or whatever you want to call it."

"We'd have noticed something."

"Maybe not. I've learned a lot about human nature in my line of work. A man can nurse a secret obsession all his life, and still look and act perfectly normal. But

Frank wasn't normal, God knows, maybe since the war."

"He was Pauline Girda's lover, I'm convinced of that."

"There's no proof. I don't think your mother's memory is all that reliable when you get right down to—"

"I don't need proof!" David's voice, raised to a shout, echoed around the marina.

Joby Ben shook his head in annoyance.

David lowered his head and said dispiritedly, "I'm not trying to convict him, he's—already dead."

A couple of shrimpers from the public docks down the road were putting out to sea with a heavy thrum of diesels; in a bulging wake, the *Denebola* rubbed against the fenders of the slip.

"Then what are you trying to do?" Joby Ben said reasonably. "Why make yourself sick over this?"

The stars were coming out, the moon emerging through the blue miles like a bald spot in space. The sun flared wildly behind them, forcing long shadows across the slopping water. David glanced up at Joby Ben, whose face looked red, violent, rubbed the wrong way.

"Do you think he killed her?"

"Hell no. But I wouldn't care if he had!"

David seemed shocked by his vehemence.

Joby Ben said, "You know what kind of background Frank and me came from. Whores and bootleggers. We were the grunts, boy. But Frank always had better things in mind, and he dragged me on up with him, step by step. I didn't have his brains and I never acquired much polish, but I've done all right. Dead or alive, I owe him." He put a hard finger against David's chest. "And so do you."

"I know that. So I want you to find Anneliese Girda for me."

Joby Ben didn't look surprised, but his mouth was set in bleak folds. He shook a cigarette out of a pack for himself, smoked it.

"David, you ought to think twice before you go messing around with the life of someone you don't even know."

"It was the last thing he asked me." David stared at Joby Ben, watching the sun disappear from his eyes, leaving them darker, appraisive, worried. "Dad told me I could count on you."

"You want some legal as well as common-sense advice, I'm telling you just to leave it lie."

"I can't," David said, with a slight aggressive lifting of his shoulders. "I'll find her myself, but I think you could handle it faster, and quieter."

"Yeah, I could," Joby Ben said grudgingly. He turned his wrist to bring up the time on his Pulsar watch. "Okay. If you're dead set. I just don't want you getting into any kind of trouble."

David smiled at Joby Ben; he was trembling a little from the sudden release of tension.

"Do you have time for a drink at the club?" he asked, belatedly hospitable.

"I don't think so. I need to get myself packed and out to the air base. Davey, thanks for the fancy sporting gun. Couldn't afford nothin' like it on my pay."

"Dad would have wanted you to have it." David felt suddenly awkward. "I looked at the will. There's a—a bequest for you. Twenty-five hundred dollars." Joby Ben seemed to flinch. "You know we've never been as rich as people like to think."

"Doesn't matter," Joby Ben said sadly. "Whatever Frank decided was right, that'll be okay."

"When will I hear from you?"

Joby Ben thought about it. "Give me a couple of weeks. And be patient."

"I'll drop you on by the Hilton," David said.

20   Joby Ben was in a terrible frame of mind when he got back to the room. Franziska had known he would be. Their room faced the street in front of the hotel, and she had been watching at the window for him. Franziska judged his mood by the way he carried his shoulders, so she had a white-rum and tonic fizzing in her hand when he walked in.

He drank half of it before he was able to speak. Franziska sat at the foot of the bed, ready to go, dressed casually for the long flight ahead: She wore a silk shirt striped in black and white, black denim pants, and half-boots. She had spent most of the day at the hotel pool, alternately swimming laps and sunning herself. She'd been pale from the long German winter, but her skin, as sensitive as litmus paper, soaked up color from the mildest rays without ever burning or freckling. Her short, freshly washed hair had healthy red highlights in it.

Joby Ben walked around the room muttering to himself, not paying attention to her radiance.

Franziska looked sideways at her reflection in the bedroom mirror, modeling her profile, playing an old and tantalizing game: With her chin cupped on one large hand, she was a knockout. When she took her hand away, revealing the full lurid heaviness of her lower jaw, the modest imperfections of other features seemed magnified. Now her nose was a millimeter too long, her mouth seemed comically exaggerated by even a touch of lipstick, her eyes were set too close together; her gaze had a dumbstruck intensity that people frequently interpreted as oafish.

Joby Ben put his drink down and began to unbutton his sweaty shirt.

"David wants me to locate Anneliese for him."

Franziska said nothing. She smiled vaguely.

"Or he'll do it himself, he says. He's all tore up inside, naturally, doesn't know whether he loves or hates Frank any more, but he's determined to set things right on his daddy's behalf." Joby Ben hesitated. "What I didn't tell you, Frank had this attack of conscience some time ago, and stockpiled a couple of hundred thousand dollars for Anneliese. How do you like that?"

Franziska said quickly and scornfully, *"Zweihundert tausend—!"*

He made a quick gesture, not to pacify but to freeze her anger at this point. "Never mind. I'll figure out a way to handle this. David won't be any trouble."

She shot him a meaningful glance at the mention of David; she was quickly trembling at the point of violence. Joby Ben as always was fascinated by this display of the power he controlled. He gestured again. Franziska sat still, but her eyes glittered.

His own face was reddening, his hands wouldn't work right as he tried to get his shirt off. "There better not be any more dumb stunts like you pulled last night." He ripped a button from the shirt. Franziska spied it on the carpet and pounced on it, came up in front of him with a shrug. Joby Ben stared at her for a few moments, then turned toward the picture window and the city of Savannah with a wide-flung gesture of dismissal.

"That son of a bitch Frank! I hate this town. That

goddam paper mill stinking up the place and makin'
'em all hog-fat and happy."

Blood pressure hazed his vision and choked him. "A
little something for me in the will, brother Frank? My
goodness. Well, *thank* you, brother! It's come just a little
too goddam late. I've already provided for my old age!"

From behind, Franziska put a hand on his brow.
Although her own temper was frequently unmanage-
able, she never liked to see him upset.

"Let's go, Daddy," she said.

"Not until I settle up a little better."

"What do you mean?"

Joby Ben reached for another shirt and pulled it on
over his head.

"Check us out and wait for me in the lobby; I need
to go down the street for a few minutes."

21 Neddie, wearing gardening gloves and a big
hat despite the absence of sun, was repotting begonias
when the gate opened and closed. She didn't look up
from the bench in the potting shed as Joby Ben walked
across the torchlit garden toward her, announced by
the screech of a peacock.

"Neddie?"

There wasn't much light where she worked. Her
movements were slow and mildly clumsy, as if the tran-
quilizers she'd taken to get through the funeral hadn't
worn off. Joby Ben moved closer. Neddie cocked her
head to catch sight of him. Her mouth turned down
pettishly.

"Well. I wonder what could still be keeping you here. Money? There's no money for you."

"I found that out already. Don't worry. I can't get out of this town fast enough."

"Then go. You can see I don't need the bother. As for Frank—why you came in the first place is a mystery. I know you always hated Frank, even when you were being so mealymouthed around him."

Joby Ben flicked sweat from his forehead with the back of his hand and said in exasperation, "Hell, I *protected* Frank, even if he never knew it. For twenty-five years he got away with murder. But I just wanted to tell you—"

Her right hand jerked; clay pots toppled. "*Hated* him. That's what I said. And all the rest of us. When Frank got involved with that little trollop overseas, you came hot-footin' it here to this house—"

"Because I knew what Pauline was like. I knew what could happen if you didn't give a good strong pull on his leash and get him back home fast."

Neddie turned all the way around to face him, and leaned against the bench.

"No. You came because you were afraid I wouldn't find out unless you *told* me. But I fooled you, Mr. Troublemaker—"

"God's sake, Neddie, now, I came here tonight in all sincerity—"

"I did nothing! Never a whisper of a mention to Frank about his pathetic fling. You see—that is the difference between people of quality and the kind of *trash* you will always be."

"Frank killed her, Neddie! And the blame is yours as much as his."

For a moment she looked, as he had hoped, terrified. "I suspected that. From the way he suffered. The way he looked at me sometimes. As if he had to speak. But

I always stopped him. I never let him feel it was important."

"Not *important?* The truth didn't die with Frank, Neddie."

"What is true, and what is a lie, doesn't matter. Because Frank is dead."

"And just before he died he told David everything."

His hands tingled, as if with a hammer he'd just nailed her to the bench. She lost focus; her jaw sagged. *"Why?"*

Joby Ben hunched his shoulders, and his face dripped. He looked up through the trees, feeling alone in the sweltering dark. And he had a long way to go.

"Reba don't have any kind of leash on David. But maybe you do. It's your turn again, Neddie."

She was sliding along the bench; he thought she'd had a stroke and was about to fall. He reached for Neddie, but she wasn't in danger. She shied from his hands, holding her own hands rigidly in front of her to ward him off.

"There's a serpent in my garden," she said blankly.

"Listen...the trouble hasn't worked itself out by a long shot. What's coming is what's due."

Neddie's hands groped behind her; she came up with a hoe that had been leaning against the bench.

"But I know what to do about serpents, don't I?"

Joby Ben backed off a step and put his hands in his pockets, sighing dismally through his teeth. Neddie raised the hoe.

"I *chop* them in the neck!"

"Shit," Joby Ben said, and bared his nape. Neddie raised the hoe a little higher, but that was it. She hadn't the courage, or the strength, to strike him. After a little while Joby Ben turned away and walked across the garden to the street, his footsteps echoing from the walls, the heights of the dark house.

22 Reba had lunch at the Edinburgh Club with Burton Bowdrie, whom she had no use for, and Mark Sams, whose opinions she respected. The luncheon meeting was at their request. They wanted to talk about David's proposed candidacy for Congress.

"If he says he doesn't want to run," Reba told them, "there isn't much I can do."

Bowdrie puffed a cigar that was making her eyes water, and smiled. It was only the twenty-fifth of April, but the continuing high, unseasonable heat had produced a midsummer crisis in the club's old air-conditioning system. The garden windows were wide open. Flies had poked through faulty screens and were crawling in plates of leftovers. There were floral centerpieces in the dining room: each table was a garden plot. Smoke hung in the air around the tables so that all of them, the men in their toney lightweight suits and the women in Easter pastels, looked like picnickers in a plague land. Reba felt damp and itchy, and somehow to blame for their disappointment in her husband.

"Honey—" It was one of the few things she loathed being called. "Honey, you'll excuse me if I assume you haven't been as *persuasive* as you might be."

"Because," Mark said, looking at the table in front of him and not at her, "you don't want to do or say anything that might upset him right now." He was a dark, slender young man with a weighty brow and nervous energy that was expressed in fits of neatness. At the table he brushed all the bread crumbs into a tidy

135

pile and tirelessly arranged cutlery and shakers into patterns that seemed to have symbolic import for him.

"I know how to talk to David," Reba said firmly. "But he won't do it without Frank. He doesn't want to. It's not—that important to him any more."

"Of course not," Bowdrie replied. "Doesn't *seem* important, when he's on his knees from the hardest blow he's had to absorb in his entire life. I understand how hurt he is; I sympathize. But it's the measure of a man to come up swinging when he most wants to lie down and die. There's been presented an excellent opportunity, tailor-made for someone of David's limited experience in politics. Right now it's family and name and connections that count more than experience. But opportunity, as we know, withereth away when it is pissed on, and it could be years before he has another opening. And God knows, I may well have passed from the scene. That's why I say, Reba, *provoke* him if you have to. Make him fighting mad. Get him off the ropes and back into the ring. Tell him he *has* to win this one, for his daddy."

"We don't have much time," Mark said. "A week at the most. David has to declare."

"Or we get ourselves another candidate. Ray Riprod," Bowdrie concluded, filling the air with clouds of disgust. "Who has already demonstrated his amazing lack of prowess in two previous elections." He looked hard at Reba. "Think what's right for both of you at this stage of your life. And that little girl, God bless her, what's her name—"

"Sharon."

"Smart as a whip."

"Yes, she is."

For a while no one at the table said anything. Except for the almost imperceptible movements of Mark's fingertips, as if he was playing a secret tune on a tiny piano, they were a still life. Monet. *Two Politicians and Woman with Chrysanthemums*. Reba thought about the time her Uncle Whit had cut his arm off above the elbow with his backyard buzzsaw. He ran a little lumber business down there in Americus, in a tin-roof shed with a dune of sawdust beside it. Reba was nine. She was playing in front of the shed and Whit was loading fresh-cut plywood into a wheelbarrow and stumbled and went back into the saw and his arm came off, like that. She was looking right at him. And she would never forget the puzzled expression on his face as he recovered his balance and saw the terrifying damage before he felt the pain.

It was that way when she looked at David now; his father was gone but he didn't truly feel the pain yet, he was still reeling away from the impact and there was a buzzsaw spinning loud in his head: He couldn't see, think, or hear.

He could be pushed, Reba supposed, into a hectic political campaign. It was a temptation; she was going a little crazy in the aftermath trying to fill his blank spaces with too much talk. Being good and patient and gentle and understanding until she was quivering with neuralgia. And drinking. Perversely, his anxiety and nerves excited in her a passion stronger than she had felt for several years; David was easily aroused but too quickly consumed in bed, and he flickered and faded while she was still in the swings of heat. His untimeliness would pass, but she felt his unspoken dismay, the further breaking of vital connections between them.

So get him involved, make him work. *Dad would have wanted you to, David*. The only stimulus strong enough for him to respond to. Burton Bowdrie was no fool. But she was reasonably certain that David would have a nervous breakdown if he tried it.

"Reba—well, honey?"

"Let's just leave him the hell alone," she said roughly.

23   When Reba got home David was there. He was packing.

"I'm going to Germany for a few days," he said.

The suddenness of it, or his eagerness, stunned her. "Why?"

"Business. There's a company I want to look at. We may buy it. Have you seen my trench coat? Joby Ben says it's raining in Frankfurt."

He stopped what he was doing and looked at her in a peculiar way, as if there was a concealed hazard in this weather report. He smiled. Reba smiled too, bewildered by his animation, by the rugged complexity of his mood. She knew he was lying about the purpose of the trip to Germany. Because lying wasn't one of the things he did well.

"Oh," she said brightly, "you talked to Joby Ben. How is he?" David shrugged. He had buttoned a shirt wrong and was folding it badly. She took the shirt from him. "I'll do that. I'll finish packing for you. I think your coat came back from the cleaner's; look in the hall closet downstairs. And why don't you make us a drink?" She had limited herself to two daiquiris at lunch, promising herself a third as soon as she was in the privacy of her own home. Now she was perishing for it.

David looked at his watch. "There's a Lufthansa flight from Kennedy at six. I've just got an hour to make National's direct flight to New York."

The thought of a transatlantic jet, a foreign country, caused a flutter of excitement.

"I'll drive you. Relax...David, why don't I go with you?"

He looked amazed. "What?"

"I said I want to go to Germany with you."

"You can't get ready in time. What about Sharon?"

"She'll stay with the Mackeys, of course. We have their kids sleeping over often enough."

"Reba, I'll just be a few days. There's no reason for you to go."

Her excitement turned to nervous apprehension.

"No reason. Except that I need to be with you. Something's scaring me, I don't know what. Maybe—we're all not used to being without Frank. Things can go wrong now, can't they?"

"No," he said, in a flat tone that caused a thickening in her throat. "It's already as bad as it can get."

His eyes looked as if they had been screwed back into his head. She remembered the night of his father's death, the rifled desk drawer, the Porsche vanished in a downpour. *He gone to Atlanta.* In a big hurry. David had never explained why to her. She was sure that his haste and secretiveness had to do with Frank. Some problem his sudden death had caused, or left unresolved. David was still trying to cope.

But for God's sake, Reba wanted to say, *why can't you trust me? There's no way I can hurt you, David!*

He was already gone, taking the stairs three at a time, agile as a kid, in a hurry again. She finished packing, her eyes stinging, trying to find something cheerful in his precipitous departure. A change of scene was always good. Maybe he and Joby Ben would paint the town red one night.

Reba carried the suitcase downstairs. David was in

the kitchen chipping at a lump of ice cubes in the sink. He had poured a beer for himself.

She put a hand on the back of his neck and said without thinking, "Ice. Frank said it was the only thing that helped, it stopped the lights flashing on and off in his head—"

Silence; her anxiety at this slip was communicated by the increased pressure of her hand at his nape. Reba clung to him as if they were bonded by a dismal electricity, and her tongue felt large and awkward in her mouth. David went on chipping at the ice and finally dropped some into an outsized drink he'd prepared for her.

When he turned to give her the glass, her hand fell away; he leaned back against the sink where the sun cut at an angle across his eyes in a blinding storm of motes that seemed threatening, a hypercomplex glare in which his filtered emotions might be dangerously charged. But he was calm enough when he reached for his tall beer. He sipped.

"How did you know about the tumor?" he asked.

"Oh, David—"

"He told you? Before he told me?" He said it as if he were weighing an essential faithlessness on her part.

"I found out by accident. During Neddie's party after the hospital dedication. I was—a little pissed and feeling sorry for myself, having a good cry up in Frank's room. He came in looking like death warmed over. He had a big bag of ice with him like that one—" She pointed out the bag in the sink, and her hand shook. "I wanted to call Mitch. He wouldn't let me. He told me then how sick he was. Said I had to—had to keep shut because it was his responsibility. Frank wanted to tell you and Neddie in his own way, his own time."

She had a way of rising on her toes in a stark balletic exercise when she didn't know what to do with her hands or the rest of her body. She seemed to be straining to take flight without wings, exhibiting to him a gooney-bird vulnerability and innocence. Then she breathed out desperately, settled flatfooted to the floor.

David turned and the sunlight hit him fiercely in the back of his head as he tilted the glass and finished the beer in a couple of long swallows. His eyes, no longer swarming, seemed lackluster.

"Come on, let's go."

"Could we wait for Sharon? She'll be home from school in twenty minutes."

David grimaced. "Cutting it too close. Tell her I'm sorry I didn't get to say goodbye, I'll call tomorrow night."

While David loaded his luggage into the station wagon, Reba went next door to ask Peg Mackey to keep a lookout for Sharon. She drove to the airport. David looked, for a time, puzzled and uncertain about this spur-of-the-moment hop to Europe, but she didn't try to talk him out of it.

For most of the way he was painfully silent, so she made descriptive conversation, as if she were talking to a blind man. She told him about the Petersons' newly decorated house, which he hadn't visited yet. She talked about a vibrant garden glimpsed in a slum, a billboard advertising condominiums in Hilton Head, a wobbling yellow bus on the expressway filled with migrant workers who gazed down at them with the stupefaction of men whose lives are consumed in the slow steerage from one green field to another.

The airport, finally. Small planes skimming too high to be heard on levels of an enormous rosy cloud that seemed half as wide as the universe. A larger plane with an orange sunburst on its tail tucked in at one of the jetways, nose covered like a sleeping swan's. David picked up his ticket while she parked, and then it was already time for him to board.

His kiss was dry, too casual for her mood.

"You should have told me about Dad," David said.

It wasn't mean, or censorious; it wasn't anything, really, except what was on his mind, and would eventually be forgotten. But she felt too blue and guilty to respond, and by the time she wanted to talk, to defend herself, he had disappeared inside the jetway.

Reba waited for the flight to leave. It seemed literally hot as hell just beyond the glareproofed sandwich glass of the observation window; the tension of heat at her fingertips made her itch all over. She felt confined in a vacuum. The orange-and-white jet pulled away and pointed itself down the field and lunged into the air in a long scarey rip of sound that made her feel suddenly hollow and weightless too. Stuck fast to the bronzy skin of glass by her fingers, she watched the plane out of sight with the unfathomable conviction that she would never see David again.

Two

24 "So you found her."

"No problem, like I told you," Joby Ben said. "If you want to order now, I can recommend the *bauernfrühstück*—"

"I'm not hungry." David fingered the immaculate heavy linen tablecloth and looked around the dining room of the Frankfurterhof Hotel, which was about half full at this hour. Joby Ben shrugged and went back to his breakfast omelette. With a mouth full of egg, which he chewed slowly, he paused to pour mulled wine from a flagon for both of them.

"You look tired. What the hell, it's a long haul from Savannah. But there just wasn't any need for you to come all this way. Try some of that wine, it's a better eye-opener than black coffee."

Joby Ben was out of uniform, wearing a tweed jacket and a mint-green Oxford-cloth shirt without a tie. It was a little cold and quite blustery in Frankfurt. David had landed, an hour and a half earlier, in thunder and lightning, but now the skies were clearing.

He tasted the wine, which was steaming, from a mug.

"Well—what'll I do?"

"Did you arrange for the transfer of funds to your company bank here?"

David nodded. "The money will be available this morning. Cash. You're authorized to pick it up."

"I'll take along a couple of my SJAs. Cash is convenient, and nobody can trace it." He cut into a broiled kidney, keeping a sharp eye on David. "Anneliese

144

Girda is about to get rich, and she'll never know why."
There was something a touch malicious in his grin, but
the grin didn't hold.

David thought about it, nodded again, and had more
wine.

"Looks like you've dropped a little weight since I saw
you last."

"Ten pounds." David closed his eyes. His head
slipped a little to one side. "Jet lag," he said half-hu-
morously, with an exaggerated clasping of his head,
pushing it up off one shoulder.

"I'll leave the receipt in your box this afternoon. I'd
show you the fleshpots tonight, Davey, but I need to be
out of town on business."

"What's she like?" David asked, not unexpectedly;
but Joby Ben went from bright to dour in an instant.
He kept eating.

"Who? The girl? How would I know? Never laid eyes
on her."

"She's—what? My age? Is she married? Does she
have kids of her own?"

"No. She's not married. I got you a suite here, the
best in the house. Catch up on your sleep while I do
the banking." He spoke more slowly, with an emphasis
he might ordinarily reserve for a jury. "And that should
relieve you of any obligation you might feel. Remember, Davey, none of us can ever be certain that Frank
was in his right mind when he—"

"Where is she? In Frankfurt?"

Joby Ben abandoned his breakfast for good. He sat
with his big shoulders hunched, a tongue working at
scraps between his overlapping teeth. They looked at
each other.

"What's on your mind, boy?"

"I want to see her."

"Jesus, I knew it," Joby Ben said under his breath.

He scratched a bushy sideburn with one finger, slid the finger up to the knob of his temple, pushed hard to force patience or encourage wisdom.

David leaned toward him.

"*See* her, that's all. I just want to know what she looks like."

"Why?"

"Curiosity. Anneliese and her mother are like ghosts to me. Maybe if I know—what she's like, where she works, how she lives, then I won't feel so goddam sorry any more."

David looked for the moment so exhausted from the emotion he'd been keeping in check that he seemed at the point of tears. Joby Ben felt a rub of sympathy he didn't try to suppress, despite his misgivings.

He said gruffly, "No need to feel sorry for Anneliese Girda. She's done real well for herself."

"Where can I find her?"

"This isn't *smart*, Davey. None of it."

David responded to his uncle's irritation with an anger that turned his lips white.

"As long as I'm here I'm going to see her. One way or another."

Joby Ben reached for his cigarettes. "I'm supposed to make it easy for you?"

He didn't say anything else. David helped himself to more wine from the flagon. He sat back with an imperial confidence that Joby Ben had to admire; he'd often admired the same quality in Frank, and tried to emulate it. But if he'd been that good, by now he'd have four stars. The princes always knew the pretenders. Although David was still young, still trying to prove himself, in a crunch you saw what he was. Maybe it had something to do with the scalding fierceness of his light eyes, or the thoroughbred muscles; maybe it was just the way he was hung. When he wanted something he would get it, and not think too highly of anyone who tried to stand in his way.

"Anneliese used to be a fashion model. Now she's part owner of a boutique. Designs some of the clothes they sell. My lady friends tell me she has talent."

"What's the address?"

"Goethestrasse, *zwanzig*." Joby Ben looked regretfully at the cooling food. "Need to be on my way." He put thirty marks on the table and shook his head indignantly when David tried to protest.

"Thanks, Joby Ben." David yawned and scratched his sandpaper chin. "I want to clean up and change my clothes. Talk to you later."

Joby Ben paused. "Conscience be damned, boy. You just remember what I told you about messing around with other people's lives."

He didn't wait for a response but walked out of the dining room and through the lounge, heading for the telephone booths off the lobby. He got into one and shut the heavy soundproof door and dialed.

"Franziska," he said, as soon as she answered, "I need you over here at the Frankfurterhof on the double." He listened to her complaint and cut it short. "You don't leave for Heidelberg until four-thirty. In the meantime there's something we better had do."

He hung up but loitered in the booth for a while, annoyed—he thought—by the way things were getting out of hand, at a time when he didn't need any more problems. David wouldn't be denied, and he was too stubborn to take good advice. Also Franziska was nerved up to the point where she could easily be unreliable if he wasn't around. Joby Ben felt that he needed to keep track of his nephew. But he had a hunch he might be turning a tiger loose on a puppy.

25 Because of Riordan/McNair's business interests in Germany, David conscientiously had taken four years of the language at the University of Georgia, and he'd made enough trips abroad to maintain his proficiency in conversational German. He also knew Frankfurt well enough to get around by streetcar or on foot, which is what he chose to do after a long hot soak in the bathtub at his hotel.

He had dozed on the plane and again in the tub, but sound sleep had eluded him for several days, and as he walked toward Goethestrasse the edges of the commercial city, almost all of it reconstructed since the war, blurred around him in a delicate haze, an illusion of softness enhanced by occasional trees so newly in leaf they seemed to be foaming, airbrushed in against the businesslike background. The air, after a cold morning, was turning mild as the harsh wind faded. Spring always happened earlier in Frankfurt than the rest of the country, because the Taunus Hills to the north blocked most of the bitter Baltic and North Sea winds and focused the strengthening sun on the plain of the city.

There were flower stalls in the plazas of Hauptwache; a German band in green leather *lederhosen* marched brassily through the crowds. Their flagrant energy was unsettling. He felt himself moving too quickly, without the desire to think, as if the temper of the place was marshaling him to fight against the slower, more subtle Savannah-bred rhythms of his body. Savannah seemed eternal, even Sherman had spared it, perhaps out of weariness as he reached the sea at last. Eternal, but losing definition through distance and time warp, sinking too fast in his conscious mind as Germany muscled in. German people had always slightly disturbed David, their passions and fatalism made a two-headed serpent. They knew what he could never fully appreciate, that it was all there to be snatched away: the magnificent industry, the prosperity, the medieval heritage recreated from ashes like a richer version of Disneyland. How many divisions of Russian tanks were on the border? It was a trauma without correlation to sin.

On a Rossmarkt bench a man had opened his shirt to the sun. His white chest was stippled, clumsily puckered, as if from old wounds. David wondered where he had been shot, and how he had survived what looked like numerous deathblows.

The fact of his continuing existence on this sunlit bench seemed precious to David, and he felt, again, a black, boiling urgency to make a connection, to know for himself that Anneliese Girda was real, and had survived his father's madness.

The boutique at 20 Goethestrasse was busy at the noon hour; looking through the small windows, he couldn't readily distinguish customers from shopgirls. He went in.

There was a tall blond woman, radiant but slightly crippled, who seemed to be running things. Fascinated, he studied the tense twist of her oval head and imagined her as a child, blundering in terror through dark woods and falling, badly, down a hill. Hurting herself in this poignant manner.

He had a dull headache from sleeplessness; his fascination was quickly wearing thin and he felt deflated, queerly disappointed, as if she were all wrong for the part he hadn't known he was casting in his mind.

"May I help you, sir?"

Another shopgirl, with glossy black bangs and a chunky face, had come upstairs to stand beside him. She had spoken in English. After hearing nothing but German in the boutique, David was startled.

"Oh, I was—something for my wife, I think. A shirt, I don't know—" The girl's cheeks got very full when she smiled. He turned in confusion to the nearest rack. "This is pretty—"

"I love your accent. From Dixie, no? I was myself studying a year at the University of Minnesota."

"How did you like it?" David asked her.

"Too much snow." She shuddered picturesquely. "What size is your wife?"

"A six, I think. She's about this tall—" He held up a hand parallel to the floor, "weighs about a hundred and twelve pounds."

"She would like stripes?" the girl said, deftly whipping a blouse from the rack. She held it against herself, modeling it for him. "This one, perhaps?"

David glanced at the blond woman. "Something that Fräulein Girda designed."

"You know about Anneliese? The designs are very popular, they sell quickly, but we have a small selection. Let me see—"

She led him to a circular rack isolated by a golden spotlight near the heart of the store, where the traffic patterns converged.

"I'm surprised to see her working in the shop," David said. "I thought she'd be busy designing."

"Yes, very busy. Anneliese comes in only two days a week now, to take care of special customers." She raised her head and saw where David was looking. "Oh, that one's Hilda. She's the manager. What color hair is your wife?"

"Dark. Not as dark as you."

"Maybe this one. In blue."

"That's nice," David said distractedly, looking around. "She isn't here now?"

"Anneliese? No, today she has her lunch, then sketches. You know, new designs to make into clothes."

"Where?"

"Oh—I think she might be at the handcrafts exhibit, in the Römer." There was a change in the shopgirl's face; a blot of suspicion in her usually merry eyes. She looked too carefully at him and David felt instinctively cautious, not knowing why. He gave his full attention to the shirt she had selected.

"I'll take this one. How much?"

Her mood changed again; she had a sale. "One hundred and twenty-five marks."

David took out his wallet and showed the girl his gold American Express card. Seeing it apparently clinched her approval of him.

She held it up. "Hilda! Charge please." She smiled at David. "Hilda will take care of you. I'll wrap the shirt. Would you like something to go with it?"

"Thank you, not today," David said.

26 He emerged from the underground in the center of the big square called the Römer with the din of multiple bells around his head. The sandstone cathedral of St. Bartholomew was behind him, florid in a pale blue arc of sky and optically unsteady, as if the flowing clouds behind its spires might send it crashing down. There was a smaller, yellow church with a tall copper spire weathered to sage green, and a forty-bell carillon in its tower. There were cafés and pubs all around and a large, aimless lunchtime crowd that seemed to be searching for a festival. If one had been promised, it hadn't materialized; they made do with lesser entertainments. Sidewalk chess with wooden pieces big as page boys, a mediocre mime troupe whose members kept popping up with preternaturally whitened faces, as if they were emerging from dungeons beneath the cobblestones.

David paused to get his bearings. The city hall, three joined medieval houses with crow-stepped gables, was in the west end of the square. A banner announced the handcrafts exhibit in the center hall. Squadrons of schoolchildren were passing in and out.

David paid his admission and picked up a catalogue. The vaulted Romanesque hall, cement walls and cold stone floors, had been partitioned into several areas. It was all potters and woodcarvers and weavers, predictably dull. He studied faces instead of artifacts.

Behind the hall there was an old courtyard, channels of brilliant sun, a working fountain. Near the fountain a woman sat on a campstool, sketching sea serpents and naiads with dense, heavenly, blue-green faces. She was about his age, but shapelessly overweight. She had an unappealing thatch of black hair that looked as if she cut it whenever she was in a rage.

The closer he came the more untidy she looked, and he felt a sharp sense of relief when a bearded man with a baby wailing in a backpack approached her first. He had another young child hanging from one hand.

"Helga! Helga, the kids are driving me crazy. Let's have lunch."

David spoke to a matron with an official-looking badge pinned to one lapel of her wool jacket.

"Is there another hall in these houses?"

"The Imperial Hall." She pointed next door. "Upstairs. But nothing's on exhibit there."

"Any old paintings? Tapestries?"

"Oh, yes."

The interior of the house she had directed him to was as modern as the lobby of a new bank, with wooden chests and sixteenth-century paintings rescued from the air raids to soften all the steel and glass angles. He went up a wide staircase to the Imperial Hall with its concave Roman ceiling and chandeliers like showers of crystal sparks. There were paintings of newly crowned kings in lancet niches around the walls. A tour group stood at one end, the guide's voice echoing dully.

He turned the other way and saw Anneliese Girda, sketchbook propped on a large glass case, peering down at something royal gleaming immensely on dark velvet. She began to draw, with a colored pencil, and he realized that she was left-handed.

From the first glimpse he had no doubts he had found her. But she was too immediate, vivid, warmer than life: His mood was one of puzzled petrification, stoniness gradually scored by a cold trickle of fear he didn't understand. She was wearing a sleeveless bush jacket with a lot of pockets over a blue-and-yellow-checked shirt, and pale blue jeans. There were touches of style without eccentricity: thin gold bracelets, cufflinks, spectacles with a hint of darkness in the lenses, a daub of beauty mark at one corner of her mouth. Her skin looked flawless at twenty feet, but that could have been another example of her art. She was not tall, small-boned, perfectly in proportion.

He took a couple of steps toward her, hesitated,

looked up at a portrait, saw a lean, diseased, self-satisfied face, looked again at Anneliese in a kind of panic.

She had unflapped the large purse she was carrying over one shoulder, opened her box of pencils, selected another. As she was turning back to her sketchbook she glanced at him, two seconds, no more. She was not unaccustomed to being stared at in public. He looked presentable, his presence was noted, she had no comment.

David was comforted; hers was a good face, beauty uncompromised by the vague tensions of vanity, avarice, discontent.

When she turned her head away, her right shoulder came up slightly, a withdrawal, emphasizing the distance between them. She bent to her work. She was absorbed. There was nothing she would ever need from him. He felt what his father might have felt long ago, having looked into similar eyes, a reminiscent face.

27   Old Sachsenhausen had been a tainted warren of early medieval houses on the south bank of the Main River until the air raids in March of 1944 obliterated all but traces of antiquity. Rebuilt with fidelity and nostalgia, Sachsenhausen was now a showplace, but its charm was too adamant and only postcard deep. It lacked the daring to be scruffy. A few of its nooky bars and cellar discos were centers of the considerable drug traffic in Frankfurt. There were some good restaurants down the stone alleys, pubs with gardens nearly empty on a weekday afternoon.

In the café, at a small square table by a doorway that was open to scarred brick and greening vines, privacy enforced by a latticework of iron topping the garden walls, David discovered that he was hungry—ravenous, as if he'd become reacquainted with food after existing for the past couple of weeks through some austere chemical process not unlike photosynthesis. He ate two fat sausages with bread and cheese and drank a stein of the local pilsner while Anneliese sat in the courtyard with her friends, a man and his wife who were the proprietors of the café. She went slowly through her sketchbook with them, pausing to match squares of fabric from her purse with the ideas on paper.

David seldom took his eyes off Anneliese. She was sitting in the path of the sun along one of the moldering brick-and-masonry walls, obviously an authentic remainder from the '44 Allied blitz, and he saw her for the most part in profile, her head alluringly modeled against the flat patches of gray cement. She never glanced toward the threshold of the café, but if she had she would have seen little of what or who was inside; the many hung and tilted windows, glamorous with massed reflection, gave light back too generously to the sky, so that only his legs beneath the table, his brown sun-warmed hands on the glass stein, were visible.

David felt comfortably in seclusion and safe in his absorption; he was absorbed as if by a stage play of such complexity that he couldn't afford to blink, let alone look away, for fear of missing some small but vital revelation that would enrich his understanding of the whole, improve his life in a way he knew he had been longing for but was helpless to articulate. It was the reverse of eating; the more he filled his eyes, the hungrier he was.

He was out of sight, anonymous, but there was a danger in that; he was losing touch with surfaces, apparent things, dreaming away objectivity. But he had no choice, he had to concentrate on Anneliese: otherwise, he was sure, her soft magic would fail to hold in this drab garden and she would fade away in a drizzle of borrowed time. He needed to magnify the commonplace into bold strokes of reality: he felt instructed by the manner in which she cocked her open hand and turned it stiffly at the wrist to emphasize a conversational point; her waste of cigarettes, a quick puff or two and then out, as if the ritual mattered and not the smoking; her laughter slyly tossed aside with a slanting motion of her head; her habit of tilting her chin high on clasped hands and looking down her nose to make a telling point.

Her style, her verve, her wit, her soul—he had imagined Anneliese to fill a void—and now that void was merely a space in which she dwelled, invisible to all eyes but his own, a space he felt prepared to enter with ease, and be welcome.

After she had picked at a salad for lunch and finished a glass of beer, she was on her way again, sketchbook under one arm.

David followed, as he had done the long leisurely way down from the Römer and across the Main. Trailing after Anneliese, he felt an innocent excitement and sense of companionship, although he didn't come within a hundred feet of her.

Anneliese dawdled, in front of shop windows and then at a newsstand where she bought a lottery ticket and talked at length with the proprietor while leafing through a couple of fashion magazines. He was stalled in front of a shop that sold armor, obsolete weaponry, and World War One memorabilia. Occasionally her voice was audible, in snatches, as traffic idled. She spoke in the Frankfurt dialect, which he found hard to understand. He wondered how good her English was.

Joby Ben had said she wasn't married, but there had to be men. Did she live with someone? He felt concerned. What kind of man would interest her? David stared at his reflection in the shop window and discovered with a slight shock that he looked gaunt and grim.

He had made up his mind to saunter closer and speak to Anneliese while selecting a magazine for himself; but when he looked around she was turning to go, with a quickness that gave him the feeling she had just been staring down the street in his direction.

She walked, at a brisk pace, toward a church with apricot-colored masonry walls. On the other side of the church was the Main, and the broad riverfront promenade, site of the weekend flea markets in spring and summer. Anneliese walked as if she had forgotten an appointment, and stopped at a phone box near the steps to the iron footbridge. There was a floating café, outlined in snappy pennants, in the water below. The river looked ashen under clouds. On the promenade near the phone box a team of acrobats was drawing a crowd. There was a kind of tense, prancing music: tambourines, cylindrical drums. Anneliese kept glancing at the ceaselessly bounding, tight-bodied young men while waiting for her call to go through.

David lingered on the curb across the street from her, not knowing what he would say once he had her attention; he had no sense of the future beyond those first moments, the closeness eye to eye. *My father gave birth to you: and here I am.*

Anneliese left the phone box and walked slowly to the edge of the crowd surrounding the acrobats. She looked at her watch. There was a patter of applause;

small young men shot one after another almost into the lower branches of the trees, turned into human balls, opened gracefully as they plummeted toward the ground.

David crossed the street. Anneliese was looking at her watch again.

A man with a child riding his shoulders bumped against her and she gave way, glancing up; she saw David. There was something flat and wild about her eyes, the expression on her face went against his benign expectations. She was frightened. It shocked him to see her like that. She tried to press her way through the bulk of the crowd, and failed. The electrifying sounds of the tambourine aggravated Anneliese, creating in her a kind of suspenseful, motionless frenzy.

David made an ill-timed decision, reaching between two bodies to touch her arm.

She jerked away, gold bracelets raking his fingertips. Her voice was throaty, not loud.

"Whoever you are, p-please! Just g-get away from me!"

This time she was able to make a path for herself between two bulky tourists who found themselves juggling precious camera equipment to avoid smashups. They glowered at David. He was compounding his first mistake by trying to catch Anneliese, as if he had some way to explain the flash fever infecting them both.

"I'm sorry. I didn't mean—I just wanted to—"

Anneliese dodged, whirled to her right, and caught a stout bearded young man in the stomach with her elbow. He sagged and sat down in slow astonishment.

David had her by the arm again, felt the frail bones in her wrist, let her go for fear of hurting her. He was aware that they had created an interesting scene, upstaging the acrobats, but he couldn't pull out of it now.

It was all going so wrong, and he'd only wanted to talk to her.

"Listen to me—"

Brakes screeched in the street, car doors sprang open, he paid little attention. Suddenly hands came down on him, he was pummeled, pushed, kneed. One sleeve of his jacket was torn loose from the shoulder. He was about to explode into a fight when a gray-haired man pushed identification under his nose. They were KRIPOs.

David stopped struggling. He was deep red with embarrassment.

One of the detectives had gone to Anneliese. She looked close to tears as she spoke to him, gesturing in David's direction. Now he realized whom she had been calling from the phone box. But why so many of them?

Another cop picked up and dusted off the bearded youth, who had his wind back and was grinning, rather enjoying himself. Even the acrobats had paused and were looking around.

"Inspector Nütterman," the gray-haired man said. He spoke in English to David. His face was nicked, like an old coin, with tiny acne scars. His eyes were black ice. "May I ask what your interest is in Fräulein Girda?"

David took a couple of deep breaths. "Oh, for Christ's sake, I wasn't trying to—all I did was say hello."

Nütterman said to Anneliese, "This is the man who has followed you for the past two hours, since the Römer?"

She nodded, staring at David. One of the cops who was holding him had pinched a nerve near the elbow; David winced and requested in German that he lay off. He said to Nütterman, trying to keep his voice at a reasonable pitch:

"It's true. I *was* following her. Because I couldn't get

up enough nerve to talk to her, that's all." He felt too unhappy to smile, but he looked apologetically at Anneliese.

She didn't respond. She had not relaxed her guard, despite the distance between them. Her eyes were steady on him. Even with the uproar, he had the curious sensation that they were all alone.

"I'm sorry I scared you, but it can't be the first time a man's come up to you on the street." He winced again at the hot pain in his elbow; the helpless hand trembled. He appealed to Nütterman.

"How about letting me go? I haven't done anything."

The inspector nodded to his subordinates. They released David.

"I hope you'll excuse us, but there are unusual circumstances. Fräulein Girda's life has been threatened. Let me have your passport."

David gave it to him, along with a business card. Nütterman looked them over, and handed the passport back.

"When did you arrive in Frankfurt?"

"This morning. On Lufthansa from New York."

"Where are you staying?"

"The Frankfurterhof. Suite 720."

Nütterman glanced at one of the other detectives, who made his way through the crowd to the street. He got into one of the unmarked cars and used the radio.

"My uncle is Colonel Joby Ben McNair, Chief of Legal Assistance, Fifth Army Corps. You can reach him at 151–5949. He'll verify everything I've told you."

Nütterman had no comment. He approached Anneliese, whom he seemed to know.

"He's a businessman, fräulein. Vice-president of the Riordan/McNair Paper Company of Savannah, Georgia. They have a subsidiary, Leybold Körperschaften, in Essen and Frankfurt. He only arrived in the country a few hours ago. I don't believe you have anything to fear from this man, fräulein. May we take you somewhere?"

Anneliese shook her head. She said something quietly, in German, that David couldn't overhear. The inspector shrugged and smiled. All in a day's work, he seemed to be telling her.

"Don't be afraid to call us if you have a good reason."

The other cops had drifted away; one of the cars left, accelerating rapidly down the long leafy street. Nütterman walked back to the remaining car, nodding pleasantly to David.

"What about my jacket?" David asked.

"Sorry," Nütterman said, his mind on other matters. He got into the back of the KRIPO car.

The acrobats had given up, the crowd was thinning out, there was space around David again. He stared at the sidewalk like a man who was trying hard to mind his own business and wanted to be left alone. He looked suddenly at Anneliese, who—surprisingly—hadn't budged. David found himself speechless again. He spread his hands in a gesture that was half angry, half contrite, turned and walked away.

"Just a moment," Anneliese said.

There was timidity in her voice; otherwise he might not even have hesitated. Anneliese saw that he was of a mind to keep going, his pride was riddled, and she took a full step toward him. But then she was cautious again. David, still stifled by his ordeal, felt, like a child, unnecessarily teased.

"I dated a man once, an executive with Leybold. Taller than you, narrow shoulders, red hair, little bald spot. When he becomes emotional he squints—like this."

She took off her glasses and screwed up her face; one

eye twitched heavily. It was ludicrous, but exact: he knew who she meant.

"Sounds like Hjalmar May."

Anneliese nodded, too enthusiastically, as if she needed to loosen up.

"And he knows you? If I asked him, he could give you a character reference?"

"If he didn't, I'd fire him." He felt, miraculously, at ease. He smiled. "You're a lot harder to convince than the police."

"I don't know how seriously they take my—my situation."

Anneliese glanced around; a few people were still deriving too much satisfaction from observing them. She flexed her shoulders tenderly, as if they were full of barbs. "They did come quickly when I called. It's the first time I've done that." Her eyes gleamed sadly through the partial eclipse of her modish glasses; David was stirred.

The sleeve of his ripped jacket was hanging down over his hand; he took off the jacket, hooked a finger in the collar, and threw it over one shoulder, then closed in protectively.

"Someone's actually threatened to kill you? Why?"

Anneliese clasped her hands in front of her, steeled herself, sighed.

"Whoever they are, they say I must know why I'm—marked. But I don't."

"How long has this been going on?"

"Nearly a month."

David was amazed, and indignant. "Why don't the police protect you?—assign a bodyguard, I mean."

"Nothing's happened. Nothing serious." She seemed to withdraw slightly from that judgment, but wouldn't alter it. "A few phone calls. The police can only do something—after the fact, as they put it."

"Look, I'm very sorry. I picked a bad time to be following you around. If there's anything I can do—"

"I have friends. They'd willingly stand guard day and night, if I asked them to. But I made up my mind not to live that way." She smiled, her teeth together. "To be f-free if it kills me."

"But they're only threats," he said hastily. "Telephone calls—that kind of thing goes on all the time."

"Three different voices so far. Three invisible enemies. Sometimes when I'm half asleep I think finally I'll see their faces, but it's always too dark." She gazed at a riverboat hauling barges. "Perhaps I'm just unlucky. It's a family tradition."

Her words scraped, as if they had worked deeply into him, against raw bone. He couldn't say anything else, but Anneliese rescued her own mood, before it fell too low, to the level of the cold river. She turned with a flourish, her hair in a tangle from breezes, glaring hotly in the photoflash of sun through the promenade trees. Her eyes were filled with speculation, and interest.

"You could never have dreamed you'd hear such a sad story when you picked me up. By the way, you're not very good at it."

"I know," David said, rubbing with a knuckle at a grin. Her presence denied the accusation. Blundering had its rewards.

"All that walking around! German men are much more direct. So are German women. What's your name?"

"David," he said, a little surprised, as if she always should have known it.

"I can fix that sleeve for you, David. I'm an expert seamstress."

"Oh. Well, you don't have to go to any—"

"If it would be any trouble, I wouldn't open my

mouth. Can we take a taxi? My feet are beginning to hurt."

As they walked toward the taxi stand in the street, they heard a pattering of applause and looked around, wondering if the acrobats had returned. But the applause was for them.

Anneliese blushed and touched his arm confidently, as if they were already good friends.

"Everybody loves a happy ending," David said.

28   From behind the wheel of her navy blue Opel Rekord, Franziska watched with rising anger as David and Anneliese got into a taxi.

Her head pounded from the venom that had pooled during a dull surveillance; confined too long, she ached in places where she needed to be supple and loose. She was Olympian in her concern for her body, fearful of the consequences of stunted reflex, and the emotion she felt upon seeing Anneliese touch David in a pleased decisive manner was too dangerous, she knew she could not afford it until other matters had been settled.

When the taxi pulled away, going west toward the Untermain bridge, Franziska put her own car into gear and made a risky U-turn, unyielding in the face of oncoming traffic, challenging and bluffing the driver of a bigger Monza, who very nearly took to the sidewalk in terror; with a grim single-handed twist of the wheel she drove fast in the other direction, blood on her lower lip where she had savaged it with her teeth. She was avid to claim a life; for now, any life would do.

29 "How's the boutique doing?" David asked.

"Not badly. But there are too many partners for any of us to make a really good living." Anneliese sat behind her desk in the workroom, using a long basting needle beneath a round illuminated magnifying mirror. David watched her hands, and then her face. "I've been to the U.S. twice since August. This last visit was the most promising. A man who owns several boutiques in Los Angeles agreed to buy several dozen lots and to do— what did he call it? The necessary promotionals. 'Fashions by Anneliese.'" She looked up with a slight smile, as if encouraging him to be impressed; then her lip curled, denying the benevolence of Fate. "Well, I may catch on but I may not. I have to be philosophical about my chances."

There was a knock at the door, and David opened it. The wry-necked blonde girl from the shop came in smiling, carrying a bottle of wine. She gave David a curious second glance.

"Hilda, this is David," Anneliese said with a casual wave of her hand. "His last name is Scottish, but I don't remember what it is."

Hilda said fondly, "Don't pay attention, she's terrible at names. Our billing was chaotic until we got her out of the boutique and into the workroom."

"McNair," David told Hilda, and spelled it.

"That's right, I remember from the credit card this morning." Anneliese glanced up and Hilda said, "Shall I open the wine?"

"Let David do it," Anneliese said. "We're working and he's just loafing."

Hilda winked at David and left. There was a tray, with clean glasses and a crystal carafe, on a chest. He uncorked the bottle and decanted some of the wine.

"Are you supposed to let white wine breathe?"

"No. Help yourself, David, I'll be through here in a few minutes."

David poured wine for two. Anneliese had begun to stitch the sleeve of the ripped jacket to the shoulder. She worked quickly.

"You didn't tell me you were in the boutique this morning."

"Yes, about eleven-thirty."

"That's a coincidence."

"How do you mean?"

"That you should be here, and that we should meet so soon afterward."

"My uncle recommended your boutique. He said it was the best. And that's what I was looking for."

"Oh, he's the one with the military here in Frankfurt."

"Joby Ben's a lawyer. Judge advocates, they call them in the army."

"Did you buy anything?"

"A shirt. I had it sent to the hotel."

"I see." Anneliese paused thoughtfully. David waited, unsure of how well she accepted his explanations. But after a few moments she resumed sewing. "This is nice goods. Expensive. What kind of paper do you make in your mills?"

"Mostly bathroom tissue."

"Oh my God, honestly?"

"Somebody has to. It's not fashionable, but it's steady."

"Yes, but think of all those trees that have to be cut down."

"The rape of the land? It's pulpwood, Anneliese. Grows like a weed where I come from. We have plantations full of them. For every tree we cut, we plant another one. We've been practicing silvaculture since 1934."

"That's very sensible. But Scots are sensible people. In some ways very like Germans." She pulled out the white basting threads, got up, and handed him the jacket. "Try it on, please."

David slipped into his jacket and buttoned it. Anneliese touched the repaired shoulder, smoothed it, gave a quick tug at his lapels to snug the collar to the nape of his neck. Then she frowned and began pinching at the material under one arm and in front.

"It doesn't fit you. Have you lost weight recently?"

"I may have. I haven't been eating. No appetite."

"Were you ill?" she asked, looking closely at his eyes.

"No. Just a—a personal problem."

Her hands lingered at the level of his breastbone, fingers lightly gripping the lapels of his jacket, as if she were reluctant to let go. Then she decided not to pry and swung around to pick up the glass of wine he had poured for her. David self-consciously touched the seam she had resewn.

"You did a good job. I can't tell it was ripped."

"Fine material, but bad sewing. It's what you get these days."

Anneliese briefly elevated her glass. "Your health, David." She had a sip. "I thought you were going to start something with those policemen," she said reminiscently. "A look came over your face. I think they would have had to knock you in the head to stop you. Beat your knees with truncheons until you collapsed.

But not before you broke a few bones yourself. Well, I'm glad it didn't come to that."

"So am I." David looked around at some of the sketches pinned to a corkboard wall. "These are terrific. Did you study design?"

"A few courses, when I was modeling. I learned the fundamentals mostly from watching other designers. I made a few trips to Paris." She stared at her sketches with a mixture of pride and worry. "There's not much encouragement to be found in this business."

There was a silence. She offered her gaze to fill it.

"Are you married, David?"

"Yes."

"You don't wear a ring."

"We decided not to."

"Do you have children?"

"A girl. She's ten."

"And you adore her. I can see it in your eyes when you mention her."

David smiled. "Sharon's great."

"You must have been staring at me in the museum for a long time. I felt your eyes on me before I looked around."

"What did you think when you saw me? Were you worried?"

"Oh no, not then. I was a model, I'm used to stares, and you seemed nice enough. But sad, now that I think about it. I felt an impulse to do something for you—anything. Is it a good marriage, David?"

"Sure. We're happy. I think Reba's happy."

Anneliese repeated the name, soundlessly, to herself, testing it.

"Have you had many affairs?"

"None. Not since I've been married."

She looked faintly disbelieving, and lowered her eyes. She pressed the glass against her lips without drinking. The tip of her tongue touched the bell and traced its roundness.

"What do you want from me, then?"

"Just—to be with you."

"What if I said that was absolutely out of the question?"

"It isn't, though, is it?"

"I have the feeling that no matter what I say, it wouldn't make any difference. You're certainly not aggressive, but you're—relentless." Anneliese seemed perplexed, and momentarily faint of heart. Then she lifted her chin. "Well...where are you staying, David?"

"The Frankfurterhof."

"I have dinner guests, from England. A charming old baronet and his wife. But they retire early."

"Where will I meet you?" David said.

"There's a jazz club in Old Sachsenhausen—the Bonhomie. Would nine-thirty be all right, David?"

30 The four-thirty express train to Heidelberg was about to leave from Frankfurt's *hauptbanhof*, the central railroad station. Franziska, unused to being pregnant, and further burdened by the hamper and campstool she was carrying, was afraid she wouldn't make it. She put one arm across the prominent mound of belly and broke into a waddling run, unsure of what the consequences would be. But nothing gave way. Around her, other dedicated playgoers were hustling to make the train. A conductor saw her coming and reached for the hamper.

"You shouldn't run like that; what if you fell?"

"Oh, I'm used to it," Franziska said, with a broad smile she intended to seem daft. "I still jog every day."

The conductor shook his head in passionless disapproval and lifted the heavy hamper up after her. Franziska took it and walked to her first-class compartment.

Just as she sat down, the train began to glide from the enormous shed. She was alone in the compartment. She put the hamper on the seat beside her, took out an apple and a copy of Marlowe's *Faust*. The Elizabethan gab was a bother, but she found the play easier to penetrate than Goethe's interminable, brooding divine comedy; and she was enamored of Mephistopheles, his casuistry. *Carpe diem*. The chains of words bound her mind, so that she didn't spend precious energy constructing scenarios of unforeseeable events.

The train began to rocket southward, through the neat greening miles between the Rhine and the heights of the Odenwald; here it was warmer than elsewhere in West Germany, the fruit trees had been in flower for a week. In less than an hour she would be in Heidelberg. There was nothing to worry about. Joby Ben would be there. At the thought of him she nudged herself tenderly, where the disjointed child of their union lay in the blank tomb of belly.

31   David returned to the Frankfurterhof at a quarter to five. There was an envelope for him at the mail desk.

Inside was a copy of the deposit slip: Slightly fewer

than four hundred thousand marks had been deposited in Anneliese Girda's personal account at the Kolner Bank branch on Reuterweg.

He studied the ticket and tried to imagine her own reaction in a day or two, when she discovered the gift of money. Shock, consternation, disbelief: He could imagine everything but joy, because he felt, desperately, that he wanted to snatch the money back. Joby Ben had been right all along. He was amazed at his self-deception. He felt like a strange kind of thief. Somehow he had reanimated rather than redressed tragedy. If he had not met Anneliese and instantly fallen in love with her, this would not have occurred to him. The money was a burden, a great bloating corpse that sickened him.

Now he realized the simple truth: There would have to be amends of greater consequence.

32 There was a tour bus waiting at the Heidelberg railroad station. The tour guide was a woman in her fifties with a youthful short haircut and frantic eyes, as if the deep vertical wrinkles in her face were the bars of a prison from which she couldn't escape.

"Your first?" she said to Franziska, looking curiously at her maternity outfit, which was black and gray: skirt, blouse, sweater. Franziska seemed about to give birth from the depths of mourning.

But her attitude was cheery enough. "Oh, no. Sometimes I feel as if I've always been pregnant. I wanted to see the play before the crowds get too bad."

The guide helped her up into the bus. "The middle seats will be more comfortable for you—away from the wheels."

"Thank you." Franziska settled down with her copy of *Faust*. The tour of Old Heidelberg lasted about fifty minutes. She seldom looked up as they went down one thriving medieval street after another, illuminated in raw gold by the lowering sun. Afterward dinner was served in the dining room of the Hotel Ritter. Franziska lugged her hamper in with her.

"Special diet," she explained, and ate raw vegetables with her tea.

At twenty minutes past seven, in the fine spring dusk, they boarded the bus again and were driven slowly up a winding, heavily-trafficked brick road toward the lights of Heidelberg Castle.

33 In a clearing off a hilltop lane a few miles north of Heidelberg, Joby Ben checked his appearance in a magnifying mirror by the last light of the sun that streamed through the rear window of his Opel Senator.

He had mounted a new nose, his favorite, which he had spent many hours constructing in a basement workroom of his house in Niederursel. It was an awesome, ravaged-looking thing with a ruddy color and realistic broken veins. Beneath the false nose he had installed a guardsman's sandy mustache, which covered a good portion of his meaty upper lip. He was wearing a pair of horn-rimmed glasses and a checked wool cap. He looked, in this face, fierce and quarrelsome, someone to be avoided.

Heidelberg, a city of two hundred thousand people, was the headquarters for the U.S. Army in Europe. Joby Ben was frequently there on business; he had dozens of acquaintances and a few old buddies from previous tours in the area. The odds were good that tonight, at the play which was being performed in the courtyard of Schloss Heidelberg, he would encounter someone he knew. And he was confident that he wouldn't rate a second glance. He was sure that he could even have fooled Franziska, if he hadn't had a dress rehearsal with full makeup the night before.

Joby Ben got out of the car, which was lit like a pyre in the clearing he had chosen for privacy. Birdsong dribbled down the ledges of trees as he changed his clothes. He took off the army fatigues he had worn to work that morning and put on corduroy pants and a flannel shirt, an older, well-worn pair of Corcoran jump boots. From the spare-tire well in the trunk of the expensive automobile he removed a chrome-steel Smith and Wesson .357 magnum revolver with a six-inch barrel. The weapon was in a shoulder holster that fitted it like a glove. He strapped on the rig and covered it with a bulky coat-sweater that had a shawl collar; the collar also concealed his clipped left earlobe, a point of identification that someone might later recall.

The sun was abruptly quenched and the clearing faded, like a very old color photo, into silver-fleshed shadows, ghost tones of violet and amber. Suitably armed and disguised, Joby Ben felt as if he had just touched down from another planet. He felt skin-deep and invisible, unburdened by age, a troublesome heart, knowledge of mortality. For a few moments he was enthralled by his potential power.

34 Anneliese locked the boutique and caught a northbound streetcar. She settled down with her newspaper and checked the Toto-Lotto numbers for the day before. She was still not a winner. She shrugged, and in the flashes of the setting sun as the linked cars angled toward Opernplatz, she tried to interest herself in the news.

But David was on her mind, and Anneliese put the paper down and stared at the familiar street, wondering about the state of her emotions when she could be so easily taken with so obviously unsuitable a man. He was in Frankfurt for a few days on business, he had slipped the leash and he wanted someone to go to bed with. He was plain about his desires, without being blunt. He'd made a fool of himself and recovered nimbly, and with honor: Anneliese respected him for that. She was even willing to believe that he didn't make a practice of picking up women during his travels. She instinctively trusted a core of integrity—if he had approached her, there must be extraordinary circumstances, an explanation for the sadness she had seen in his glances, which she would hear in time.

Anneliese knew, but didn't care, that her judgment had been crowded out of shape by his presence—the truth was she hadn't had the full use of her senses since being hit, at some time during the afternoon, squarely in the back of the head by a big soft mallet. She was fascinated, excited, impulsive—she had been ready, impatient for this man for many months. She felt a subtle chill of loss, a minor ache, and wished that she had invited David to dinner. He was married, he would inevitably leave Frankfurt. Their affair had to be brief, and all the more pleasurable for lack of time. Perhaps she could still give him a call, just as soon as she got home...

She left the streetcar at Grüneburgweg and walked toward her flat. It was a prosperous, immaculate neighborhood of three-and-four-story homes and some small apartment houses near the Palmengarten. Two blocks north of Anneliese's flat at 90 Oberlindau stood several recently built high-rise apartment buildings, across Grüneburgplatz from the headquarters of the U.S. Fifth Army Corps in Frankfurt. Four children were playing with a remote-controlled racing car near a phone box on the corner of Parkstrasse and Grüneburgweg. In the box the phone was ringing. Anneliese glanced at it, happily preoccupied, thinking about preparations for dinner, and crossed to the north side of the street.

She saw, without looking directly at it, a gray-and-black Citröen CX-2400, moving slowly toward her but a block away, near the thoroughfare of Reuterweg. As she reached the opposite curb she heard the car speed up with a quick screech of tires, and thought of the children.

Anneliese looked back. One of the boys had ventured into the phone box; standing on his toes, he lifted down the receiver. The Citröen, with its somber colors and tinted windows reminiscent of a hearse, had swung to the opposite side of the street and was bearing down on her.

The near-side back door was flung open. Anneliese turned all the way around, facing the car, and took a step back, to a brick-and stucco wall fiercely struck by the lowering sun. Her angular shadow flew up the wall and out of sight. A tape was playing in the car. She heard a snatch of an upbeat popular song: ABBA. "Take a Chance on Me." She saw the faces of men, split by black bars of sunglasses, turned toward her. The thin young man in the back seat, his hair in wooly disarray, leaned to the open door and lobbed a bomb.

Anneliese screamed and instinctively jerked her face aside, throwing up her hands. The bomb hit the brick wall beside her head with a glassy *pop*. Most of the red paint, laced with bits of glass, struck her hands and dress. But globs of it splattered her hair and got into one eye, momentarily blinding her. The car sped away; she wasn't aware of its going. Anneliese sobbed in fright and distress. The remains of the big light globe that had been thrown at her littered the sidewalk. There was a heavy splotch, like an open wound, on the brick wall.

"Are you Fräulein Girda?"

Anneliese fumbled in her bag for a handkerchief to wipe the smarting eye. Dripping paint, she looked down at the boy on the curb. All of the children had abandoned their game and were watching her. She trembled uncontrollably.

"Y-yes," Anneliese said.

"There is a phone call for you."

"W-what did you say?"

"You are wanted on the phone."

"W-w-where?"

He turned and pointed gravely at the phone box. "There."

"What happened, Fräulein?" one of the other boys asked. He couldn't resist a mess, and was poking at the sharp remains of the paint bomb on the sidewalk. "Did they hurt you?"

Anneliese tried to answer him, and couldn't. She was shuddering too badly. She looked around for help; there was no one in sight but the children. In the phone box the receiver dangled from its steel cord. Her nose ran from the paint fumes. She blotted it with the stained handkerchief, making a worse mess of her face. Then, because she could think of nothing else to do at this moment, she crossed the street and picked up the receiver of the telephone. She had a glimpse of her reflection on the steel surface of the equipment. She bit down hard on the handkerchief she had knotted around her hand, trying not to scream. A car drove by and Anneliese turned away from the street, as if ashamed to show herself.

Dimly she heard someone call her name.

"W-what—who is it?"

Silence then, the charged silence of a long tunnel, an open line. Anneliese braced herself against one side of the phone box, streaking it with paint from her hand. Streetcars whined distantly on Reuterweg, a nervous mother called her child off the street. Anneliese began to sob.

Still she continued to hold the receiver to her ear, unable to let go, as if it were a lifeline.

35 Traudl Hecker, standing near a window of a tenth-floor apartment in a building two blocks from the phone booth on Parkstrasse, could see Anneliese clearly with binoculars, though the sun was gone from the street.

Traudl was a hardbitten beauty with the charred eyes of a waning firebrand in a face flat as a stencil, which would, nonetheless, swell with extravagant emotion at the slightest provocation, until she burst into tongues. Fluent in six languages, she owned as many bogus passports. In the past several months she had gained thirty pounds and her hair had changed from brown to gold to red and back again. Traudl Hecker was the most hunted woman in Europe, considered to be the most dangerous. Tears streamed down her cheeks as she wept for Anneliese, even as she contemplated her anguish in the phone box and wondered if she had broken yet.

Traudl put down the binoculars to rest her eyes, leaving her face imprinted with owlish false spectacles. She spoke into the phone.

"We could as easily have killed you, Anneliese."

"What—are you s-saying? Who *are* you?"

The slight stutter she remembered so well. Traudl said patiently, "You must recognize my voice, Anneliese."

"No! I don't know who you are. W-why are you doing this to me?"

Behind Traudl the door to the room opened and Jürgen Sollmann came in. She offered him the binoculars. He stood beside her, a head taller, and looked at their quarry in the phone box.

Anneliese's teeth were chattering; Traudl could hear them over the phone. She wiped her wet cheeks with one hand. Her own voice was steady and without passion.

"Very well. Perhaps you don't remember. It's been five years since you last saw me, and ten years since we all took a vow—"

"Oh my God—it's Traudl, isn't it? Traudl Hecker!"

Traudl felt an instinctive twinge of dismay at hearing her name spoken aloud on any telephone. She talked more quickly, wanting to get this over with.

"I tried to stay out of it, Anneliese, because of what

you meant to me. I told the others that you couldn't be involved, no matter what rumors we heard. But now there's no doubt that you've betrayed us."

"This is crazy! I have nothing to do with *any* of you any m-more—"

"Last month two of our comrades were double-crossed and killed. The heroin disappeared, the money disappeared. But you know where our money is."

"M-money—?"

Jürgen lowered the binoculars and said in disgust, "What a waste of time."

Traudl continued, as if she were instructing a dull-witted child, "One million marks that belong to the Tribunal. Our war fund, Anneliese."

Her stammer was pronounced, angry. "I'm t-t-telling you, I don't know what you're t-t-talking—"

"You made a mistake today. You deposited some of our money in your personal account at the Kolner Bank. Nearly four hundred thousand marks."

Jürgen looked again at Anneliese. She was holding her head with one hand. He had begun to worry about the time she was taking, about the police.

"That's not true," Anneliese said in a weary, deliberate voice.

"We knew about it almost as soon as the deposit was made."

"How could you, when I don't even know mys-s—"

"There are only a few of us," Traudl said. "But we have many *sympathisants*. Anneliese...you mean nothing to me any more. There will be no more warnings. I'll call you again. You will then tell me where we can pick up our money, all of it." Jürgen, searching with the binoculars, had noticed a flickering of blue lights several blocks away, on Reuterweg. He nudged Traudl.

"If you fail us, Anneliese, I'll kill you myself."

Anneliese took a quick sharp breath. "Why should

you want to kill me? Stop s-saying that! I haven't done anything!"

Traudl hung up. Jürgen continued to watch the on-coming *panzerwagen*. It passed the intersection with Grüneburgweg and continued, racing, north. He looked back at Anneliese. She was still standing in the phone box, holding the receiver of the telephone. Two boys were outside, keeping her company.

She hung up finally and crept out of the box like an accident victim leaving a wrecked car and continued toward her flat, walking hesitantly and with a diffident weave, as if she were trying to establish dance steps for a persistent tune in her head. Anneliese's fingers picked at the tacky paint everywhere in her hair, on her face.

Jürgen surrendered her and turned to Traudl.

"Was she frightened?"

"Yes." Traudl put the telephone on the floor. In this room of the apartment, which they had occupied for three weeks, there was also a mattress with a blanket, a lamp, a chair, a stray cat, an Israeli-made submachine gun.

He said ruthlessly, "We should pick her up now and finish with her."

Traudl's face swelled, toning to purple beneath the eyes, and subsided. Her voice was composed, but it was law.

"She won't resist us any longer."

Traudl and Jürgen looked at each other. A failed intellectual turned gunman, he had sulky dark good looks, the settled-in sensuality of a balding man. During the unhappy weeks they had lingered in Frankfurt, he had been losing hair as fast as Traudl gained weight.

"You said she couldn't steal from us. But she did."

"No. I'm convinced she wasn't directly involved. Perhaps someone has a hold on her." The cat, a gray-and-white tabby, arched against one of Traudl's boots;

Traudl picked her up. "We were the victims of rich, arrogant criminals, who also happen to be businessmen. The sort of people Anneliese knows well. I think I shocked her when I told her it was heroin they stole."

"She could be more afraid of them than she is of us. We've done this badly." He brooded over the possible consequences. "Either she'll alert her friends—or she'll run."

"We've made it obvious to Anneliese that no matter how far she runs, we'll find her. Who knows how long the money is intended to remain on account? Weeks, months. It won't be missed right away. If she turns it over to us, she'll have time to make—arrangements. But if she talks to her powerful friends, if it's apparent that she knows more than she should, for their own protection they'll kill her immediately. When she's calm, when she can think it through, she'll realize her best hope is to trust me."

"There is this—bond between the two of you, that the rest of us are not privileged to understand."

Two sets of eyes appraised him. The room was growing dark. The cat began to lick her fur. Jürgen wavered from Traudl's flat and unsparing gaze, looked around the room.

"We've stayed too long. I can feel it."

"We'll move soon. The money first." Only a year ago the Tribunal had been at full strength: fifteen *anarchistische* Marxists, nearly matching the known membership of the *Rote Armee Fraktion,* the more notorious RAF, who also practiced the "politics of despair." Kidnappings, bombings, audacious jailbreaks: After each sortie the Tribunal had been reduced in size. Six of them were now serving long prison sentences; two had been recently murdered, by gangsters taking advantage of their inexperience in the major leagues of dope dealing. Now there were Traudl, Jürgen, Chris, Ernst. And they were desperate, although not for themselves.

"The money," Traudl said again. "Money is our key to the prisons. Manfred has already gone crazy in isolation. Who knows how long the others will last? There'll be another Stammheim, more state-sanctioned murders, unless we act quickly."

The cat was now dissatisfied, restless; perhaps Traudl had squeezed her too tightly. Traudl put the cat down, experiencing a twinge low in the back as she did so, regretting the extra poundage that made her feel awkward and uneasy. She had always hated what was soft and indulgent in the world; her new craving for food was like a scary disease. For much of her life she'd had the rigorously compacted body of a gymnast. For a while her favorite disguise had been as a sixteen-year-old boy. Now she passed for a matron of forty on streets where newspaper-sponsored wanted posters still featured her narrow silhouette and shoulder-length hair, the beret she had adopted in homage to Patty Hearst.

Traudl had eaten only an hour ago, but she was ravenous again. Food was a substitute for inaction, hunger a symptom of vacillation. She was still at odds with herself in the matter of Anneliese. How sincerely Traudl wanted to believe in her former friend's innocence, how badly she'd been fooled! Even so, Traudl knew she could never have permitted Anneliese to be physically tortured.

She licked her lips in remembrance of Anneliese's panic, the weakening protestations of innocence. The money that rightfully belonged to them would be released as an offering, and soon; then Traudl would have to kill her, but it could be done mercifully. Forgivingly. Unlike nearly everyone else in this world, Traudl never forgot a debt, an obligation.

36 On that sultry noon in Savannah, Reba let herself into the garden of the townhouse on Governor's Square feeling like the resident haunt checking in for work a little early. She'd taken her last Percs at six A.M. after a torturously sleepless night, and they were just wearing off, leaving her with a slightly nauseated, one-foot-in-limbo feeling. Reba hid her eyes behind dark and oversized lenses, but she didn't think she'd fool anybody who looked closely: She was in miserable shape today.

Sharon had spent the night with Neddie; the two of them were on the Greek porch. Sharon rocked while Neddie unpacked rare old porcelain and bisque dolls from a trunk designed to hold her collection. Sharon didn't seem caught up in the spirit of the event. She sprang out of the chair as soon as she heard the gate and saw her mother.

"Did you talk to Daddy?"

Reba felt her smile pulling her face out of shape.

"No—not yet. Are you and Neddie having a good time?" She forced her way through the palpable heat of the garden to the foot of the stairs. Neddie glanced at her.

"Sharon and I always have a good time, when we get to see each other. You're not taking her away from me already, are you, Reba?" She held out a doll to her granddaughter. "Look at this little lady, Sharon, she's an authentic Bye-lo doll, more than a hundred years old."

Sharon said, with a bland lack of enthusiasm, "Grandma says I can have any one I want for my next birthday."

"That's nice," Reba said.

"Reba, is anything the matter? Your eyes are just slits this morning."

"I must have an allergy."

"Oh. Why don't you see if there's some black coffee left in the kitchen?"

Reba shrugged and went on up to the porch. "Do you think you and Louellen could look after Sharon for three or four days?"

"Mom."

Reba said, with a flash of temper, "Don't start." Neddie's good eye narrowed.

"Why?"

"Because I've been thinking—I'd really like to join David in Frankfurt. Surprise him." She put a conciliatory hand on the back of Sharon's head. Sharon edged away, eyes grimly downcast.

"Is that a good idea, Reba? Bothering him when he's away on business?"

Reba's nails gripped the sore palm of her right hand. She made a deliberate effort to keep her tone light.

"You've said that before. What makes you think I'm ever a bother to David? He's my *husband*. We have a marriage. And I miss him."

Neddie fussed with the fragile dress of the doll she was holding.

"I certainly don't think David has any quarrel with the kind of wife you've been—"

Reba ignored the slight emphasis on David's name, but discouragement was already setting in: she was always too many points behind in the private reckoning Neddie kept on a tab somewhere in her mind.

"It's a feeling I have, a feeling that he *needs* me right

now. Don't you—can't you make the effort to understand?"

"If you're going to fight," Sharon said unhappily, "can I go someplace else?"

Reba reached awkwardly for her daughter again, and Sharon relented, leaning against her.

"We're not fighting." Reba stared at Neddie, who had obligingly assumed a rather vacuous expression, meant to convey that she was indeed trying to cope with another of Reba's irrational moods.

"I don't like the way David left here. I don't know what was on his mind. He said it was a business trip, but I—I don't think so. You see, he's not at the hotel, I've left messages, he hasn't checked into the office, I can't get hold of Joby Ben—"

At the mention of Joby Ben, Neddie's face changed; something claimed her attention so forcefully that she seemed snatched from the presence of Reba and Sharon. Reba was about to go on, but realized she wouldn't be heard. She watched, perplexed and a little frightened, as Neddie turned and went to the doors of the library. She fumbled there to let herself in, dropping the old doll she'd been holding. The door closed behind her.

"What's the matter with—"

"I don't know. Maybe she—you wait here, I'll go see if I can—"

Reba handed the dropped doll to Sharon and went in. She heard Louellen singing gospel in the kitchen. Neddie wasn't in sight. She crossed the library to the hall and caught a glimpse of Neddie moving through the parlor, which had seen little of the light of day since the wake for Frank. Reba intercepted her there.

"Mother Riordan?"

Neddie sighed.

"What's the matter? Don't you feel well?"

Neddie trembled in Reba's grasp. She raised her

head. She looked dazed in the dim light. She turned, distraught, as if casting around for the body of her husband. There was something senile and pathetic in her actions.

"Gone."

Oh, my God, Reba thought. *What is David going to say?* "Yes. Neddie, why don't we—"

"I was sick. Old before my time."

"What? What? I can barely hear you."

Neddie raised her hands, capturing Reba's face. She had strength, and anger, despite the weakness of her voice. Reba was afraid to move.

"That's why I couldn't go. How could I face Frank? How could I win?"

"Mother Riordan," Reba said kindly, "I don't understand what you're trying to tell me."

In the kitchen, Louellen's voice hit an unexpected, lovely high note. Neddie took a fresh purchase on Reba's face. She moved her own face a fraction closer.

"That's all I was ever afraid of. *Her.*" Reba felt a little sick from Neddie's breath, and shrank from the vile contempt she had expressed. But Neddie wouldn't let her go, and for a giddy few moments Reba imagined that Neddie was on the verge of clawing at her face. Then, unexpectedly, Neddie stepped back, hands falling to her sides.

"But it's twenty-five years! How can she hurt me now?"

"I'm sorry. I have no earthly idea what you're talking about."

Neddie gestured vaguely, her hand heavy with pain.

"Oh—never mind, Reba. What were we talking about? Of course you know I'd be delighted to have Sharon! Why don't we go into the front room. I don't believe it's too early for sherry."

"No, it isn't, but I'd rather have that coffee you—recommended."

Neddie called to Louellen, then took Reba by the arm. In the front room they sat as far apart as possible on a black horsehair sofa that had always been so forbidding and uncomfortable Reba thought of it as a Seat of Judgment. She watched Neddie, anxiously; but Neddie seemed to have come around, and was in full possession of herself. Neddie mused silently until Louellen served them. After two sips of Bristol Cream she said to her daughter-in-law:

"What plane are you catching?"

"The three o'clock to Kennedy. Then TWA to Frankfurt."

Neddie nodded stiffly.

"I really *have* to go. I just wish I could help you understand how important it is for me to have my marriage work."

"Why shouldn't it work? You have David."

"But marriage isn't so—so final as all that, Mother Riordan. It isn't like the grave. For me—it's always been a process of catching up. Trying to redefine myself, in favor of everyone else's expectations. Always on the short end, I guess. Resenting it."

Neddie poured more sherry into her tiny glass. In profile her chin came up, rather defensively.

"I have always wanted to love you. But I can't. Forgive me."

Reba's eyes teared; she didn't know if it was pain she felt, or humiliation. She put her cup and saucer down.

"Better run, still have to p-pack."

Neddie didn't move. Reba went awkwardly past her, then hesitated and turned, expectant as always.

"I can make a difference to David, now; don't you see?"

"Yes. Yes, just go."

Instead Reba went back to give her a kiss. It only brushed her cheek, rasping lightly, falling like a leaf past a monument in the park.

"It's all right...Neddie."

"Don't we hope so," Neddie said, not looking up.

37 At seven-thirty, with the sky a nearly starless navy blue overhead and a cloud-flecked line of sunset visible in the west, the outdoor floodlights of Heidelberg Castle dimmed and a figure in medieval costume stirred on an open-air stage hung like a vast cocoon in one walled corner of the courtyard.

From his vantage point on a battlement of the west bastion, Joby Ben raked opera glasses across the cobbled yard, which was packed with spectators, many of them standing. Franziska had camped where he had told her to, on a grassy knoll just inside the main entrance to the seven-hundred-year-old castle. The knoll was crowded too—with blanket-sitters, mothers diapering babies, families disposing of the last of their picnic dinners as the stage lights, mounted in nearby trees like alien buds, warmed and focused on Faust's study. Appreciation rippled through the audience; the advent of the drama, like a painful birth, worked to still their incredulity, their careless murmurings.

The hamper that Franziska had brought with her sat between her feet. Her hands were folded on her protuberant belly. Joby Ben smiled and watched the play, for nearly twenty minutes.

At ten of eight he heard someone coming cautiously along the parapet; a shoe scraped stone. He put down the glasses and closed his eyes, so he would be able to see better in the velvet dark. A hand was placed on his shoulder. Joby Ben turned.

She was a pretty, folk-naïve blonde in her mid-twenties, with a rabbity upper lip and round steel-rimmed glasses. Her eyes looked timid, wearied by the burden of the prescription lenses she had to wear. She seemed, for a moment, airily unreal, as if he had been charmed by the actors into believing only in the life of the drama they were enacting.

But when she spoke, her breath smelled of spicy bratwurst, a hasty meal that hadn't set too well on a nervous stomach. She held out her other hand, modeling a Tyrolean hat on her fist.

"I think this one should fit you."

Joby Ben took the hat from her and substituted it for the cloth cap he'd been wearing.

"Thanks. You got the time?"

"Any time," she said, and backed away from him with a little nod and a defensive bunching of her shoulders. She smiled then and returned the way she had come, along the parapet. Joby Ben raised his opera glasses and glanced at the play again, then relocated Franziska. Satisfied, he put the glasses away in a pocket of his bulky sweater and took nearby steps down to the courtyard.

Patience was required to get through and around the crowd without antagonizing anyone or drawing unnecessary attention to himself. The actors' voices seemed to boom at this level. Franziska didn't look up as he paused beside her. He tapped her shoulder twice with the spread fingers of one hand, bent down to take the hamper. Her cold hand grazed the side of his face; she fumbled with his clipped earlobe for luck and then let the hand fall back to the shelf of her lap. Joby Ben continued on his way, down the wide dim alley from courtyard to driveway, a distance of about fifty yards. Others were leaving temporarily, or returning from the portable toilets along the drive. He came upon divergent paths, grassy spaces, trailers that served as dressing rooms for the actors, another trailer from which the lighting for the play was controlled. Apprentices in tights or jeans were lounging with cigarettes on broken walls. There was an unexpected patch of fog, as if someone had been experimenting with a theatrical effect. He looked for policemen, and didn't see any.

He skirted the east walls of the castle, finding it dark again, except for small footlights placed between boulders on a green. A big drumlike flood was tilted toward the heights of the castle. The narrow path led abruptly down to a parking area where about twenty cars and recreational vehicles belonging to members of the theatrical troupe were parked in a rectangle about half an acre in size.

Within this compound, picnic tables and grills had been set up. Joby Ben smelled sizzling meat. There was an outlet road on the far side of the compound, winding downhill to the starry river. As he approached the parking lot from total darkness he encountered more fog at hedge level, where the cold air of the mountain and the humid air from the river came together.

Joby Ben squeezed cautiously between a Winnebago camper and a van, glancing at the driver's seat of the camper as he went by. He saw the blonde again. She was looking through the high windshield at a picnic table where three young men and a woman sat silently, eating. All of them wore Tyrolean hats. He couldn't see if the blonde was holding a weapon, but he felt reasonably sure she had a submachine gun close to hand.

Before announcing himself, he made a quick reconnaissance of the compound, looking for trouble spots. Across the way a squat bearded man, his back to Joby Ben, was grilling meat. His dog, a tethered shepherd, was growling about something. The man quieted him by throwing down a handful of smoking pork. On the river side of the compound a couple leaned against a car, caressing each other in a way that was sufficiently sensual to arouse the voyeur in him. No one else was around.

It wasn't a great setup, but it would do. Obviously the RAF felt that this location placed him at a disadvantage, which might make them somewhat less than homicidally suspicious, their usual state of mind.

He stepped boldly out from between the camper and the van and plunked the picnic hamper down at one end of the table. They all looked up at him.

"Hello, cousins," Joby Ben said.

He looked from one face to another. Because they were obsessed with disguise, he found them only vaguely familiar, although Fifth Army Corps was plastered with their most recent mug shots. The RAF, in the Baader-Meinhof days, had bombed the Abrams Building twice.

On his second try he recognized the spokesman for this small group, with whom he had had shadowy preliminary dealings. His name was Felix. He was tall and surprisingly tanned and was suffering from a bad cough. The girl next to him, then, had to be Friedelind Schmid, the resident intellectual and glamor girl of the movement; her popularity with a university generation immersed in radical chic rivaled that of Traudl Hecker. She had wonderful bones and that thrill-mad wanton look of minor European movie actresses, but her mouth was spiteful and she ate peasant fashion with her hands: an obvious affectation, because her background was one of money and quiet social distinction. Joby Ben couldn't name the other two men, and didn't care about them. They looked like the kind of pretentious middle-class dropouts easily recruited by zealots to serve as foot soldiers in the revolutionary army. One of them got up to turn the sausages on the grill. He gave Joby Ben a narrow-eyed, over-the-shoulder look he had stolen from a Clint Eastwood film.

Felix cleared his throat. "Hello, who's this, Mr. Smith?" He coughed again, a hacking dirge that raised drops of sweat on his reddening brow.

Joby Ben said, "I thought you'd get rid of that asthma after a few weeks in the desert."

Felix, as if he were afraid he'd been belittled, coughed harder. Friedelind put a protective arm around his shoulders. Joby Ben watched the fog creep closer, and kept talking.

"You're thinner, too. Maybe Arab food don't agree with you." He opened his hamper. One of the soldiers looked as if he were about to go for his gun. Joby Ben gestured peaceably and handed Felix a wrapped sandwich. He could feel eyes on the back of his head, and wondered if the blonde in the camper had him pinned down with her own weapon.

Felix brought himself under control and carefully unwrapped the sandwich, after examining it from all angles for possible booby traps. Between generous wedges of German dark bread he found new money, a packet of deutschemarks a quarter of an inch thick. Felix, expressionless, rewrapped the sandwich and placed it beside his plate.

"That's a gift," Joby Ben said. "It's show-me money."

Felix nodded, and gestured wanly in Friedelind's direction.

"Show him."

Friedelind removed a head of lettuce from a vinyl tote bag and passed it to Joby Ben. He peeled away a couple of leaves and came to a fist-sized plastic bag stuffed inside the hollowed-out head. He untied the bag and sampled the contents. It was pure heroin. He looked at Felix.

"That's good. I can handle all you've got."

"That's all there is."

Joby Ben winced and looked at the table. He began to smile, torturously. He looked up, wide-eyed, staring at Felix.

"Now, I can't believe that. I can't believe you'd call in a top expert like myself just to handle this miserable poke—" He batted the head of lettuce off the table. "It shows poor business judgment. It shows you're not *serious!*" Felix hung his head patiently, clasping his hands. "But you're dealing with a serious man," Joby Ben continued, really angry now and struggling not to lose control of his voice. "And I didn't come all the way to Heidelberg to get jerked off by a bunch of so-called revolutionaries!"

He glanced around the table. Only Friedelind met his eyes, and lifted her shoulders indifferently as she gnawed the meat from a sparerib. Joby Ben put two fingers on the pulse of his right wrist and willed himself to settle down. He tried again.

"I know you've got more than this. The PLO stole plenty of it, and they've been passing it out to terrorist organizations all over the goddam—"

Friedelind tossed the bone aside and flared at him. "Don't call us terrorists. The government and the newspapers have created terror, and we're all victims. We are political, of the people, liberators. Not common criminals, like you."

"Oh, excuse me, honey. I always thought mailing a businessman home to his family piece by piece was a criminal act. But then, I don't have your education to explain how blowing up an airplane full of tourists is going to make a better world for us all."

Friedelind turned to Felix with a dark look of anguish and said, "It's demeaning to sit at the same table with this vulture."

Joby Ben threw up his hands and contrived to look over his shoulder at the windshield of the camper. The blond girl wasn't there. Maybe she had gotten antsy and gone to the bathroom. He hoped. He turned back to Felix and said earnestly,

"Let's say you had some ideas about taking my money and keeping the stash, selling it yourself. I'll tell you something: You may be good at hit-and-run, but in my line of work you'd be up against the *Kriminalpolizei* as well as the U.S. Army's CID drug-suppression teams. On the street, their informers would make you in an hour."

Felix had another coughing fit and braced himself against the table. Joby Ben sneaked a look at his watch. Seven minutes had passed since he left Franziska. There was no way to stop what was coming, and here he was bogged down in futile arguments. Tension had him by the nose, and the balls.

"We know we have to be careful," Felix conceded. "About how we proceed, and with whom. Our comrades in the Tribunal—"

"They're not our comrades," Friedelind said jealously. "Any coalition is impractical as long as the ideological differences—"

"Can't you shut her up?" Joby Ben said with a desperate laugh.

Felix put a hand on Friedelind's wrist, a request for cooperation which she sulkily acknowledged.

He said to Joby Ben, "The Tribunal received a gift equal to ours. Through trial and error they contacted a—a businessman, like yourself. But things went wrong. They were double-crossed. Two members of the Tribunal were killed. The heroin disappeared."

Joby Ben nodded thoughtfully. "That's a bitter pill to swallow." He had counted off about another minute and a half in his mind. He opened the hamper again and took out six more of the wrapped "sandwiches." Snow-white fog hung all around the compound now. If they noticed it, they were liable to panic. And if they panicked, they just might run, leaving his corpse behind.

"Okay. I'm on the table. All I'm worth. You could shoot me in the head right now and make off with the money. But I figure—you'll be getting more gifts like the last one, and you'll need me to turn them into hard cash." Desperation forced him to be indiscreet. "So where's the rest of your stash? Did you bring it?"

He was watching them closely, eagerly, and he saw the sudden cold suspicion in Felix's eyes. But one of the soldiers had glanced too quickly at the charcoal grill and the puffing, splitting sausages; when he made no move to rescue the meat, Joby Ben suddenly realized where the remainder of the heroin was hidden.

At that moment Franziska came around the left corner of the camper, hunched over a submachine gun. She had discarded her false belly and wraparound skirt and was wearing black shorts and a long-sleeved black knit top. The submachine gun was a prototype silenced weapon being developed by the Armalite Company; it had cost Joby Ben four thousand dollars on the black market in arms that centered around the military's Rod and Gun Club in Frankfurt. The weapon was eerily quiet as Franziska fired livid ecstatic bursts at the RAF terrorists, who seemed to respond with comic-strip balloons of blood, blank red language of astonishment. The only sounds came from deformed slugs thudding spent into the metal of vehicles nearby. The terrorists slumped back into their chairs, agape, or forward into their plates. They were all briefly convulsed, like people helpless with hard laughter.

Joby Ben tapped Franziska on the arm and pointed at the camper. She went inside with the steel nozzle of the submachine gun uppermost, saw a similar weapon posed jauntily against the steering wheel. She heard the toilet flushing in the head, crept toward it, and from an angle pumped a dozen slugs through the thin metal door.

In her absence Joby Ben had tipped over the charcoal grill, loosening the false bottom; he stuffed hot one-key bags of heroin into the hamper as fast as he could snatch them from the coals. His fingertips were seared, but he wouldn't feel the pain until later. He had already retrieved his money.

Franziska reappeared, the machine gun at her side, to stand calmly by as he worked. Her eyes were on the bearded man dimmed by fog across the way. The dog was on his feet, ears pricked alertly, but he didn't bark. The lovers Joby Ben had observed earlier were standing groggily toe to toe and tongue to tongue; she had opened his pants and was frantically pumping away at him.

As soon as he had the heroin stowed, Franziska dismantled the submachine gun and placed the pieces in the hamper. Five minutes later, as the castle courtyard emptied for the interval, they were driving down the mountain, music on the radio of the Opel Senator.

Franziska peeled off his fake mustaches, which had begun to itch. Her fingers under his nose smelled of fire and powder. When he glanced at her, her eyelids were heavy; she seemed half asleep or dazed, drunk from the killing.

"I caught the other one in the bathroom. Was it a man or a woman?"

"Woman," Joby Ben said, his throat so tight he could scarcely talk. His pulse was much too fast, and his heart wouldn't slow down either. "Blonde. Cute little thing. Probably a new recruit. She must have been shitting her pants holding that gun and wondering if she'd have to use it."

"It was a little like opening a can of spoiled tomatoes under pressure. Blood burst through every jagged hole in the door."

"You're getting to where you like it too goddam much," Joby Ben said, chafing at a traffic light. He had to hold the wheel tightly to keep from trembling. He felt as if blood pressure was distorting his face, like the face of a slain terrorist: Passersby looking in would see his ears fly off, his forehead rudely leveled, blood gushing down his chin. But the moment of agonized empathy passed; he wanted to scream from the sheer relief of getting away with it again.

As the light changed and he headed for the autobahn, Franziska snuggled against him with a faint smile.

"I was a little thief, who wanted money. You were a gambler, and you needed a lot of money. Together we make a third person, who's not afraid of anyone or anything. Do you know what I think? The money's not so important any more. Nice...but not as important as what we do to get it."

38 By a quarter to eleven David had a headache from the smoke and the extra beer he'd ordered while waiting for Anneliese to show up at the Bonhomie. The club in Sachsenhausen specialized in pretty good imitation fifties rock-and-roll, and it was packed. He was wedged in at a small table in the gallery to the left of the main-floor bar; from there he could see the stage and club entrance, a doorway with a heavy velvet drape over it. The raspy honk of alto sax, the bowlegged bumble of bass. "Move It On Over." Music and drink gave him a hectic pulse, and he was still a little stoned from transatlantic jet lag.

It had occurred to David that Anneliese simply didn't intend to come. The possibility of not seeing her, tonight, made him uneasy, but he rejected the idea that she'd had second thoughts and dismissed him completely. Because he wouldn't let her, and although Anneliese knew very little about him yet, she had to know that much.

He sipped more of his beer and closed his eyes. His father, at a moment in time that seemed as distant as galaxies, had through murder committed magic, enclosing, confining him in a strange foolproof machine, which had conveyed him, first at an unnoticeably slow speed, then explosively, here—where he badly needed a countering magic, the heart of Anneliese. His previous conscientiously tended but unprovocative life seemed snatched away by the mad energy of this fated universe. Peeping through the din and youthful bodies of the Bonhomie, he saw his life as a receding glossy blur at one corner of his eye. Though he turned his head quickly he couldn't catch up to it, bring it back into focus. David felt momentarily soulless, and dizzy. He fretted over Anneliese's absence, a pathetic murmur in his heart; anticipating her touch and closeness, he had drunk too much and now wanted relief—air, space around him.

He got up and went down to the alley and leaned

against the outside wall beside the entrance to the club until his head cooled.

And still she wouldn't come.

39   After two hours in bed with Franziska, Joby Ben needed, was long overdue for, a prostate massage. He ached fiercely as he stood looking out at the moonlit garden of his house in Niederursel where he chose to live, as they say in the army, "on the economy," and away from the enclaves of his fellow officers on Hansa Allee or in Bad Vilbel.

While he was trying to get his pipe going, Franziska came quietly up behind him, naked and still humid from their labors. She put a hand inside his dressing gown and her head against his shoulder.

"Maybe we should bury the stash for a week or two, and not keep it in my car," he said.

"How are you disposing of it this time?"

"The less you know, the happier you'll be."

She shrugged. "You seem worried."

"Worried? What've I got to worry about? Level Two's run several spot checks on the 97th Pharmacy this month, the Turk's in pretrial confinement, K-54 and the CID have buttoned up every pizza parlor in town, and the 42nd MPs just brought in another brace of drug-sniffing dogs. Those nosy mutts can find an ounce of stash in a carload of detergent powder."

"And as Chief of Legal Assistance, you know what they're going to do before they do it."

"All I'm saying is, they may put the parking lots off-schedule and turn the goddam dogs loose looking for dirty cars."

"Drive my car for a while. I'll drive yours."

"Yeah. Just might do that."

Franziska nudged a little closer to him and placed her lips against the back of his grizzled neck.

"David and Anneliese were together this afternoon," she said.

He bowed his head wearily.

"Jesus. That kid. As if I don't have enough on my mind."

"It took him a couple of hours to get up the nerve to approach her. But Anneliese is very nervous these days—"

"What's she got to be nervous about?"

"And she called the police."

"The police!"

"There was a big, you know, 'hassle.' But David got it straightened out, and they went off together. Arm in arm."

She pinched him suddenly, his crippled earlobe. Joby Ben jumped and brushed her away irritably.

Franziska said from behind his back, "What do you think David will do now?"

Joby Ben ground the stem of his pipe between his teeth.

"Tell her everything he knows."

"I think so too."

"After he's eased his conscience and made life hell for Anneliese, then maybe he'll go home where he belongs."

"You shouldn't have let him come to Frankfurt in the first place."

"I tried to discourage him. He wouldn't listen."

"It doesn't matter. In a way I'm glad it happened."

Joby Ben turned around and looked carefully at her.

"How's that?"

Franziska didn't reply. She preened herself in the moonlight, which gave her nakedness a soapy, post-erotic glaze; but her heavy jaw looked thuggish in profile, her mouth had a familiar twist to it. She was working up to something unpleasant, Joby Ben knew that, and he had a black taste on the side of his tongue, where glowing pipe tobacco had bitten it.

"No need for you to take an interest in those two. Leave 'em alone."

"I don't *have* to do anything to them. It will happen regardless."

"What'll happen?" He squinted furiously, trying to intimidate her, but she had drained his balls until they hurt and he just felt old and abused. "What've you been up to?"

"Creating a diversion." Franziska thought of an appropriate American expression, and squared her shoulders proudly. "Taking the 'heat' off of us."

Joby Ben backtracked, hoping for better information. "So what's Anneliese got to be nervous about?"

"The Tribunal believe she had something to do with their recent misfortune. I 'told a little bird,' no? With her background, they naturally would be suspicious."

"Suspicious? Those crazy bastards will kill Anneliese!"

Franziska rapped back, "It was always Anneliese you wanted, wasn't it? But you settled for me. Why? Because you knew you weren't good enough for her?"

"What the hell are you talking about?"

"Sometimes it makes my flesh crawl when I think of you hanging around, watching us all the time we were growing up. Were you so impartial? How many of your little gifts of money did you leave where *Anneliese* would be sure to find them? I grew up with my head down and my eyes on the ground, the nuns thought I was so shy and studious! And what did you get out of it? Did your charity appease the guilt you felt for your marvelous brother? Or was it a form of masturbation?"

"You've got a rotten mouth tonight! All I ever did was keep an eye on the two of you, making sure nobody gave you a hard time."

"I went to jail!"

"You deserved to go."

"Oh, thank you very much!"

"Shut up, I need to think. Do you have any idea of what you've done to Anneliese?"

"Isn't it your nephew you should be so concerned about? After all, they'll kill him too—if he happens to be in the way."

He recalled then what he'd said to Neddie in the garden before leaving Savannah; the words had just popped out. *What's coming is what's due.* It seemed to him now like a self-fulfilling prophecy. If he'd really wanted to, he knew he could have kept David from lighting in Frankfurt. Joby Ben stared at Franziska, surly and dismayed. This was *her* fault. In his mountain family there had been anger, grievances, feuds, bloody fights, but all of it in the open. There were few sins beyond the pale. Drunkards were cared for, thieves excused; incest went unremarked. But no member of the family had ever conspired to betray another to outsiders.

In a fit of petulance he smacked Franziska backhanded in the mouth. Franziska sulked happily, blood on her lower lip. Hitting her restored some of his faith in the relationship.

"Looky here—I don't care what goes on between you and your sister, but that boy is *family*. Understand?"

"His father killed my mother. And I never did anything about it *because you wouldn't let me!*"

"All I ever did was take real good care of you, and now we're almost rich. So what else do you want? It's a terrible thing, what Frank did, but he paid, don't think he didn't, all the way to his grave."

"Oh no, thanks to you the son of a bitch never got what was coming to him. But now I think David will pay for his father!"

He didn't hit her again; he didn't feel the necessary rancor, only a sick sense of inevitability. He decided to reassess the blame for what David had blundered into. The craziness that Joby Ben had touched off in Franziska by taking her to Savannah was clearly out of control. But he couldn't have done otherwise. She was correct about their relationship, they were one person—or rather, like Siamese twins hopscotching a minefield. He only knew for sure they didn't need this additional cloud of disaster around their heads, which she had brewed from her resentment, a hotheaded and not wholly understandable desire for revenge.

Joby Ben went to the telephone and dialed the Frankfurterhof Hotel. It was a few minutes past midnight. No answer in David's suite.

Franziska, supple and conciliatory, came to perch on his knees. She played with her swollen lip. Then she took his pipe from between his teeth and smoked it.

"What are you going to do, Daddy?" She seemed content that nothing much could be done.

"In the morning," he said, "I'll yank David up by the scruff of the neck and put him on the first plane home." Franziska snuggled down and smoked his pipe. "Why the hell do you hate Anneliese so much?" he asked. She withdrew the pipe. Smoke wavered from the perfect, lascivious O of her mouth. He placed a hand at the back of her neck and began to squeeze rhythmically. Her big bold jaw waggled up and down, her teeth clacked together, her eyes opened and closed like those of a ventriloquist's dummy. She could hold one eye shut while raising and lowering the lid of the other. Hoodwinking. Her face came to look altogether artificial. She made noises that prickled the hairs on his own neck, but said nothing that could enlighten him.

40   David returned to the hotel and, outside the door to his suite, heard the phone ringing; but he was too slow with the big awkward key, suspended from a ball of brass with a rubber ring around it, a design that the hotel had adopted to discourage guests from walking off with the keys.

Having let himself in, he turned on a small lamp in the sitting room and left the jacket of his suit over the back of a chair. The door to the bedroom was closed. He had bought a newspaper, which he glanced at, standing up in the center of the room while he rubbed the back of his neck. He had a headache and still felt, despite a long cold walk home, as if his lungs were packed with the cigarette smoke he had inhaled at the Bonhomie. His stomach was a little sick because of that smoke, and his sinuses were glued shut.

He sensed, rather than heard, the stealthy turning of the brass knob on the bedroom door behind him. As he looked swiftly around, the door fell open and Anneliese stood, barefoot, in the space, looking wide-eyed at him, without her boots much smaller than he remembered. Her hair was in a tangle like exploded rope; her face, caught up in the soft wildness, was as indistinct as a kitten's.

As he stared at her, she gathered focus and glanced at her wristwatch. A shadow of displeasure crossed her face.

"It's after midnight. Where've you been so long?"

"Where have I been? Well—you—I thought—"

Anneliese looked past him. "Did you lock the door?" Without waiting for a reply, she put a hand to her head, turned, and went back into the bedroom. He saw her sit tensely on the edge of the bed, breathing hard, still clasping her forehead. Her feet didn't quite touch the floor. The comforter on the bed was in disarray. David followed her, still tingling from surprise.

"I was waiting for you—at the Bonhomie."

Anneliese said with a pained smile, "You don't give up so easily. Couldn't you tell I wasn't coming?"

"No. I didn't know what to think. What—how did you get in here?"

"I charmed a chambermaid. Told her you absolutely had to have some sketches by morning. She let me into the suite to leave my portfolio."

She inclined her head in the direction of the big flat leather portfolio, which was leaning against one wall of the bedroom.

"I fixed the lock on my way out so I could sneak back in once she was off the floor."

"Why didn't you call me?"

Anneliese had begun to tremble. "David, I tried! No one picked up at the Bonhomie. Are you sure your outside door is locked?"

"Yes. What's the matter? Did you get another of those phone calls?"

She made a gesture as if to shield herself. "Worse, this time. They could have k-killed me. They said they *would* kill me unless I give them back their money, but I don't have the slightest idea—"

David, taking an aimless turn around the big bedroom, stopped short.

"Money? How much money?"

She turned her face to him, pushing the hair off her forehead, offering a mild, stunned smile.

"A million marks! And I'm supposed to have deposited f-four hundred thousand marks in my b-bank account today—" Overcome by the absurdity, she choked on a laugh and missed the sudden bleakness in his eyes, the rigid guilty set of his mouth. "It's so ridiculous. In my whole life I've barely earned that much money. But Traudl says they've been watching me, keeping an eye on my account at the bank—"

David, rigidity giving way to a soft cramp of panic, sat down in a chair, as if he'd been speared through the middle. "Watching—Traudl—who the hell are *they*, and why—"

"I buy lottery tickets every week, I've dreamed of winning—" She shrugged to expel this shade of avarice. "But—*four hundred thousand* marks! And for some reason—" Her voice coarsened to a rasp. "They think I've stolen it."

"Anneliese, what are you talking about?"

"The Tribunal."

"What's that?"

"A Red Army splinter group. Some of them were with the old group, the Baader-Meinhof Gang. I don't know if you've heard—"

"Hell, yes. They're political terrorists."

"They threw paint at me, instead of a bomb—"

"Where? When did it happen?"

Anneliese hurried through an explanation.

"I went home afterward. Well, I had to get off the street. There was nowhere else. I called Hugh and Emily and made excuses; then, after I cleaned myself up— God, what a terrible mess!—I got dressed and left with my portfolio as if I had a business meeting. I rode the subways for an hour, until I was sure no one could possibly be following me. I was afraid they'd be watching all of my friends. But nobody knows anything about you, David." Her voice gave out; she sat rubbing her head, soft scrubbing motions, as if she could still feel the paint sticking to her skin. "Please forgive me," she whispered. Her mouth made motions too; she might have been a fish consuming the last of the oxygen in a thick cold sea of terror. "Is there—something to drink?"

"The hotel sent up a bottle this morning. Scotch, I think."

David lunged up and went in search of it. In the sitting room he thought to check the outside door, was reassured by its thickness and the solid locks. He broke ice out of a tray from the refrigerator, poured shots of Clan MacGregor over the cubes, added water.

In the bedroom Anneliese took the glass in both hands and sipped, with a vacant air, now rubbing her bare feet forlornly together.

He touched her shoulder. "Anneliese, I'm sorry. I know how scared you must be." She turned her face toward the warmth of his hand, eyes downcast. "I had no idea you'd run into all of this trouble—" She looked up; he held his tongue. "If there's anything I can do to help—"

"I only wanted a place where I'd feel safe for a little while. But...no. I can't involve you in my problems."

"Then I think we should call the police."

"I wanted to. But it's futile. Nothing's happened to me, you see. Nothing criminal. I was splattered with paint. That's all."

"But you know who they are. They're terrorists. The police must be after them."

"The KRIPOs, the BKA, everybody. But I can't afford to tell everything I know, David."

"Why?"

Anneliese moved slightly nearer, as if willing his arm to slide around her shoulders. David sat down beside her.

"Twelve years ago I was a student at the Free University, in Berlin. We were political activists, in open rebellion against what we called the 'Auschwitz generation.' I steeped myself in Marx, Hegel, and Lenin. Some of my friends were already becoming notorious: Ulrike Meinhof, 'Red Rudi' Dütschke, Traudl Hecker. At first I was as militant as they were, eager to be at the front of the barricades. But when they turned to bombs, the following year, the pleasure some of them took in destruction frightened me. That's when I began to rethink my philosophy, to understand myself a little better. Then I got out."

"But you don't want the police digging up your past."

"Several years ago Traudl escaped from a police trap. She was wounded and exhausted when she came to me. Try to imagine what it was like for her—five thousand police were looking for her, the government had paramilitary units in the streets. Armored cars, machine guns. Our civil liberties were trampled in the process, and that made me furious. So I—I took a great risk, I helped Traudl get away, to Belgium. I could still be put in jail for doing that. I could be jailed for a *very* long time."

David felt a shiver of apprehension, and a defiant pride in her.

"You won't be. How many terrorists are there?"

"Only a handful are still free."

"I think the best answer is for you to go away for a while."

Anneliese was boneless in his embrace, incapable of movement.

"It would seem so. Yes. But the RAF and the Tribunal have many sympathizers in the Federal Republic." She told him what had happened to her the night of Otto Kolner's party. "Now I know it was Traudl— that whiff of perfume. She must have put on weight. She said today that she'd been t-trying to stay out of it, that she didn't believe the rumors about me. What rumors? My God, it's just impossible! How could anyone link me with them?" Anneliese was beginning to have spasms, centered at the diaphragm, as if breathing was painful and words were a knife-edged torture. He held her close. "And the m-m-money. I don't *have* f-four hundred thousand marks, David, God is m-m-my—"

The telephone rang, two nerve-jangling bursts. Anneliese flinched badly.

"It rang before. I was s-sleeping."

David turned his right wrist and looked at his watch. "It's just seven-thirty in Savannah." He put a hand protectively against the side of her face, pressed her against him, got up to answer the phone. But it wasn't a transatlantic call.

"David McNair?"

David hesitated. It was a young woman's voice, musical, like that of a crystal angel, and brimming with good cheer. There was considerable background noise. Rock music.

"Who's this?" he asked. Anneliese looked around worriedly.

"Please, it's so important, may I speak to Anneliese." She wasn't asking if Anneliese was there; she had already assumed that. He felt suddenly short of breath, dull-witted.

"Speak to—" David glanced at Anneliese, who was rising from the edge of the bed. "*Who* do you want?"

"Anneliese. She's nowhere to be found tonight, so I thought naturally she's with you."

"No. I haven't seen her."

Anneliese closed her eyes in sudden fright; David reached for her and drew her to the phone, held the receiver so they both could hear.

"Oh. You're sure you haven't seen her?"

Anneliese's mouth fell open, but she didn't utter a sound. She held onto David with both hands, listening.

"Yes, I'm sure. Who is this?"

"Well-l," she said merrily, "I was much mistaken then. I'm sorry for the bother. Good night."

David hung up. Anneliese said earnestly, with all the color gone from her face, "That does it." She pushed rudely at him, as if he was a heavy door she needed to pass through. David gave way, then caught her and turned her around. Her cheekbones stood out sharply; the pupils of her eyes had shrunk to points of light in a void, they seemed incapable of seeing him.

"Who was she? Traudl Hecker?"

"Hilda."

"Who's that?" With her head down she was still shoving at him, trying to turn him, as if to a dreadful point of view she couldn't face herself.

"In the shop. She brought the wine this afternoon. If I trusted anyone on this earth, I trusted...Hilda."

Her breathing deteriorated into small sobs. David felt a spasm coming and tried to hold it off, hugging her, murmuring, but Anneliese's hysteria broke over him in a devastating, violent stutter, worse than vomiting.

"They—*Nah!* Nah—nuh—nuh—know about you. They knowwww—oh—*ohhhhh*—ohhhhh—ahhhh. Huh—*huh!*—huh—help. Help. Me. David."

41 In the bar on Fresgasse the tall wry-necked blond girl stood thoughtfully by the wall telephone, unable to move very far because of the mass of customers jamming every corner and alcove. Her foot was stepped on. Over all their heads she caught Traudl Hecker's eye in a dark booth near the open rear door, and gestured apologetically.

Traudl left her companions and came to Hilda's rescue with a stein of beer. Traudl was wearing frumpy clothes and a wig with a million frizzy curls of reddish hair. It looked like a rabbi's beard. She smoked a Gauloise. She was wearing bifocals. She looked seedy and a bit past it, like a lecturer on obsolete social questions at Goethe University.

She put an arm around Hilda as if to protect her from further damage from the mob; Hilda was momentarily tongue-tied, thrilled by the attention. She tried to be worthy of it.

"He said he hadn't seen her. But something about his voice—I think she could be there now. In his room."

Traudl nodded. "What's this American like?"

"Oh, *very* good-looking. I had a feeling Anneliese was already crazy about him, and she told me they'd just met."

Traudl drank her beer with a crooked smile. "Well, I wouldn't want to interrupt her fun for the evening."

"It's so amazing! I had no idea that you and Anneliese were—"

"I'm sure it isn't something she would want to talk about now. But, yes, we were very close once." Traudl winced and held the side of her jaw, as if she was getting a toothache. "I think we'll move on now. I don't like staying too long in one place. We'll find another bar. It's been weeks since I've had an evening out." Hilda nodded understandingly. "Perhaps you could call your husband and have him join us. His new book on Sartre is the most brilliant analysis I've read. I'm eager to discuss it with him."

Hilda said, paraphrasing the popular philosopher, "Violence, like Achilles' lance, can heal the wounds it has inflicted."

Traudl gave her a squeeze of approval. "It's so good to know," she said, "that there are still people like you in this miserable world."

42 The Hotel Lindener Palace in Bad Kulmbach was located on sixty choice acres overlooking the extensive *kurpark* and the forested Taunus mountains to the north. The hotel was the largest in the famous old spa, a favorite of European royalty in the nineteenth century, and it offered complete facilities for the utilization of its radioactive sodium chloride medicinal springs. Even at six in the morning, with clouds of vapor drifting across the green parkland, there was activity in and around the hotel: riders on horseback, elderly bathers moving ponderously through the mists and heated waters or half-buried in mudpack like soon-to-be-extinct members of the species.

The indoor pool was a rococo marble pavilion with big northeast windows; at sunrise the windows were alight, an intense pale gold that hurt the eyes. A couple of old men with the lumpy wattled bodies of sea lions were swimming nude laps in the slippery darkness of the pool; but David was going all-out, using a racing crawl, and had been swimming like that for nearly fifteen minutes. He was gasping for air, sounds of distress echoing above the soft slap of water.

When he couldn't manage his strokes any longer he floated to the side of the pool in five feet of water, clung there with the waves he had made rippling against his chest. He stared red-eyed at the undulating surface of the pool, breathing painfully, heartsore because he hadn't been able to outswim his fear, and as he closed his eyes wearily he was overwhelmed by images of the sea, by the sight of his father falling, at the end of a taut line, from out of a monster wave.

His right hand cramped, fingers curling into a hard ball. David groaned and threw himself up and out of the water, lay naked and face down on the frame of tiles around the pool. He thought he heard his father's voice, plain as yesterday.

"Whatever you do, David—"

David looked up, aghast, at the sad drowned face hanging over him.

"—don't punish yourself."

He lunged up in terror, almost falling back into the pool. A hand reached for him, caught him at the elbow. Steadied him.

"I said you shouldn't *punish* yourself." The voice had changed, acquired a German accent. "You get muscle cramps, like in your hand. Gentle, steady exercise is best, even for a young man like you."

David saw him more clearly then. A superficial resemblance to Frank McNair—the big angular body, dark hair plastered over a high forehead. But this man was older, wrinkled, he had a pot belly in the sling of white towel with which he had draped himself.

The old man was afraid he'd been misunderstood; he smiled and released David.

"Did I startle you? I'm sorry."

"It's all right."

David, down on one knee, took several deep breaths and got up, the nightmare dispelled. He toweled off, found his terrycloth robe and put it on, went back through the underground passage to the bathers' elevator. He took the elevator to the sixth and top floor of the hotel. His heart was still beating fast, but he'd achieved the rush he'd been looking for, the surge of peak vitality from extraordinary physical effort. And, for the moment, he enjoyed peace of mind. He let himself into the warm, richly furnished room where Anneliese was sleeping, on her stomach, arms outflung, half-draped with a blanket.

He dried his hair again in the bathroom, brushed it, hung the robe up, and got back into bed, but not to sleep. Just to sit crosslegged and look at her, to touch her carefully, taking a delicate sensual inventory: the cap of a shoulder with its sheen of bone under a fading coppery tan; the velvet rack of ribs and pale underarm, fragile as the inner ear; a soft smothered breast with a faint rose trim of nipple; the boneless indentation of her long back. She'd been restless for most of the night—the four and a half hours, really, since they'd checked into the Lindener Palace—and now she was at it again, moaning, grinding her teeth, moving her legs beneath the sheet, a jerky kind of supine running. She began to murmur and then to cry, woke up with a startled fling into his arms.

David soothed her. The aftershocks of awakening dwindled in her body. She seemed surprised to find herself naked, and shyly tentative in her adjustments to his own body. They had peeled, unselfconsciously, at two A.M. in the nearly dark room, in a state of rapt exhaustion, still thrilled by the momentum of their escape, and she was unconscious a minute after getting into bed. He held her now around the waist, he was boldly erect against her thigh; her heart beat glancingly against his chest.

"David..."

"What's the matter?"

"D-dreaming—first time in years so bad—m-my mother, you see—s-she was dead, half-buried, and I was trying to—"

The image was too vivid in his mind; he saw his father with a shovel in his hands, but could not imagine the expression on his face. In his anguish David had never been more aroused, more desperate to possess a woman.

"I've got you, you're okay, just don't think about it. It'll go away."

He began to kiss her, with a sweet but restrained ardor; to caress her, his touch light, hands skimming vibrantly over the deep and sensitive places of her body, causing a magnetic prickling heating her blood, and his. The tightly-curled mound, pressed down warmly in sleep. Anneliese snug in the saddle of his hand, riding him instinctively with voluptuous shifting movements of her body, discovering, little by little, the state of his own excitement, her eyes opening and closing, as if she needed brief spells of privacy, a delay in their coming together.

"Where are we, David?"

"Bad Kulmbach."

"That's right—that's right." Only her body was under tension now; she no longer stuttered. "And we're safe here, aren't we?"

"You're safe, Anneliese. I swear I'll never let anything happen to you."

With her sex in the palm of his hand he began, ecstatically, to weep; from relief, from a strange kind of despair.

43 Getting off the early TWA jet at Rhine-Main airport, Reba felt as she always did after a flight of long duration, gritty and numb, eyes swollen and dry, her rump like a sack of lead. She was still a little dubious about the wisdom of her decision to follow David to Frankfurt; but she was humming with pleasure at the prospect of actually being there. She'd been in a serious rut for too long, needing to do something glamorous or eccentric, and this was it—David, surprise— but most of all she needed to prove to herself that she had a will and freedom of her own.

There were watchful policemen with submachine guns in the glassy, echoing terminal building, a reminder that the West Germans weren't fooling about their aversion to terrorists. Reba was carrying all the luggage she'd brought with her, a suede garment bag and a matching carryall that could be crammed under most airplane seats; she traveled light wherever she went, and from first class to the taxi stand took a matter of minutes at six-thirty in the morning.

"The Frankfurterhof," she said to the driver, settling into the Mercedes diesel; the taxi fleets in Frankfurt were luxurious compared to the slovenly wrecks on the streets of most American cities.

Reba smiled, trying to visualize David's expression when he awakened to find her snuggling against him. She couldn't suppress a fit of giggles and looked up to find the driver watching her curiously in the rear-view mirror. Well, if she didn't want to scare David half to death, she needed to do some fast repair work. She went to her purse for comb and brush and cleansing lotion and didn't look up again until the taxi was crossing the Friedensbrücke on the way to the center of the city.

44   Joby Ben, wearing his dress greens, cooled his heels by the reception desk while the assistant manager he'd sent up to David's suite took his time returning. He felt conspicuous in full uniform in this place, since it was Army policy not to unnecessarily remind the citizens of the West German Republic that they were still heavily occupied by a foreign power. But he had a meeting on base at ten-thirty with some brass from USAFE.

He'd spent nearly five minutes on the house phone trying to get an answer from the suite, then concocted a story about his nephew the diabetic in order to insure some cooperation from the management. While he waited he looked around the reception hall, which was small and unimpressive for so distinguished a hotel. A couple of Japanese businessmen were looking at the cultured pearls in a jeweler's display case. A prim and overweight woman in a tweed suit, wearing heavy tinted horn-rimmed glasses, was standing at a writing desk nearby, trying to compose a note. She had torn up several previous efforts.

"Colonel McNair?" Joby Ben turned to the assistant manager, who had come down the stairs from the second floor. He wore a severely dark cutaway and a carnation.

"Did you find David okay? He can be forgetful about those insulin shots."

The young man shrugged delicately. "I'm afraid he's not in the suite. The bed hasn't been slept in."

"That so?"

"Perhaps he didn't spend the night here."

"Or else he checked out."

"I'll look into that. But there's luggage in the suite. I noticed a large leather portfolio." He described it with his hands. "Of the sort advertising artists use to carry their work."

"Or fashion designers," Joby Ben said thoughtfully.

The assistant manager went into the office and came back shaking his head.

"No. He hasn't checked out, sir."

Joby Ben scratched his head. "Well, he's got me worried. But I guess he'll turn up. Thanks for your help."

He bought a newspaper from the concierge and went to the phone boxes in a small lobby opposite the reception hall. He called Franziska.

"He's not here and he didn't check out. There's a big designer's portfolio up in the room, I don't know about his clothes.... Yeah, that's what I figure. Anneliese is with him, and they're on the run. She must have had a bad scare. Well, I need to get moving, I've got a full schedule this morning....I don't know yet how I'm gonna find him, have to give it some thought."

He left the hotel by the Bethmannstrasse door, crossed the street with the folded newspaper under his arm. He walked to the corner of Kaiserstrasse half a block away, where an Army staff car and driver were waiting for him.

In the front seat of the gray-and-black Citröen CX-2400, which was parked across the Kaiserplatz about two hundred feet from the main entrance to the Frankfurterhof, Traudl Hecker took off the tinted horn-rimmed glasses she'd been wearing in the hotel. The thick lenses were hurting her eyes. Jürgen Sollmann was behind the wheel, and there were two young men named Chris and Ernst in the back seat. They all had a good view of Joby Ben as he leaned down to speak to the driver before getting into the staff car.

"There. You see?" Traudl said to Jürgen.

"Yes. Yes, it could be our 'Mr. Jones.'"

"Take him out of uniform, give him a false beard—"

"A racketeer, highly ranked in the U.S. Army, dealing in drugs."

"I overheard him talking to the manager," Traudl said. "He's the uncle of David McNair."

"Anneliese's new friend."

"Not so new, perhaps. What's this?"

As Joby Ben was leaving, the taxi with Reba in it had pulled up in front of the hotel. Reba got out quickly, calling to Joby Ben, but a streetcar, westbound to the railroad station, was going by and he didn't hear. Traudl got out of the Citröen as the staff car turned right onto Kaiserstrasse.

"Follow him," she said to Jürgen. "I want to know more about this woman."

Reba had returned to the taxi, and a porter appeared to help her with the luggage. Traudl sized up Reba as she trailed her to the reception hall of the hotel. She was about thirty, slender, almost gaunt from certain angles; she had a high-caste forehead and stunning length of hair, nearly to her waist and full as a foxtail. Her eyes were light and curious, she moved with a trained dancer's blissful stride. Traudl, who had once been that thin and now felt as if she were wading through her own suet, envied her. Traudl had never coveted luxuries but she knew the value of things, and she guessed that Reba's simple traveling dress, a silken tasteful blue, was a three-hundred-dollar item; the diamond on her finger, if perfect, was worth a hundred thousand marks. She drew the worshipful attention from staff that money, particularly hushed money, always got.

"Good morning," Reba said to the smiling clerks at Reception. "I'm Mrs. David McNair."

45   Due to the miscalculations of Allied bombardiers, the stone office building of the I. G. Farben Company had survived the great air raid, and the Army had taken over the complex in '45, at a time when nothing but hazed rubble could be seen from the front steps of HQ to the main railroad station, a distance of more than five miles. Now it was called the Abrams Building, surrounded by a pleasant park which had been a part of the old Rothschild estate.

Joby Ben's overcrowded offices, a maze of partitions and cul-de-sacs crammed with filing cabinets, was on the first floor west. He supervised more than fifty lawyers, secretaries, and clerks, and most of them were already at work when he checked in, after a working breakfast at the officers' club, at eight-thirty.

His secretary, a petite blonde wearing fatigues and boots, followed him into his office with a sheaf of overnight communiques from JAG-O in Washington. He dropped his attaché case on the desk and read through them.

"Bernie in?"

"He had to go to the Mannheim Confinement Center this morning: that rape case he's trying."

"Okay, tell him collateral investigation is definitely required by 95-5 on that helicopter crash at Bitburg. What's new on the PX warehouse job?"

"The CID wants to work a deal, as usual."

"How many informers do they think they need?" Joby Ben pulled at his lower lip, giving the matter some thought. "I'll talk it over with Major Cummings. Later. Right now see if you can get me Roland Hahnwald at the BKA in Wiesbaden."

When his secretary left, Joby Ben sat down and opened his newspaper. The murder of the five RAF terrorists in Heidelberg was all over the front page, in red ink. The accompanying blurred photos of the victims didn't resemble very closely anyone he remembered meeting. He yawned, put on his reading glasses, and scanned the story. Surprisingly, his telephone buzzed. He'd been expecting the usual half-hour delay, due to the glitch-filled telephone system.

"Yeah, okay...Hello, Roland? Colonel McNair. How you this fine mornin'. Does your T-department have a line on who shot those Red Army kids down there in Heidelberg? Yeah, that's kinda what I thought. Looks like a serious family feud, considering what happened to the Tribunal last month. Hell, let 'em kill each other off, it'll make life easier for you boys. Listen, what I need today is a big favor. My nephew got in town yesterday from the States. He was at the Frankfurterhof and then he took off, probably with a German girl named Anneliese Girda. But he neglected to leave me a forwarding address, and there's a family emergency requires his immediate attention..."

46 A buffet breakfast was served on the glass-walled terrace of the Lindener Palace Hotel, with a view of formal gardens and early-flowering shrubs and trees, coaxed into bloom by the moist warm air from surrounding springs. Anneliese had given her dress to the hall porter for a quick pressing, and felt at least respectable; when the spa shops opened at nine-thirty she could do something about her severely limited wardrobe. The day promised to be sunny and almost hot. They chose a table by the windows, where, still so full of each other, they ate sparingly. From time to time David reached across the table to take her hand.

Anneliese seldom had talked to anyone about her sad childhood and her mother; but with David it was easier, necessary.

"Mother didn't neglect me on purpose. She had a career, she traveled. When she was with me, when she took the time, she was wonderful. I remember that much. I think she really loved me. Franziska, that's another story."

David poured another cup of coffee from the silver carafe on the table.

"Who's Franziska?"

"My sister. Half-sister, ac—"

His hands jerked, and he poured hot coffee on one wrist. Wincing in pain, he used a napkin.

"David, did you burn yourself?"

"No, it's okay." There was a red mark the size of an egg yolk on the back of his wrist.

"Are you sure you're all right? You look as if—"

David shrugged. "I didn't know you had a sister."

"You don't know very much about me at all, why should that be such a shock?"

"It isn't," David said with a determined smile. "Tell me about Franziska."

Anneliese felt slightly uncomfortable and overstuffed on half of a small omelet; she wished they could be outside, walking where there was a breeze and the direct warmth of the sun on her face. She didn't particularly enjoy reminiscing about her sister.

"Well—she's six years older than I am. She was—is—illegitimate. She always resented that, resented me, because I had a father, even if he didn't stay around for very long. I could never be friends with Franziska. I'd think I was getting along with her, then—pow!—she'd do something crazy-mean."

"Like what?"

Anneliese pointed out a couple of still-visible scars on her right arm near the elbow.

"Those are tooth marks. Franziska did it when I was ten. You should have seen the blood."

"What was the matter with her?" David said, staring at the marks, having an excuse to touch Anneliese again; he was always fascinated with anything that had to do with her physical self. Such modest imperfections gave her permanence, strengthened her reality in his mind.

"Mother made her that way. Franziska was always running away to find Mother. When she did, Mother would beat her and send her home. She had lovers, and didn't want to be bothered. Franziska never said a word against Mother—she just took it out on the rest of the world. My grandparents couldn't manage her, so she spent most of her time in boarding schools. That's where she was when Mother was killed. Poor Franziska. She must have been so lonely."

"Do you ever see her?"

"Occasionally we bump into each other. We have nothing to say. She was in trouble a few years ago, and went to prison. Something to do with extortion. Now I think she's getting on well enough. There's a man she lives with, an American. I've never met him."

Anneliese broke a croissant and buttered half, then put it down untasted. She looked, uneasily, over her shoulder at the partly filled terrace room. She looked back, seeing their reflections blazed in glass, not quite true likenesses, as if silent impostors were closing in and mimicking their every move. Her throat closed. Her heart missed a beat.

"Well. I had such an appetite. Two bites and it's gone. I've got the worry bug again."

"Don't, Anneliese. Nobody's going to touch you."

His assurance, which was all the more affecting for its futility, and his expression of grim-jawed bravado, brought her to the point of tears.

"I wasn't thinking about...the threats, being killed. That all seems unreal now, as if it happened to someone else."

"What's wrong, then?"

"It's just that—you listen so well, you care so much, I haven't had a man like you before. I'm afraid to find out—that I can't keep you."

"Don't be. I'm not going anywhere."

"That isn't realistic, is it, David?"

The sadness in her voice caught him unprepared. Their hands met again, were anchored in each other; Anneliese felt that incomparable surge of longing to make love to him and be oblivious of everything else. She turned her face dizzily from the glitter of the window glass. His face had broken out in dark sunspots, she blinked to clear her eyes.

"Things can be worked out," David said.

"That sounds—unpromising, somehow." But then she was faint-hearted, bewildered, unwilling to doubt or deny him. The sadness in her chest felt like a wrong bone; a second, unbeating heart. Anneliese saw in his eyes that some of her feelings had sneaked over to him, through the intricate structure their hands had made. She smiled, she couldn't hurt him.

"It suggests arrangements, when all I want to do is dream, and enjoy you, and not be practical at all." Unexpectedly shyness dried her up, but David squeezed her hand, his face relaxing softly. She blurted, "I'm not religious, but I wonder who sent you, and why, when I needed you so badly."

Was it too much to say? He seemed, for an instant, to have glimpsed something distasteful in her. His teeth, visible through parted lips, were on edge. All the strength was gone from his clasping hand, or so she imagined. Anneliese felt suspended, disavowed. Then, before she could react, he was on his feet, brightening, drawing her toward him.

"Finished your breakfast? Good. Let's get out of here, it's too beautiful a day to waste. And we've got a lot to do."

"Really! What?"

"Everything we've always wanted to do, all of our lives, and saved till now."

47 The taxi let Reba off in front of 20 Goethe-strasse. She stood for a few moments on the sidewalk looking at the smallish display windows of the boutique and the collections they were featuring, most of which came from Saint Laurent. She followed a stylish German woman wearing a Robin Hood hat into the boutique and browsed until a salesgirl with bangs and plump cheeks came over. The girl glanced at the boutique's shopping bag Reba had with her, which was white with a diagonal plum-colored stripe and gold lettering.

"Good morning."

Reba smiled and pulled out the shirt David had bought the day before; she had found it in the suite at the Frankfurterhof.

"I believe my husband was in yesterday—"

"Oh yes, I remember him. You must be Mrs.—let me think now—McNear! Your accent too is charming, like your husband's. I studied in the U.S. I'm very good at recognizing regional accents. 'Fi'ty-turd street.' That's what they say in New York City. 'Fi'ty-turd street.'" She looked crestfallen. "But you're returning the shirt?"

"I like it very much. I wanted pants to go with it."

"Of course! And you take a six? This way."

"What time yesterday was David in?"

"Midmorning. And then of course he came back with Anneliese, in late afternoon. Do you know Anneliese?"

"I'm afraid I don't. Tell me about her."

The girl gave her a quick searching look. Reba was still smiling.

"Well, she's a very talented designer—"

"I've seen a few of her sketches."

"And she is part owner of this boutique, although she doesn't spend much time here." Gold bracelets jangled on her wrists as she sorted through a rack of pants and made a selection. "The navy is stunning with that stripe, no?" She held a pair with thirteen-inch cuffs to the blouse, which Reba had draped over her arm.

"Umm. How old is she?"

"About like you. Do you want to try them on?"

Reba didn't answer. Her head was bent, her eyes narrow as she fingered the material of the pants.

"Do you know where I could find her?"

"Anneliese? She has the workroom across the alley. But I don't think she's coming in today. Someone else was asking, an old customer, and Hilda said no, definitely Anneliese would *not* be in."

"I'm sorry," Reba said. "I have something of hers she might like to have returned. Also I think she has something of mine."

She straightened and handed the pants back to the shopgirl.

"These won't do. I'm more the Geoffrey Beene type."

"Geoffrey Beene?"

48 Reba went walking, and covered several blocks before she roused herself from the daze she was in.

Unfamiliar with Frankfurt, she was totally lost, and uncaring. She looked up and saw a park and crossed a busy street to get to it. There was a low-lying lake. She stood staring at ducks and a miniature, fairy-tale castle on a small island and rippling reflections and thought about what David had done, was doing to her, and wondered why he had chosen to go off the deep end in so trite a way. His last trip to Germany had been eighteen months ago, so obviously he wasn't pursuing some irresistible affair he'd begun then.

Anneliese... Blank. Reba didn't know her last name, hadn't thought to ask in the shop. The business card with the portfolio in the suite had said simply, *Fashions by Anneliese. Twenty Goethestrasse.* Maybe she didn't have a last name. Maybe she was one of those.

He could have met her on the plane, flying over from New York. Champagne cocktails in the first-class lounge. Flirtation. *I'll be at the Frankfurterhof.* Reba half believed this, because there was nothing else to believe. Her stomach ached from coffee and no breakfast. Had Anneliese spent the night with him? Then they'd slept on the floor. And why should she leave her valuable sketches there? Where *were* they? When would they be back? David had left most of his clothes, taking only a small bag and his shaving gear. It made no sense. She'd felt so damned clever, flying over on the spur of the moment to cheer him up, and now she

228

was crying. Moping beside a dank little lake, utterly alone in a city she didn't know at all. *David, why?*

A man had come along, and was standing next to her. Standing too close in a park with a lot of acreage. He wore a raincoat on a fair day. He had curly dark hair around a spreading bald spot, thick dark eyebrows. He was good-looking. A little like Maximillian Schell. Not as old as the bald spot suggested.

Reba sensed that he was going to speak to her, try to pick her up. Her skin crawled; she wasn't having any of *that*. She turned and almost blundered into a thickset woman with frizzy reddish hair and bifocals. She was also wearing a nylon raincoat. And she had a gun, which she was holding, as if she were a subspecies of flasher, inside the unbuttoned coat. She let Reba see a little of the gun.

Reba stood absolutely still, but she wasn't afraid. There was nothing to be afraid of—she'd just gotten off an airplane, the park was full of people, the whole thing was preposterous.

"Mrs. McNair," the woman said, "I think we should have a talk about your husband."

49 David tagged along while Anneliese put together a wardrobe, which took her less than an hour. She was a quick and decisive shopper, and everything she put on became at once so perfectly a part of her she might have designed the clothes herself. She wore pants especially well, French-cut brushed corduroy jeans; she wore with them an unbuttoned checked shirt over a sleeveless knit pullover. Because they thought they might spend part of the evening in the gambling casino, she also chose a semiformal black sheath dress. She refused his money and paid with her credit card.

The balance of the morning they explored, in a rented Audi, the valley of the Lahn River, rich in vineyards and wine cellars.

In Heyl, a bright-yellow eighteenth-century stagecoach drawn by a storybook four-horse hitch conveyed them, swaying, laughing and tumbling into each other, down a brick street narrow as an aqueduct. Light and shadow fleeing by; Anneliese clutching her stomach in protest and falling back into his lap, her head bobbing up for still another kiss; the hooves of the horses, broad as kettledrums, clobbering the old brick to a fine rising dust. The choice cellar that they toured was as extensive as a catacombs, burial vaults for casks of great wine. David got exuberantly soused on samples and expertly underplayed the tottering drunk as they visited a plot of ruins baking in the sun—pieces of a wall, a Roman arch, all that was left of the conquerors' estate. Her cheeks glowed, the laughter wouldn't stop, she knew she loved him.

After lunch David took a long nap on a hillside overlooking the gracefully curving river. There were Paisley patches of wildflowers in the long coarse grass, beaten sideways by the spring winds that swept the valley. Gliders soared overhead, their spindly shadows breaking across the rim of the hill. She sat beside him for a long time, wide-eyed and dreaming. With each broad airy stroke of a glider over the place where she, motionless, was hoarding time, the sun fell; the afternoon went all too quickly.

When David's mouth opened and he began to snore, she teased him under the chin with a handful of grass until he took a deep gasping breath and looked strangely at her.

His face was too somber. She touched him, hopefully.

"Why do I make you so happy—and so sad at the same time?"

"My father—"

"What, David?"

Suddenly he was struggling not to weep.

"Died. Two weeks ago."

"Oh, David, I'm sorry! I knew that something was wrong—you must have loved him very much."

"There was nobody like him. There never will be."

He looked at the sun, much lower in the sky than he remembered. Another glider came by, only about fifty feet overhead, enveloping them in darkness; David turned his head to watch it climb, bank serenely out over the river. He pulled Anneliese down to him. She pressed his fingertips against her lips.

"What do you look like with a beard?"

"A bum. What do you look like—"

"Hmm?"

"Naked."

"You have a short memory," she chided.

"Refresh it."

"We'll take the baths together when we get back. A lovely sauna."

"Then?"

"Then—everything." Her face was in the hollow of his neck. She kissed his throat. "David, I truly believe what we're doing isn't wrong. Not yet. But it could be."

"Why?"

"An act of love is selfish—all-absorbing. That's all right if there could be only the two of us. But there are others who loved you first, David. And I'm too late."

"No," he said, tightening his grip on her as if he was afraid she would slip away, like the glider shadows.

"David, people do outrageous and unforgivable things, all in the name of love. And in the end no one profits."

"We don't have to talk about it yet."

"I told you I was a worrier. I worry because you're a good man, David. I don't want anything to happen to that goodness. It can be a fragile thing. Irreplaceable."

He played with her hair and sighed, too content to take her seriously.

"Let's have one more day as good as today was. Then we'll think about it."

"Of course."

In the last full light of afternoon, David's eyes closed. She smiled, holding him. He began to breathe deeply again, dozing off. She put her lips next to his ear.

"What liars," Anneliese said softly. "Soon we'll tell any lie we have to—just so it will go on one more day."

50 They had put Reba in a windowless bathroom and wired her to the plumbing, where for most of the afternoon she listened to distant flushings, the pipes draining throughout the apartment building. When the men came in to relieve themselves they pulled the shower curtain first. She was lying in the bathtub on an air mattress that took up a lot of space but made her captivity halfway bearable, but she couldn't get comfortable and the showerhead dripped on her bare feet, which were bound together. The gag they'd improvised, a gauze pad fixed in place with heavy transparent surgical tape, wasn't too stifling, but her jaws ached from being clamped together for long stretches of time.

She had seen three men so far, including the balding, glowering sexy one who had been in the park. His name was Jürgen. Chris was thin, young enough to have complexion problems, very blond, with a long face and watery blue eyes that sagged tragically at the corners. Ernst was bushy-haired, narrow in the hips like a chorus boy. With his olive complexion and dazzling teeth, he looked more Italian than German.

Traudl had visited three times to help Reba up, to give her water and food, a chance to sit on the toilet, a few minutes' freedom from the maddening gag. Each time she came she had a different look. Reba wondered how many wigs and pairs of glasses the woman owned. Apparently she was obsessed by the need to constantly change her appearance. She couldn't spend two minutes in the bathroom without staring anxiously at herself in the mirror. Also she had a mammoth toothache on the left side of her jaw. She was lopsided under the ear. She carried oil of cloves with her and frequently dipped a finger into the bottle to massage the bad tooth and surrounding gum. It gave her fleeting relief.

"I can't see a dentist," she explained when Reba asked her. "Every dentist in West Germany has a copy of my charts. I would be instantly recognized by the crowns of my teeth. You see what it's like for us."

She sounded paranoid to Reba, even though Traudl had explained, at great length, who they were and what they hoped to achieve. The Tribunal. Revolutionaries. Reba remembered the comparatively mild ferment of her own student years. They sounded harmless enough. But the hysteria that their little band apparently had promoted among members of the West German government was difficult to believe, leading to violence and more violence. Nevertheless Traudl had assured

Reba, often, that despite her present circumstances she was in no danger.

"Then why can't you let me go?" Reba begged, breaking down after hours in the cramped tub.

"Shh, shhh! It isn't possible. Not until we have Anneliese Girda."

Reba wept. Traudl reached for the gag; the walls of their hideaway were thin. Reba jerked her face sullenly aside.

"Let me cry, goddammit! I won't scream. I just want to get it out of my—system."

Traudl helpfully wetted a face cloth and handed it to her.

"You *know* I can't help you. I—I missed my husband, I got on a plane and came here, and I don't know what the hell has been happening to me since."

Traudl leaned toward her, reeking of cloves. "Too loud. You *must* keep your voice down."

"I don't understand what David has to do with that woman! I never heard of her until I got to Frankfurt." She sniffed and snuffled into the cloth, and was done. Reba never shed her tears for very long. "Are you going to hurt David?" she said at last, having tried before to work up to this crucial question.

Traudl's lips were compressed. "We'll try not to, Mrs. McNair."

"Oh dear God!" Reba wailed. Traudl was quick with the gag. Reba sank back into the tub, staring fearfully at her. Traudl returned the look, not without compassion. Then she wordlessly left the bathroom, a fist to her jaw, tears of pain running down one cheek.

51 In the casino of Bad Kulmbach, Anneliese saw a different David, the gamesman, who seemed determined to break the house, first at roulette and then at chemin-de-fer. He was neither inexperienced nor untalented, but he played by rote, without flair or intuition; she gradually observed in him the temperament, the rigidity and competitiveness, of those who would ultimately repel through some fatal chemistry the will-o'-the-wisp gods they needed to attract.

For the time he concentrated on his cards David largely forgot her, and Anneliese had mixed feelings about his neglect. In a way she was grateful for the time to breathe deeply and stand apart, see him unblurred by sensation. Her head felt almost normal, which was a welcome change. The casino was crowded, three deep at some of the tables, the roulette balls made chipper sounds coming down out of the slots in which they flew around the opalescent revolving wheels. Other women during the evening had also studied David frankly, perhaps knowing he wasn't going to pay attention to them. He was solid, calm, good-looking, assured. *Manly*. The old-fashioned word, humming to the pluck of strait laces, suited, endowed him, as it suited so few others of his sex.

Anneliese felt both thrilled and dismayed by the certain knowledge that she wasn't a passing fancy. But they were together now partly through circumstances she had exploited, because she was scared and needed him, and abrasive questions demanded answers. There was Reba: a presence tonight, the unseen wife. David had avowed a good relationship but hadn't mentioned her since. What was his marriage really like? And the child he loved: How could she not be on his mind? He must have thought about them today, once, a hundred times. It would be inhuman of him not to think of family, and of home, no matter how absorbed he was in her. Anneliese felt a bruise of jealousy—that glamorous ache—a possessive stiffening of the backbone. She was amazed, she wasn't like that, she wanted to lay hands on him and drag him from his chair and up to the room, shut them both away from all distractions and prior claims, confirm the indestructibility of a passion neither had imagined only a single day ago.

After a while, bored by cards, she went away to play roulette by herself. *Rouge et noir.* She won over six hundred marks without caring very much, which was probably the best way to succeed at roulette.

David pushed his way in beside her, looking disgruntled. "I've had it."

"Did you lose?"

"Oh, ten thousand DM. My limit." Earlier that afternoon the Casino's management had arranged the line of credit with his Frankfurt bank. "Let's get some air."

Anneliese dropped her chips, uncashed, into her purse, and they walked outside onto the broad terrace. Other couples were in the gaslit formal garden, there was symphonic music from the nearby *Kurhaus*. Brahms. She still felt shocked by David's casual acceptance of ten thousand marks lost in a couple of hours, and wondered if he could afford it; or was he rich to the extent of someone like Otto Kolner? It was a new prospect, she hadn't considered his resources before.

"It seems like so much money," she said timidly, as they strolled along the terrace.

David hunched his shoulders and contrived to look

destroyed. He turned his pockets inside out and faced her, guilt-ridden, chin trembling. Anneliese grinned and joined him in the pantomime, burying her face in her hands, then pleading, her gestures broad, for him to come home with her. She rocked a pretend-baby in her arms. David, consumed by anguish, shook his head and staggered away, one hand on the concrete terrace railing for support. Too late, it was all over, his misspent life had come to this. Anneliese followed, snatching at his sleeve. David tugged free of her, dipped a hand into the inside pocket of his jacket, whipped out a cap pistol and loudly blew his brains out.

He did it so quickly and convincingly that Anneliese, who hadn't seen the toy gun before, was shocked enough to let out a genuine cry of fear. Then she whirled and ran away from him, into the garden. David caught up.

"Hey, wait, I'm still in one piece."

"Where did you get that?"

He glanced at the little fake pistol in the palm of his hand.

"While you were having your hair combed out, I was playing with some kids in the game room. One of them had an extra gun, and I gave him a couple of bucks for it. I thought I might lose tonight, and I wanted to be prepared." He chuckled. "It went off with a pretty good bang, didn't it?"

Her heart was racing; she stared resentfully at him, and wouldn't let him touch her.

"Anneliese, what's the matter?"

"I hate guns! Even toy ones, they aren't funny."

"It was just a joke, I never gave it a thought. I grew up with guns," he said, somewhat on the defensive.

"I know. Children do, in America." She sighed, bleakly, and relented. "But I grew up with real violence. With murder. The consequences went on and on.

My grandfather grieved, and died. I had to be placed in an institution for children with nervous disorders. For two years I couldn't sleep without a light on. I wet the bed. I stuttered. As you know, I still do when I'm upset."

"My God," David said, and couldn't say anything else. There was an expression of real horror on his face, and Anneliese felt obligated to comfort him. She shuddered; it was too cool in the garden without a wrap. She put her bare arms around him, inside his jacket. Silently they commiserated. They had spoiled each other's good time.

"I'm sorry," Anneliese said. "You were only clowning. I know I'm making too much of this. I shouldn't be bothered any more. I shouldn't."

52 Her fear was like a beast that threatens only when it's hungry; in their comfortable chamber on the highest floor of the hotel, it seemed safely locked out for the night—out there beyond the narrow chiaroscuro of parted windows. As she rolled her head from side to side on the pillowless bed, Anneliese had glimpses past her lover of the starched unmoving curtains, like thin white whorls of lacy, sectioned bone, through which was blackly revealed a hypnotic depth of sky; firmament. Destiny. When she looked straight up she saw him, his gravely enthralled face juxtaposed, the dark and well-shaped head nodding gently from exertion, then moving down and down until their foreheads met, withdrawing as she flicked her lavish tongue across the closed lid of an eye, along the corded angle of jaw.

Above them on the ceiling, no longer well defined in the midnight room, there were half-clad Greeks in profile, men with the wedge-shaped torsos of gladiators, austere temples rounding into the pale blue Olympic heaven. His body like theirs, welts of muscle in the clenching belly, thighs supple but very strong, the swayback plum-decked cock with its single wicked and meaty eye, cocksure in the thriving flower; Anneliese imagined, in conceit and thrilled contentment, that he screwed her like a god. At least he had marvelous control. She leapt from one climax to another, subsided in a kind of humming, resonant delirium. She slept. She held her man, and fought through her dreams to keep him.

53 The next morning, early, there was a bicycle race, the start of the famous (Anneliese said) and grueling Trans-Taunus, with nearly three hundred cyclists entered. They were starting from some arbitrarily chosen point within the maze of paved roadway in the *kurpark,* which, even before a bleary sunrise, was continually in an uproar. Aficionados had taken over Bad Kulmbach. The finish was at the mountain village of Lüttring, some eighty miles, most of it nastily upgrade, from the spa. The course totaled one hundred and fifty-nine miles of winding road.

They dressed hurriedly and descended to the *kurpark* as the milky morning mist was evaporating in the pooled body heat of the crowd, which was unruly in a good-natured way; but not a single flower bed had been trampled, out-of-bounds markers were scrupulously observed. The police had little to do, and seemed eager themselves for glimpses of the major names of international bike racing. Obviously it was a big media event: there was television coverage. Helicopters flapped overhead, the loudspeakers roared announcements.

David looked over the extremely thin, lightweight bikes, which seemed so frail he could crush one between thumb and forefinger. The athletes, for the most part, were of medium size, wiry rather than muscular. Trainers and team managers, wearing important-looking patches on their windbreakers, oiled and pummeled and rubbed down their jittery stars.

It seemed impossible that a race could be organized out of this chaos, but officials on an observation platform made demands, flags were waved meaningfully, the many athletes were left alone by the roadway in some predetermined order, looking almost hypnotically charged up; at the crack of a smoky starter's pistol they dashed away, getting deceptive speed from what looked like minimum effort, the scything sounds of their passing bikes lost in cheers.

In little more than a minute the blacktop lanes in the heart of the park were empty. The crowd stayed on for breakfast, which consisted largely of beer and sausages bought from dozens of vendors.

"Is that all there is to it?" David said, with a last glimpse through the park trees of flashing colors and big numbers as the trailing cyclists swooped over the crest of a hill and into the town of Bad Kulmbach.

"Now we go to Lüttring for the finish," Anneliese said, tongue between her teeth; she was making notes in a program she'd bought.

"When will that be?"

"Oh, hours from now. It's the climax of the Festival Lüttring. Very exciting, don't you think?"

"Oh, yeah. Hell, I don't know how much excitement I can take! Did you see that blowout? I thought the fella was going to get grass stains all over his white shorts."

Anneliese flicked her rolled-up program at him, missing the tip of his nose by a calculated half-inch. She said scornfully:

"I suppose your idea of sport is huge, beefy men hurling themselves at each other in order to possess a ball that's pointed at both ends. Incomprehensible! Do you want to go to Lüttring, or not?"

"Sure," David said. They grinned at each other, pleased with their playful spat. "What else is going on there?"

"Something you're bound to enjoy. Guns. It's a marksman's fair. Crack shots from all over Germany compete for prizes. David, let's have breakfast, I'm starved."

"Beer? At eight o'clock in the morning?"

"I was thinking of champagne with fresh peaches, to start."

"Fantastic."

*"Fan-*tastic," she repeated, smiling, fondly mimicking him.

54 Reba couldn't remember when she'd passed a more miserable twenty-four hours. Her nearly sleepless night trussed up in a bathtub had seemed unendurable, but somehow the limited freedom she now enjoyed was worse, because, although she wasn't tied, she couldn't move without permission, and she'd been bluntly warned not to speak at all. The world one hundred feet from the nose of the motionless gray-and-black Citröen sedan went about its business with all apearances of normality; cramped between Chris and Ernst—who obviously didn't bathe very often, despite what she'd heard about the German fetish for cleanliness—she was alternately bored and terrified by premonitions. She would nod off, then snap awake whenever one of the terrorists spoke in German.

One by one the others got out to relieve their own tedium by walking around the barren, shadowy concrete floor of the building across Grüneburgplatz from Fifth Army Corps headquarters.

She was allowed to leave the back seat only once, with Traudl guarding her, to urinate in a low crouch in a cold corner of the unfinished and deserted structure. Apparently the builders had run out of money well short of completion. There was a rusty fence around the property, a padlocked double gate at the base of the ramp to the two parking floors; the terrorists had broken the lock and replaced it, so that the gates would swing open at a firm nudge.

In the car there were infrequent whispered consultations she couldn't understand. But once Reba heard her husband's name and looked up just as Traudl, in the front seat, cut her eyes away from her. Reba didn't know what that meant but feared the worst. Traudl was a different person this morning; her toothache was murderous, it had swelled her face with poison, puffing her eyes behind sunglasses as big as yellow-tinted headlights. *I used to have hair as long as yours,* she had said wistfully to Reba, and today she was wearing a long fall that made her seem younger. She also had a beret with her that she tried on from time to time, to take her mind off the toothache. There was a disaster in the making, Reba was certain of that. The others were keyed up and smoked too much, the car was filled with the sour breath of used-up cigarettes.

The U.S. flag flew over the buff stone building across the way and MPs patrolled the parking lot, so Reba assumed they were near an important military base, but she didn't know which one. Nor did she know why they had been waiting, for what seemed like hours, watching the entrance to the base.

Then, in midday brightness, his face as familiar to her as the full moon over the bayou back home, Joby Ben came outside wearing fatigues and carrying an attaché case. He stood on the steps looking impatiently up the drive as if waiting on a car, and Reba drew in a sharp breath. Traudl gave her a quick, noncommittal glance, sucking on a cloves-saturated finger. Jürgen started the engine of the Citröen.

"Why?" Reba said, and Chris pinched her painfully in the ribs to remind her to be quiet. They all sat staring suspensefully at Joby Ben as if he might do something unprecedented, like rise straight up in the air and disappear over the treetops. Presently a civilian car, a classy Opel Senator, drove up and he jogged down the steps, threw his attaché case into the back, and got in.

Jürgen drove down the ramp to the gates and bumped gingerly through them, turned right and picked up the Senator as it left the base through the east portal on Bremerstrasse. A woman was driving the car. Traudl twisted around in the seat and said to Reba,

"Who's that he's with?"

Reba shrugged helplessly. "I don't know. I really don't know much about Joby Ben." Bidden to speak, she had to rattle on. "What does Joby Ben have to do with—with the Tribunal?"

"He's a thief and a murderer. Involved with Anneliese in the conspiracy against us."

"Joby Ben? You've got to be—"

"Now *listen*. Before long, I think, this man will lead us to Anneliese. And your husband. Then there's going to be, without a doubt, a bloody lot of trouble. I brought you along today because there's a chance Anneliese and your husband may be separated when we catch up to them."

"David. Call him David." If he had a name, Reba thought, a flesh-and-blood identity, then they might hesitate to kill him no matter what they thought he'd done.

"Very well. David. None of us know him. It's to his advantage if you see him first, without Anneliese. Then we can take him aside before we deal with the others. I'm sure that your—that David is in no way responsible for the plot against us. So he may well survive. But only if you're smart, Mrs. McNair."

55 Joby Ben changed his clothes in the car on the way to Bad Kulmbach, putting on a blue golfing shirt and khaki pants, a pair of scuffed Adidas sneakers. The spa looked nearly deserted at one in the afternoon. Franziska had a beer in the outdoor café of the Lindener Palace while Joby Ben went inside to verify the information that the BKA had passed on to him about his nephew. He was back in a few minutes, and ordered a beer for himself while he cased the lawns, gardens, and tennis courts of the hotel without seeing David or Anneliese.

"My hunch is they went to the festival. That's where everybody else is today. We can probably find them up there if we look around."

"All right," Franziska said indifferently, toying with the heavy gold-link chain around her neck. "I don't feel like staying around here until all hours."

They got back into the car; this time Joby Ben drove, taking a pleasantly winding, little-used road north toward Lüttring, passing through upland villages where the Trans-Taunus bicycle caravan had already been. The air was crisper in the mountains, the trees on the brown slopes a mixture of tall pines and tawny green cedars, some of them almost as enormous as cathedrals.

"Have you noticed the gray-and-black Citröen behind us?" Franziska asked.

"No." He checked the rear-view mirror as they rounded a walled curve. The Citröen was well below them, traveling at a moderate speed. "Why?"

"It's a distinctive car. And expensive. You don't see many of them in this country."

"Who needs it? Germans make the best cars in the world."

Another curve, and they had caught up with the stragglers, the also-rans of what was here not a race but a crucible of the spirit. Casualties were frequent by the side of the road, men with fierce cramps crying helplessly, or lying gray with exhaustion, their chests barely moving. Their car was routed slowly and carefully around other riders straining to push their fragile machines over the summit and into a waiting pillow of clouds. A helicopter circled overhead, fell away to the left, went whirling beyond the peaks of trees like a runaway buzzsaw.

Franziska said, "I never knew just how you felt when I found out that your marvelous brother was a murderer."

Joby Ben scowled. "You saw some pictures in an album. It was twenty years after the fact. I made you a bargain, and I've kept it. We've earned a lot of money, Franziska. Enough to keep us on a good-sized yacht in Cannes for the rest of our lives."

He glanced at her to see what was working in her face. She looked like a cat with a well-used rat in her jaws. She gave her head a shake.

"It amazed me when I saw him, there in his coffin. Of course the art of the undertaker is to produce a bizarre freshness, a look of haunted youth. Still, he looked much the same as he did when I spied on him in my mother's bed...did I tell you? He was a wretched lover."

"How would you know? You were all of eleven years old at the time."

"I knew—by the expression of disgust on my mother's face."

In his irritation Joby Ben drove too fast; a motorcycle cop sailed up on his left and motioned for him to slow down. A mile later they were detained at an intersection, rerouted to Lüttring. Spread out before them in the valley were the front-runners of the Trans-Taunus and their mechanized entourages, bright gaggles of spectators beside the road.

Franziska yawned and looked back again, at the gray-and-black Citroen idling over the brow of the sun-streaked hill above them. She studied it thoughtfully, unable to make out who was in the car, although she counted at least four heads.

Without letting Joby Ben see what she was up to,

she reached into her purse and put her hand on the butt of a .38 caliber Walther automatic, to be reassured that the gun was where it needed to be, positioned for instant use.

56 Lüttring was a hillside village high in the mountains; part of it was quite old, with half-timbered houses and a twelfth-century wall with spear-point towers that roughly divided the old and new towns. About three quarters of a mile above the village, reached by a winding road, stood an immense castle-fortress through which an entire river flowed and fell, in a spectacular drop, down the other side of the mountain. The woods nearby contained stag and roe deer and, in the more inaccessible areas, wild boar.

The cobbled main street of Lüttring, Kerstingstrasse, began at a lower square that was surrounded by historic buildings and a medieval church, jogged crookedly uphill for several blocks, and then joined the fortress road. There were charming side streets, too narrow and steep for automobiles; some of the little streets had stone steps down the middle. On both sides of Kerstingstrasse there were *gasthäuser,* sidewalk cafés, and the expensive shops that catered to the people from Frankfurt who could afford to maintain weekend homes in the area.

To the left, traveling up Kerstingstrasse (which was closed to auto traffic during the Lüttring Festival), the view beyond the short side streets was of parkland, where the contests for marksmen were in progress; rifle shots crackled almost continuously on the firing ranges. To the right, where the sunless streets seemed like tunnels and were blocked at the lower end by the old town wall, the last five-hundred-yard stretch of the Trans-Taunus race was marked, through many twists and turns and archways, with blue-and-white pennants.

From one of the dealers in antique firearms in the gunsmiths' bourse at the edge of the park, David purchased a boxed pair of mid-nineteenth-century German officer's 14-bore percussion holster pistols. After a considerable wait for a table at one of the cafés on Kerstingstrasse, he opened the walnut case and looked at the weapons again. They were more than a foot long, with plain half-stocks and steeply angled, fluted butts, oval German-silver wedgeplates, brass-tipped steel ramrods.

David had also bought a quantity of copper percussion caps, some gunpowder, and balls for the muzzle-loading pistols. He held one in each hand, sighting a high-flying hawk, eager for a test firing. No one in the café or on the street paid attention. Lüttring was filled with guns today, they were carried openly everywhere.

"They're beautiful," Anneliese conceded. "If you can admire that kind of beauty. Put them away, David? Please."

"My dad collects antique firearms," David said, preoccupied with cleaning some tarnish from the maker's name, which was engraved around the hammer of one of the pistols. "I'd like to see if I can find—"

The sun was on their table, the draft beer was warm and oddly tasteless, flies buzzed them. A German band played on a little octagonal stand set up on a level few feet of Kerstingstrasse, their instruments bobbing like brass balloons above the heads of the fun-seekers surging restlessly by. The sudden realization of what he was saying caused David to jerk his head up. Anneliese had been contentedly watching his face, seeing dimensions in shadow which she hadn't yet fully appreciated. The sun penetrated to the bone, he blinked and squeezed out tears, she beheld the anguish of a burning man.

"My God, I bought them for *him*. As if he was still alive."

"It'll take time, David. A very long time."

There was a concerted roar around them in response to a loudspeaker announcement. Customers finished steins of beer, hurriedly paid their bills and left, some of them leaping over the café balustrade to the street, which was rapidly emptying, draining downhill toward the old town.

"What's going on?" David said as he was jostled. It seemed to him as if there was a panic on. He hadn't paid attention to the announcement. His assumption struck a corresponding panic in him. He leaned at an angle in his chair, wondering what to do, what move to make. Anneliese laughed.

"It's the finish—the tour is close by." She took his hand. "Come on, we'll miss it!"

"No—wait." David resisted being unseated, held her firmly in his grip. She wanted to run away too: He looked startled and unnerved, desperate. Anneliese sat down again slowly and touched the side of his face. In him decision cracked like a cyst. He felt a bitter blind Judgment overtaking them; but he had to speak.

"There's something I want to tell you," he said. "About my father."

57 Joby Ben found no space in the car park at the foot of Kerstingstrasse, but Franziska said she would wait for him in the Senator.

"All the crowding at these festivals nauseates me. You go and see if you can find the lovebirds."

He left the car double-parked in the shade of two black oak trees and crossed the square. Some children went running by him, on their way to the finish line of the Trans-Taunus. Volleys of gunshots echoed flatly from wall to wall down the hill. She heard band music and a voice from a distant loudspeaker, which was punctuated by shouts and cheers from the unseen crowd. Joby Ben started up the long slope of Kerstingstrasse, his diagonal shadow sawing jerkily through walls and doorways. A helicopter smothered all other sounds; she saw it reflected clearly in the windshield of the car.

Franziska glanced around the car park, but there were too many trees in her field of vision, she couldn't locate the gray-and-black Citroen that had followed them to the limits of the town. She wasn't sure it mattered anyway. She leaned back in the reclining seat, purse in her lap, and closed her eyes. Her hand was on the butt of the Walther in her purse. She wondered what it would be like to shoot David McNair, quickly, five or six times in the stomach, as soon as she laid eyes on him.

58 The Citröen, its motor running, was on the other side of the car park, behind a temporary signboard, where Franziska probably wouldn't have seen it even if she'd left her own car to have a look around.

For the past half hour, as they trailed Joby Ben and Franziska to Lüttring, the members of the Tribunal had been arguing, sometimes angrily, about the strategy they should follow, revising their plans several times.

"I say he's meeting Anneliese here," Traudl insisted, as she and Jürgen Sollmann got out of the car. "She's always had a passion for the tours."

"Then she'll probably be in the crowd at the finish," Jürgen said, watching Joby Ben as he continued up Kerstingstrasse. "He doesn't look as if he knows where he's going. Can we afford to have him get away from us?"

"No. If Anneliese isn't at the finish, it's because she's in bed with her lover. There's a way to bring her to us. We'll cover both possibilities."

Traudl turned to the car. In the back seat, Chris and Ernst were taping Reba's ankles and wrists together.

"Chris?"

The blond young man nodded and began pulling on a pair of thin leather driving gloves. Jürgen opened the boot of the Citröen. He and Traudl removed three semi-automatic shotguns in leather cases, and vests filled with extra shells.

Traudl got into the back seat to talk to Reba, who had seen the guns and was quaking with fright. Traudl put on her beret in a businesslike fashion. If she had any nerves it wasn't apparent. Her voice was distorted by her swollen jaw.

"If you lie down on the floor and keep still, nothing will happen to you. Otherwise I can't make any promises."

Ernst finished taping her ankles and backed out of the car. Reba nodded weakly. Traudl pressed a wide strip of tape across her mouth and pulled Reba down, wedging her into the floor space between the leather seats. She got out and shut the door. Chris took over at the wheel. Traudl picked up a hooded shotgun and put it over one shoulder.

"Win or lose," Traudl said to Chris, "we all meet at the Bethlehem bridge. Six o'clock."

Chris drove slowly away. Traudl glanced at Jürgen and Ernst. "Baby, let's go," she said with a tight grin. The two men walked in the direction of the Trans-Taunus finish line. Traudl stayed where she was, waiting for Chris to do his stuff. Joby Ben was no longer in sight.

The Citröen drove through the square and turned into Kerstingstrasse, which was clearly marked *verboten* to automobiles. It idled there, nose pointed uphill.

In the back seat Reba lay as still as she could, not because of what Traudl had said but because she felt so nauseated she thought she was going to vomit; and if she did, she would surely strangle on it.

59 A bee buzzing through the open window of the Senator annoyed Franziska. She opened her eyes and batted the bee away from her and saw golden streaks of cloud in the blue sky, trees moving lazily in the late afternoon breeze, sunbursts in the west-facing windows of the town. She also saw the Citröen sitting low and ominously at the foot of Kerstingstrasse, heard its tail-pipes bubbling as the engine was revved. And she could just make out the figure of Joby Ben in his golf shirt as he toiled the last few blocks up the deserted business street. She bolted out of the car with her purse in one hand as the Citröen fled from her with a lavish scream of burned rubber on brick.

60 They sat alone, at the table of the sidewalk café, within a mazelike clutter of abandoned tables and chairs, in a castled setting slowly devoured by shadows; and in those quaint sawtooth shadows pressing at his back, David sensed the monster of his father taking shape while he groped in a fever and stumbled, shackled by secrets, desiring, even this late, to plead his humanness and acquit him.

"Just before he died, he told me about a woman he'd

been in love with, twenty-five years ago. I guess it isn't enough to say he loved her...he was obsessed by her."

The remaining sunlight was a crystalline bowl in which Anneliese's face seemed isolated, like a fabulous candle flame, steady, burning at a graver temperature, refining her features to a childlike simplicity of brow, lash, and tepid vein: the eyes of a disquieting, shocked young beauty. This was nearly the face his father must have seen, by firelight. David felt grotesque, voyeuristic, lover and murderer in one. As if he held a live grenade, he wanted to hurl the confession at her, explode the past and free them, through some miracle of purification, in a new intensity of the light they were rapidly losing.

But he was distorted by his father's presence, unsure of his own skin and afraid of the face she was seeing and must soon recognize. He slumped lower in his chair with a shiver of hallucination and lowered his head, unable to speak any more; nothing formed in his throat but lumps of grief. He swallowed them as if he were swallowing blood. His right hand cramped painfully.

In his pitiable anguish Anneliese had glimpses of the heart that were new to her, and thrilling. She was puzzled, not knowing how to help him. The crowd some distance away cheered, a hoarse, sanguinary sound. Somewhere else a car, its back wheels locked, accelerated with a supremely arrogant, skin-prickling howl of horsepower. David shivered again.

"Hey, David! How you doin' today, boy!"

David turned, startled. Joby Ben was standing near the center of the street about two blocks away, waving at him. At that moment the Citröen came hurtling up the hill behind him. Joby Ben jerked his head around to look at it, then hopped nimbly to one side, close to a stone wall, giving the speeding car plenty of room.

But as the Citröen approached him it went into a

controlled rear-end skid. Joby Ben hollered and tried to run but was caught between the car and the wall and dragged in a shower of sparks to a shop window, which shattered. The Citröen straightened out, wrecked the bandstand that had been left in the street, and boomed on past the café; David had a quick glimpse of the blond maniac behind the wheel as he scrambled over tables to reach the street.

He ran to where Joby Ben, his clothes ripped and smoking and bloody, had fallen away from the low sill of the broken window.

Franziska had appeared, running hard uphill, and was bending over Joby Ben, lifting his head from the pavement, speaking to him quietly and urgently. When David approached she looked up, wild with rage, eyes slashing through him as she located the Citröen. Windows creaked open overhead and David glanced up to see a few elderly faces, toothless as muffins, and babes in arms. One of Joby Ben's hands fluttered on the brick, he gasped for air and foamed blood. Although he was muffled by shock, he still recognized David. His lips formed the semblance of a grin.

"Told you...not to mess with...other people's lives."

Above them Chris made a screeching turn and drove at them again. This time Anneliese was in the way; she had lagged well behind David, and seemed oblivious of the present danger.

"Anneliese! Watch out!"

Quick as a snake, Franziska pulled the automatic from her purse, turned, and fired two accurate shots past Anneliese at the oncoming car. Chris swerved, lost control, drove through the sidewalk café where David and Anneliese had been sitting, and came to a dead stop, the Citröen wedged up to the windshield in a stout doorway.

In the street below them, Traudl Hecker unzipped the case of the shotgun she was carrying.

Anneliese looked from the wreck of the car to the woman with the shotgun and saw something familiar, although afterward she couldn't be sure what had sparked an almost instant recognition. Traudl was almost eighty yards away, and she was very heavy. But the beret was a symbol, as defiant as a name tag. The set of her shoulders, the purposeful stance, the graceful movements of her hands on the shotgun, the cynical, quizzical tilt of her head, everything recalled to Anneliese the night she had been assaulted in Otto Kolner's bathroom.

She cried out: "Traudl! No!"

Franziska, hunched over Joby Ben, whipped her pistol around and snapped a shot at Traudl, who ducked into a doorway working the pump action of her shotgun. She was a little out of effective range.

Franziska leaped over Joby Ben and grabbed Anneliese by the hair, putting Anneliese's body between herself and Traudl as she cruelly dragged her sister up the street.

"You know them, so I need you. *Run,* you idiot! Before we're both killed!"

"Franziska, don't—*David!*"

David was still on one knee beside Joby Ben, appalled by the blood, the jagged edges of bones. Joby Ben, sucking wind through his chest with every breath, blinked sadly at the sky.

"Not...doing so good, Davey. Get 'em...away from here. Fast."

David glanced at Traudl, who was advancing cautiously with her shotgun, leveling it at him. He opened the walnut case and picked up one of the heavy, long-barreled antique pistols. When she saw it, Traudl flattened herself in another doorway. David looked up at the faces in the windows and shouted in German:

"Someone get a doctor—the police—this man is dying!"

Then he ran after Franziska and Anneliese, who had just turned into a side street. He heard the stunning, echo-flattened report of Traudl's shotgun and a shop window at his elbow disappeared in a sharp dazzling avalanche.

On the terrace of the café, Chris had forced open the door of the Citröen and was getting out, holding a bloody head with one hand. David saw the halting way in which he moved and paid no further attention. Carrying the case in one hand and the unloaded pistol in the other, he caught up with Franziska and Anneliese, still tingling from the aftereffects of the near miss, the back of his head feeling naked and vulnerable.

Below them in the narrow street, two blocks away, a crowd was jammed into the bottleneck created by the intersection of two streets, one of which was fronted by the eight-foot-high wall of the old town and a massive tower with a tunnel for the roadway. Blue-and-white pennants crackled in broad angles of orange sun. There was a din of loudspeakers and a palpable current of anticipation attracting new faces to the fringes of the crowd, pulling them from every doorway along the route. Everyone was looking in the same direction; periscopes were aimed at the tunnel where the front-runners of the tour would come flying down the last long stretch to the finish line.

Franziska was still leading Anneliese by a halter of hair, as if she were a balky pony. David smacked Franziska on the shoulder with the back of the hand in which he held the officer's pistol.

"Let her go, you're hurting her."

Franziska dropped her hand to Anneliese's arm and glared around at David.

"Where is she? The one with the shotgun?" She shook Anneliese. "What did you say her name was?"

Anneliese stumbled on the downhill cobbles; Franziska yanked her upright.

"Traudl—Hecker." Anneliese looked blank, as if her whole face had gone numb. She said softly, shaking her head, "I knew. I just *knew*. Now what is she going to do to me?"

There was a streak of blood on one of Franziska's cheeks, probably Joby Ben's, and David flashed dismally on his uncle dying unattended in the street. He caught sight of Traudl at the top of the street, the mask of her oversized amber sunglasses catching a ray of sun. She stalked them patiently with her shotgun at port arms, working her way through the people hurrying to high stoops to catch a glimpse of the racers.

An elderly man carrying an heirloom shotgun stepped out of a shop behind Franziska. She caught a glimpse of him in a bay window, whirled, and threw down on him with the Walther. David went cold, certain she would kill the old man, but her reflexes were admirable and in a split second she realized he was harmless. He tottered backwards into the shop again, huffing with fright, and Franziska pressed on, yanking Anneliese over and around obstacles.

"*Everyone* has a gun! Anneliese, use your eyes. Where are the rest of them?"

"I don't know! I only know Traudl—"

"My God. That woman. She's the worst of them by far."

"Here she comes!" David warned. They had reached the crowd lining the tour route, a wall of flesh that seemed as impenetrable as the stones, marked with zigzags of fresh mortar, across the way.

Franziska didn't hesitate. With Anneliese in tow, she wedged her way between bodies, silencing protests with an emphatic show and jab of her automatic, heedless of the potential consequences if a policeman should glance their way. David bulled in behind her and suddenly, as the beer-drinking crowd began to chant with excitement, they found themselves on the road, in a space quickly filled by bicycle racers churning full tilt and at swooping dizzy angles from the deep gloom of the tower tunnel on their left.

David had made fun of the sport, but this was a different, very deadly matter: the cyclists, only four hundred yards from the finish at this point, were sprinting downhill at speeds of more than sixty kilometers an hour, and they had almost no room to maneuver. Their narrow, graceful machines sliced past the fugitives like whirling blades.

Somehow the first group of cyclists just missed them as the crowd shouted warnings: Then Franziska, leaning deftly away from one of the bicycles, thrust her right hand out too far for balance. Her wrist was clipped and the Walther automatic went spinning far down the incline. A bike ran over the gun and the rider tumbled into the front line of spectators, knocking two of them down. Within moments the road was piled with wrecked bikes and athletes flung into the wall or crowd, skidding bloodily to the bone on asphalt.

The policemen on hand were village auxiliaries, slow to react. Franziska pushed Anneliese through the tunnel, dodging the tour stragglers as they approached. On the other side of the tower they ran, and didn't stop until they reached the forest midway between the town and the castle-fortress at the top of the hill.

61 They hid there, depleted, in a little depression in the hillside, a cove of earth-bank strapped by roots and furnished with a crisp sponge of pine needles.

The evening sun glimmered like uncertain flame across their humid faces. Anneliese was out of breath and holding her side. Traudl kept lifting her head for foxlike glances at the forest in their vicinity, which was crisscrossed by trails. They heard and glimpsed people moving all around them: teen-agers, couples holding hands, picnickers on the way home. Birds twittered brightly overhead.

For the first time since he had been on the run, David had a couple of minutes to think; but his mind was uncooperative, running backwards like a wildly reversing film through his recent panic. Seemingly irrelevant details were most vividly repeated: a blind, frost-blue eye like an exclamation mark in a crowd of stares; a racer sitting dazed in the street, a liplike imprint of blood on his cheek as if he'd just received a sticky kiss of death; a three-legged dog standing absolutely still and looking mournfully over one shoulder at them as they fled; a shop window aflutter with little green and yellow birds; Joby Ben's wristwatch broken open, revealing cogwork secrets, bits and pieces of static time. But he couldn't make any sense of what had happened.

Franziska reached over and tapped him on the knee. "What do you have there?"

He stared at her. The bad sister. Tooth marks on

Anneliese's arm. He saw no resemblance between the two. What did she have to do with Joby Ben? *There's a man she lives with, an American. I've never met him.*

David glanced at the pistol he was holding, then opened the walnut case and showed her the other one.

"One shot each?" Franziska grimaced in disappointment. "Load them anyway."

The strident *hee-haw* of police sirens rose from the streets below. David looked hopeful.

"I think we'll be okay now."

"Is that so?" Franziska turned to Anneliese. "Do you know how many of them there are?"

Anneliese tried to speak, but her tongue was stuck to the roof of her mouth.

"You're not going to start stuttering again, are you?" Franziska said in disgust. She slapped her sister. "Get hold of yourself and try to think!"

Anneliese's color had been poor, but now she turned green and crawled awkwardly away to vomit. David glanced at her hunched shoulders, the animal thrust of her head, the splayed jaw and sick glass of her eyes, and in a rage of sympathy he grabbed Franziska.

"Leave her alone!"

Franziska shook him off. "Shut your mouth. I know how to handle this one." She pulled a tissue from her sweater pocket, put an arm around the shuddering Anneliese and wiped her mouth for her.

"Anneliese—you know they intend to kill us, don't you?"

Anneliese nodded, and retched again.

"What the hell," David said, "the police are all over the village. They'll help us now."

"What a good idea!" Franziska gave him a look of such loathing that David felt a pinch of fear. "And while we try to find a sympathetic policeman, someone we have never seen before will blow us to bits. These are trained terrorists we're dealing with. They've been to school, you see, in Yemen and Iraq. They're as mindless and deadly as attack dogs...and they know the three of us on sight by now."

She turned away, murmuring in Anneliese's ear. "Deep breaths. That's good. This is no time to be weak."

David bit his lip and began to load one of the antique pistols.

"Why did they try to kill Joby Ben?"

"Never mind. He's a good man, compared to what your father was."

David, disturbed by the unexpected reference, fumbled the copper-fulminate cap and caught it between his knees.

"What about my father?"

Franziska had risen from a crouch and was gesturing at him.

"Keep quiet!"

She motioned to a young man moving softly and slowly off-trail about thirty yards away. David couldn't see his face, but he had a semiautomatic shotgun in one hand, and his finger was on the trigger.

Franziska pulled Anneliese toward her, forcibly turning her head until she was looking at the intruder.

"Tell me if you've ever seen him before." She glanced back at David. "Hurry up with that pistol. And do it right!"

The young man obviously was searching for something. At intervals of a few feet he paused to look around, as if he were seeing in the broken brush signs of headlong flight to their place of concealment. He was standing largely in shadow and evening haze, further obscured by the massive trunk of a cedar tree. Birdsong accompanied the strong red death of the sun. The young man looked out, lifting his head to follow a patter of woodcock wings into the airy upper forest. He resumed his walk toward them.

"I don't know," Anneliese whispered. "The one who threw the paint bomb at me was thin, and his hair was like wire—this could be the same man."

"No more talking," Franziska commanded, her voice barely audible. Her back-stretched hand trembled slightly as she waited for David to lay the loaded pistol in it. He glanced at the shotgun and thought of the consequences if she missed with the unfamiliar weapon. He gave it to her anyway and began at once to load the other, for himself.

The young man paused again fifteen yards away, a little uphill and directly in front of Franziska and the long steady barrel of the German officer's pistol. He gave no indication of having observed them; the hand that held the shotgun was noticeably relaxed. But he was, unexpectedly, smiling as if in triumph. David looked up frantically at the young man's guileless tea-colored eyes, then rammed a big ball down the muzzle of the pistol he held clenched between his legs. It had occurred to him that there might be another one, coming as stealthily from a different direction, to catch them in a crossfire.

Apparently this was also on Franziska's mind; he realized that she was going to shoot the young man now, and worry about identifying him after.

But before she could pull the trigger a piercing trill from a branch high above the young man's head attracted him; looking up, he trilled and wheedled back convincingly.

Franziska lowered the heavy pistol and bowed her head. David, looking around, was satisfied that there were no terrorists creeping up on an unguarded flank. In a matter of moments the young man had lost his sinister aspect; he was simply amusing himself with bird calls.

After a while he wandered off and they took a breather. Anneliese crept into David's arms and her nails bit into his back. Franziska got comfortable with her ankles crossed and stared at David with a balefully curious eye.

"We're lucky for now," she said. "But it will be cold in these woods tonight."

"Why are they trying to kill us?" David said.

"Because Joby Ben and I stole a million dollars worth of heroin from them. And we killed a couple of their comrades in the bargain." She flicked pine needles from the hair below her ears, and grinned at Anneliese's reaction.

"Franziska, my God, is that why they think—because you're my—"

"Well, no, I'm sure it's because I ratted on you, Anneliese. 'Ratted.' That's the right word, isn't it?" She said this to David, who didn't respond. Franziska got up, stretched, and shook herself in a self-confident, arrogant way. She pitched the heavy gun she'd been holding butt-first to David. "They're almost ready to close the fortress for the night. We can hide in there for a week, if we need to. Unless you want to take your chances in the town. No? You don't like that idea any more? Then come along with me, lovebirds."

62 For more than half an hour Reba was helplessly stuck, face down, in the wreck of the Citröen.
The front seat had rolled back like a vise, squeezing
her shoulders and hips between hard and soft leather;
the hump of the differential was solidly and after a
time excruciatingly positioned in the pit of her stomach. She heard voices in German, which she didn't understand. A good many people glanced into the car
without seeing her, and a policeman had climbed into
the front to open the glove box with the ignition key.

When she felt his weight pressing into the seat, Reba
squealed behind the tape over her mouth. But there
was a loud clatter of metal tables and chairs as the
owners of the café sorted through the ruins, and the
policeman didn't hear her. Until a wrecker's cable was
attached to the bumper and the Citröen was yanked
from the café door, no one thought to look into the back
seat.

Her rescuers needed a few more minutes to get her
out with a pry bar. When the front seat was forced
forward on its track, Reba was lifted, doubled over,
from the car. A knife sliced through the tape binding
her hands and feet; every movement she made brought
jabs of needles, long shooting pains. Her hair had been
dusted gray by powdered masonry drifting through the
polished lace of the shot-up windshield. Someone cautiously lifted her head by the jaw; she was a tough-
looking matron with a Peter Pan thatch of silver hair
and unexpectedly warm brown eyes.

The woman peeled the surgical tape away and Reba gasped through her parched, bleeding lips, the evening air burning at the back of her throat. The sun was below the rooftops but there was a false hectic glow of dusk in the street, from the amber and red lights of wrecker, fire truck, ambulance, and *panzerwagen*. Half a dozen men, some in uniform, pressed around her, interrupting each other with urgent questions in German.

Reba had no idea of where she was. The effort to concentrate stunned her. Her eyes wouldn't focus, and her head rolled from side to side.

The matron broke a capsule of smelling salts under her nose. It stung; faces leaped sharply into view.

"Could I have a drink of water?" Reba asked meekly.

One of the KRIPOs switched to fluent English. "Who are you, fräulein? What were you doing in that car?"

"Kidnapped," Reba said, licking her sore lips. She felt a little ridiculous. Looking past the cop, she saw Joby Ben being lifted, on a stretcher, into the waiting ambulance. She started up, hands flailing wildly at the hands that tried to restrain her.

"No! Is he dead? David! Where's...Davidddd!"

It took three of the husky policemen to hold her back. The matron deftly prepared a syringe. The KRIPO who had spoken in English stopped her.

"In her state, even the mildest sedative might knock her out for hours. We need answers, and we need them now."

63 The castle-fortress of Lüttring, one of the largest and best preserved in Europe, had several unusual or unique features. It stood high and apart from the village, although at one time the walls of the old town had continued as far as the fortress itself—as protection against the long and forested south slope of the mountain, from which a siege could easily be maintained. The fortress was surrounded on three sides by a swift river and a man-made lagoon. The river, which provided fresh water in all seasons, coursed through the elliptical fortress yard, dividing the outbuildings and east gate from the main castle.

Instead of the usual isolated Bergfried tower, a customary feature of German castles, Lüttring consisted of three residential towers with helm-roofed superstructures, joined by inner walls, each of which had a covered walk on top. This complex was built on a spur of palisade which overlooked the steep falls of the river and a blue valley starred with the lights of neighboring villages. In the late sixteenth century, long after the principal construction of the fortress was completed, a chapel and a large *palas* had been added by heirs of the dynasty of Hohenstaufen, who liked to be wed and entertain in a big way.

The outer buttressed wall was thick and high, made of stones worked so carefully that no breech had occurred in more than six hundred and fifty years, despite intermittent hostilities such as the Napoleonic Wars. The wall enclosed an area of nearly twenty acres.

The southeast-wall walk, which faced the village, was unroofed, and wide enough to drive a pair of mid-range Mercedes trucks along it. Wooden scaffolding for a festival-climaxing fireworks display were being hammered together by workmen on the high wall when David, Franziska, and Anneliese approached the castle through the paved outer ward.

A few tourists were on their way out, crossing the central drawbridge over the river. The iron portcullis was still up and the inner-wall door, a massive eight feet in width, stood open. But a guard heard their footsteps on the bridge and came toward them smiling, waving his hands across his chest, palms out, to indicate that it was closing time.

Franziska waved back breezily. She had picked up a knobby hardwood walking staff along the way. With it she pointed out the double-headed eagle painted on the entrance door and chatted in English with David and Anneliese until they were across.

The guard pointed at the posted closing hours as Franziska walked by him, pretending to be enamored with the architecture. A couple of naked light bulbs cast large wraparound shadows in the vaulted arch of the inner wall.

"I'm sorry," the balding guard said in English, pausing and turning away from Franziska to admire Anneliese. "Too late today. Vhy not coming back tomorrow, please?"

Franziska turned with her elbows high and poleaxed him; the hard wood against his bare skull made a sound like billiard balls cracking together. Anneliese moaned; the guard sagged into David's arms and Franziska ran to tug the door shut. The crossbar fell into place with a noise that reverberated around the walls.

Franziska popped the light bulbs with the tip of her staff. Then she turned to the wheel that lowered the portcullis, but found it difficult to budge. She swore and put her back into it.

A steel guard-hut stood just inside the wall, in the courtyard. It was wired for telephone and electricity. There was a potbellied stove inside, a heater, an army bed, a shelf with food and a few dishes on it. David stretched the guard out on the bed. A blushing lump had risen on the back of his head.

"Do you think he's hurt badly?" Anneliese said.

David put his ear to the guard's open mouth and heard a restful breathing.

"No."

"David, look." She took his arm and showed him the wall-mounted telephone. Outside, Franziska was still fighting the wheel. "Ring the district police," she urged him. "They'll come and get us."

David nodded and picked up the receiver, scanning a list of numbers taped to the side of the telephone. He found the number for the police and dialed.

64 The Hesse state police already had their hands full, trying to cope with the disorder at the finish of the Trans-Taunus bicycle race.

Three ambulances had already taken the most grievously injured racers to the nearest large hospital, in Bad Kulmbach. Others received treatment from local physicians and nurses as mangled bicycles were thrown into flatbed trucks. Irate cyclists argued, in five or six languages, with tour officials about the outcome of the race. Bookmakers huddled, looking worried. A great many people were just milling about, voraciously consuming food and drink. As the setting sun turned the fortress on the heights to a blood-red mirage, television lights came on in the dusky square.

Traudl Hecker, carrying her shotgun upside down over one shoulder, stayed as far away as possible from the TV minicams while she tracked down Jürgen and Ernst. They were having draft beer under the awning of a café that had a good view of the square. Traudl thirstily helped herself to Jürgen's stein, then treated her aching tooth with oil of cloves.

"They ran into the forest," she said. "Either they've slipped back down into the village"—she gestured hopelessly at the crowds—"or else they went higher."

They all looked over the rooftops at the fortress. A light was flashing from one of the towers; it was only a little brighter than the evening star. Traudl stared at it, mystified. Then she leaned across a table and borrowed a pair of Zeiss binoculars from an Austrian tourist. She isolated the light and concluded that it was a reflection of the sun from a casement window that someone seemed to be cranking in and out, monotonously, for no good reason other than to catch the last rays of the sun. It could have been a crude signal. Traudl handed the binoculars to Jürgen.

"What do you think?" she asked him.

"I don't know. What happened to Chris?"

"The car crashed. He was hurt. But he got out of the car okay. I couldn't help him. I don't know what happened to him after that."

"Well, it could be Chris. He could be trying to signal us."

"Then they're in the fortress; but he needs help."

"Let's have a look," Jürgen said.

65 The police telephone circuits were busy.

"That can't be," Anneliese said. "You can always call the police. Can't you?"

"Not if everybody else is calling at the same time."

"David!" Anneliese screamed.

He turned just as Franziska picked up an old bread knife from the top of the stove. He hadn't been listening for her, hadn't sensed her presence in the hut. The black blade of the knife was very sharp; over the years it had been whetted to about half of its original size. It flashed toward his throat.

And missed, as he jerked his head to one side. The blade caught the telephone cord an inch below the receiver, and sliced through it.

Franziska withdrew the knife and stood back, studying his reaction. David had instinctively raised an arm to protect his throat and turned sideways, ready to lash out with the severed telephone receiver.

Franziska laughed uproariously and began to cut the telephone cord into two-foot sections.

"What the hell are you doing?"

"By now they will have located Joby Ben's car. They'll look it over very carefully. There's more than a million dollars worth of uncut heroin in that car. I don't want to have to answer for it."

She handed the pieces of cord to the astonished David, pointed the tip of the knife at the guard on the bed.

"Tie his hands and feet to the bed frame."

She leaned over the guard, who was snoring lightly, slipped the blade between his paunch and leather belt, and jerked. The belt parted easily and the guard's brass key ring jangled to the floor.

Franziska pocketed the keys and began pulling food off the shelf. Tea, half of a greasy blood sausage, the dark butt of a loaf of pumpernickel. She thrust the sausage under Anneliese's nose, and laughed again when Anneliese recoiled. She began to pare big chunks of the sausage and pop them into her mouth. She chewed with great zest, frowning at the halfhearted way in which David tied the unconscious guard.

"That's a good knot? I thought you were a sailor." David glanced at her, mum with dislike. "Oh, yes. I know all about you. From Joby Ben. Now why don't you get serious, do I have to do everything myself?" Franziska popped restlessly outside the hut and popped in again, satisfied with her quick reconnaissance. She peered critically at David's final knots and gave a grudging nod.

"Better eat up now, you two. Maybe we don't have another chance for a while. There's only a little light left, and the castle's not electrified. That's the right word? Good idea if we become familiar with this place, before dark."

"Why?" Anneliese said.

"The portcullis would come only halfway down. Maybe that doesn't matter. But I would have liked the protection of the portcullis. A place like this, there are always ratholes. For the rats to creep through. I think we had better not sleep too soundly tonight, if we want to wake up in the morning."

She licked the sharp edge of the knife with her tongue, just showing off; but her eyes drilled into David.

66 The workmen had gone off to their supper in the village, leaving long ladders against the outer wall of the fortress; they looked, in the sober light of the moon, like elements of a giant web connected to the ashen stones. Each of the three terrorists took a ladder, climbing one-handedly, clutching his shotgun. The moon rubbed shadows everywhere. The night air was sharp enough to lance a boil.

Jürgen was the first to reach the top, and he helped Traudl over the high-embrasured parapet. On the wall-walk there were cartons of fireworks, mortars, high scaffolds wired for colorful explosions, a giant catherine wheel stuffed with sparklers; in the dark these frames echoed the shapes of the trebuchets, ballistas, and other primitive siege-engines on display in the open spaces of the ward below.

"Have you been here before?" Jürgen asked Traudl, as he pumped a shell into the breech of his shotgun.

"Long ago, on a school outing." Traudl recalled that day, and, wistfully, the young teacher she'd been having an affair with at the time. She gazed down over the roofs of the granary, forge, and kitchen, at the spring-fed river the color of boiling mercury in its steep-sided channel. She wondered if they should search the outbuildings. But the signal, if that's what it had been, had come from one of the residential towers in the castle itself.

"I wonder where Chris is?" Ernst said.

"If he's here, he'll be watching for us." From the dull monotone of pain she had endured all day an excruciating high note emerged, causing her body to vibrate and dance. She resorted to her bottle of oil of cloves, which was nearly empty. Jürgen had turned and unzipped his pants and was pissing against the parapet. Looking again at the acres of the fortress, the numerous buildings, Traudl felt a grinding in the pit of her stomach.

"Let's go," she said.

They went down the stairs in the angle tower nearest them and, staying in the darkness at the foot of a long storeroom wall, walked single file toward the river. The bridge was down. They would be totally exposed for a minimum of five seconds while sprinting across the paved yard and the bridge, and she couldn't see past the entrance to the tunnel through the drawbridge tower. The portcullis looked like a half-sprung trap, waiting for them. Traudl's skin crawled. But that was the way in. The river, pouring in and out of the fortress through iron grates, blocked access everywhere else, unless they went back and hauled the heavy ladders up the outside wall and used them to reach the narrow windows high in the tower.

She looked helplessly at Jürgen, whose face loomed over her shoulder.

"Baby, I'm not as fast as I used to be."

He grasped her shoulder reassuringly. "I know. I'll go. Cover me."

Jürgen handed her his shotgun, drew a 9-millimeter Parabellum Beretta with a sixteen-shot magazine from a holster inside his vest, and sprinted out across the yard to the bridge.

Traudl held her breath, but there were no gunshots from the dark beyond the portcullis. In a matter of moments he had vanished into the mouth of the tunnel.

67 From the drawbridge tower the approach to the castle was through a terraced park, where in summer heraldic crests bloomed on the small oblongs of lawn. The first building on the right was a chapel with a two-story loggia; the *palas* took up most of the remaining space in front of the three widely separated residential towers. In late medieval times the occupants of the fortress had been penned into nearly windowless, dark rooms, with cattle and horses, with sheep and pigs and dogs. Most of their available space had been taken up for the storage of food, and of weapons needed to defend them from countless besiegers. Through the long winters they had been driven nearly mad by the suffocating smoke from cooking fires, by the cold, by the stench of sulfur and gunpowder and manure; by the bleating and lowing of their miserable animals.

Gracious living arrived perhaps two centuries later. The castle was now a museum of Renaissance refinement: leaded glass casement windows, frescoes and paintings, rare carpets from Persia, salt-glaze tiles on the walls, elegant porcelain stoves to heat the bedchambers, suits of mail and gowns of silk.

Franziska had found a flashlight in the guard's hut; it was some help as they prowled the rapidly darkening halls and stairs of the castle, but they encountered locked doors at unexpected turns, for which she couldn't find keys on the guard's ring. On other doors the old locks were hard to open, even with the proper keys.

And they quickly discovered that almost every sound

above a whisper traveled phenomenal distances within the walls.

A couple of times Franziska was certain she heard footsteps other than their own. Finally she removed her shoes and went off unarmed to investigate, leaving the light with David. She was better off without it, she said. She would only call attention to herself.

They had chosen as their refuge a large second-floor chamber in the tower immediately behind the *palas*. It had good solid chateau furnishings, a fireplace, touches of luxury in the tapestries and flocked wall coverings. There were two fully-clothed mannequins in the room, a lady and her maid in front of a dressing table. In the moonlight that came through a pair of small windows, their frozen-piquant faces seemed real enough to get on David's nerves.

Anneliese was shivering from the cold; she sat on the edge of the square canopied bed, her bare feet off the stone floor. She rested her head against David.

"My c-crazy sister. My God. What has she d-done to me this time?"

"Do you remember the way out of here?"

"No. D-do you?"

"I think so. I'm not sure. We've toured everything but the dungeons. I think Franziska's been leading us around in circles. Keeping us busy. And scared. So we won't think about leaving."

"Is it safe to leave?"

"I'd feel safer on the outside than I do with your sister."

Anneliese raised her head. "So would I. David—you didn't know Franziska before? She knows so much about you. You n-never met her?"

"No. She was another one of Joby Ben's little secrets. He must have been hungry, moonlighting in the drug business." His tone was bitter. "You never know about

people, do you? Even your own family. You don't know
a goddam thing about them, until it's too late."

She held him tightly. "The way Franziska looks at
you f-frightens me. I don't know why."

David unbuttoned her shirt and put a soothing hand
on her breast, filling his cupped palm with her nervous
heartbeats, the shapely, timid nipple.

"Traudl Hecker doesn't want you. She wants Franziska. Don't forget that."

"But David, where did all the money—"

He kissed her. They were both worn thin from nervous exhaustion; the solutions of sex invited both bliss
and clemency as he made a place for himself beside her
on the bed. But something as subtle as a change in the
moonlight in the room, the wing-brush of a bad angel,
caused him to look up from the gentle cleft of Anneliese's bosom. The two mannequins in the room had
become three. The third one grinned fiercely at him.

David snapped upright on the bed and aimed his
flashlight. Anneliese gasped, closing her shirt front
with one hand. Franziska, isolated in the beam of light
like the Madonna in a triptych, gazed chastely at the
floor and came closer. David wondered how long she
had been standing in the room, doting malevolently.
Her ability to glide around unheard and unseen spooked
him. He had conceived, on short acquaintance, a real
hatred of Franziska.

"Go ahead," she said to David, making a suggestive
pumping motion with one hand. "Maybe it's just what
she needs. When she gets this overwrought, she sounds
just like Porky *puh-pee puh-pee puh-pee*—you know,
Swine."

Franziska leaned past David and took a soft swipe
at Anneliese's nose. Anneliese cowered, rubbing frantically where she'd been touched.

"What's that?"

"What does it smell like?"

"B-blood!"

"That's right." Franziska held out her hand for David's inspection. Two of her fingers were dark with the coagulating blood.

"Did you hurt yourself?"

"How sweet of you to ask. It's not mine. Someone stood dripping on the floor of the great hall, and not too long ago."

David thought back to the blond driver of the Citröen, who had crept out of the wrecked car with his head pulped by the accident—or by one of Franziska's well-aimed shots.

"The terrorist in the car that hit Joby Ben."

Franziska nodded. "Creamed him. Isn't that what the GIs used to say? 'Shee-it, we *creamed* the mother.'"

"You don't have any feeling for him at all, do you? Jesus Christ. You've got the emotions of a codfish."

"Oh, no. I have *real* feelings, Mr. McNair. As real as yours, or anybody's. And I never forget an injury." She turned to Anneliese.

"The money you've been wondering about? I think I can explain."

From a great distance they heard the sound of a massive crossbar falling. Anneliese jumped, and looked horrified. Franziska stood twisting the gold chain she wore around one finger, looking thoughtful.

"What's that?"

"What I've been expecting," Franziska said. "They've got in."

68 Chris was sitting inside the door with his back to the wall when Jürgen put a light briefly on his face. Chris had wrapped a handkerchief around his head hours ago; it was soaked and stiff with blood and cerebral fluid. Blood had trickled beneath his shirt and down one sleeve to his hand. His face had the greenish cast of a hardboiled egg yolk just beneath the skin. His lips and hands trembled. The pupil of one eye was wildly dilated.

Traudl and Ernst came running through the tower tunnel. Traudl knelt beside Chris. Jürgen, shielding the light with one hand, gave her a glimpse of him. Traudl caught her breath.

"He used everything he had getting the door open for us," Jürgen said.

"Where are they, Chris?" Traudl asked the injured man.

He raised a hand and pointed across the courtyard.

"Poor Chris." She kissed him on the forehead and stood up. Jürgen flashed his light inside the guard hut. The old man, bound and gagged, stared at them from the bed.

"This one doesn't know anything."

"No more lights," Traudl cautioned. "Their eyes will be better than ours in the dark."

69 David said to Anneliese, "Coming in, I noticed fireworks on one of the walls. What time would they set them off?"

"Midnight, I suppose."

He held his Rolex watch so he could read the time in the sparse light available.

"It's a quarter past nine. If I can get to the fireworks and set them off, it ought to bring a lot of people running up here."

"David, please don't leave!"

Franziska, who had been standing near the chamber door, came back to them. She touched David urgently.

"You may have something there. It may be a chance."

"No," Anneliese protested, clinging to David.

"It's a *good* chance, Anneliese," he said confidently. "All I have to do is follow the walls around—even in the dark I can't get lost." He pressed one of the officer's pistols into her hand. "If you have to fire this, use both hands to hold it steady. Brace the barrel on a table or the back of a chair if you can. The trigger action is reliable and not too stiff; just keep pulling back firmly." He took the other pistol and, before she could protest again, he kissed her and melted away through the door.

Anneliese threw the pistol on the bed and tried to follow him, but Franziska caught her roughly and put a hand over her mouth.

"Let them concentrate on David. He has no idea of what it is to be hunted by such people." Anneliese squirmed; Franziska squeezed a nerve on the inside of her elbow to make her stop. "I sent him off to be killed. And when I tell you why, you're going to be happy that I did."

70 From a small clear window near the top of the drawbridge tower, the three terrorists studied the layout of the castle by moonlight and divided it, as they'd been taught to do in a course in night reconnaissance tactics, into rigidly defined search areas. After muted discussions, they had decided it made sense to split up. Separately they were less prone to blundering into a costly trap, although they had a considerable edge in firepower. Anneliese, Traudl felt, would not be good for anything. She didn't know what kind of courage David McNair had, if any, but he was a young man and his reflexes were impressive; she'd just missed killing him by inches.

The woman, of course, was dangerous, although she'd probably lost the gun she was carrying earlier: Traudl had had a glimpse of her running without it. And the woman had nerve. She might come up with a devastating surprise. It was practical to assume, Traudl told the others, that they were expected.

71 David opened a hefty door in the center tower and stepped out on the covered walk. Rather than bear the scraping of the door across the high sill again, he left it open a few inches. The long wall curved only a few feet from the edge of a cliff, split like a dragon's claw, from which the river dangled and writhed in the descending dark like the tattered remains of a knightly pennon. A jumbo jet angled deafeningly down toward Frankfurt, striking sparks that continued to burn colorlessly across the wall of the sky. It was light enough for him to see the rafters overhead, the occasional gaps in the steeply pitched thatch-and-lath roof, as he hurried toward the northeast tower.

Here he found the door stuck fast, or locked. But they had come this way only about an hour ago. He leaned against the door with the cold iron handle, like the handle on a pitcher, pressing into his stomach. He trembled, indecisive. He couldn't double back, he already knew that the door to the opposite tower was locked. It would be easy to reach the courtyard, but that was wide open, and they had shotguns. He felt safest on the walls, and it was the quickest way to get to the fireworks.

David leaned over the parapet and looked up at the tower. He saw embrasures spiraling toward the roof like a thin, narrow stairway; they were perhaps five feet apart, with drain holes interspersed. One of the embrasures was just below a window that looked big enough to admit him. It appeared to be, from his per-

282

spective and allowing for the distortion of the moonlight, like an easy climb once he got to the roof of the
walk. The problem was, for one and possibly two minutes he would be as obvious as a fly on a wedding cake.

Still, it seemed worth the risk.

David tore a strip from his shirt and tied his officer's
pistol to his belt. He tested the wooden railing on the
inside of the walk. Then he stepped up on the railing,
grasped a roof beam that stuck out a foot beyond the
thatch, and pulled himself up on that. He balanced on
the narrow edge and made a running lunge up the steep
thatch, which had been weathered to the crusty slippery texture of thin ice. He seized the backbone of the
roof and threw himself across it, straddling it like a
horse. Then he shinnied toward the tower.

There he stopped, flattened low along the roof line,
and surveyed the courtyard over his left shoulder. He
saw plots of shady light and inky shadow, the softened
angles of buildings and walls, a cat running across the
paving stones.

He stood up, holding the rounded tower in a wide
embrace, and tilted his head back to look at the in-
dented window he hoped to reach. It was about fifteen
feet above him. He took a deep breath and began climbing.

72 In the Renaissance chamber of the center
tower, Franziska stroked Anneliese with one hand and
inflicted pain with the other, whenever she threatened
to get out of control.

"Twenty-five years ago, David's father came to Germany. His name was Frank. He was our mother's last lover."

"Last—?"

"Don't twist around like that, you'll make it more unpleasant for yourself. Anneliese, I tell you this for your own good. Father and son, they'll only make another victim of you. Yes, I said *last*. He concluded the affair by strangling mother."

"That's c-c-crazy—and you're lying!"

"When I got out of prison I had nowhere to go, no work, no hope. Joby Ben stepped in then—I suppose he thought I'd be properly grateful. But I taught him a few things. He wanted to be very rich, and I showed him how. One rainy afternoon when I had nothing else to do I discovered a photo album that belonged to Joby Ben. I still think it was no accident. He wanted me to see the album, which was filled with snapshots of his brother. I had last seen Frank McNair in Mother's bed, in a hotel room in Hannover. Four days before she was murdered. Are you crying? Have I convinced you?"

"No-no. What does *that* prove?"

"It was him, all right. Anneliese, he died of a brain tumor two weeks ago. But before he died he confessed his crime to David."

She felt in Anneliese the inevitable stiffening of disbelief, the will to resist the truth. Franziska held her more tightly, pinning her to a bedpost.

Anneliese said softly, dumbly, "Nuh. Uh. No."

Franziska put her mouth close to Anneliese's ear, taunting her.

"Have you made love to David? Was it heaven? How does it feel now?"

Anneliese was trembling. She made little meaningless sounds of protest, but she was obviously incapable of full voice. The sounds turned to dry sobs. The muscles in her arms jerked spasmodically. Franziska glowed with pleasure, sensing what she'd always hoped for; a final, terrible, bone-breaking fit, the destruction of her pretty sister.

"Mmm-mm-mother."

"Think of how ugly it was, Anneliese. You saw, don't you remember? Mother was naked, with dirt thrown over her. And her neck was broken." Franziska thrust herself again and again at Anneliese, feeling all of her sister's heaving bones. Her temperature was shooting up. "Let me tell you the worst of it. I saw his cock once. My God! It was like a weapon—for hurting women. Do you know what he did, that night on the mountain? He *raped* her. *Then* he broke her neck. And she was in the dirt with her head all twisted round *and his fuck was running out of her!*"

With a strength Franziska hadn't known she possessed, Anneliese shoved her away. She raked at Franziska with her nails and jumped off the bed, stood with her feet widely planted, hooked hands against her face as if she wanted to rip out her own eyes.

"Da-day-dav—"

With her thumb, Franziska flicked a drop of blood from her forehead.

"He's the flesh of his murdering father. And he's going to die tonight."

73 The pieces of the leaded-glass pane that David punched out with his fist clinked dully on the ledge inside. He was clinging to the tower he had climbed with one bare foot wedged into an embrasure, the other atop a bas-relief crown underneath the window; he had found a slight purchase for his left hand in a chink between stones. His shoulders and chest were above the lower level of the window. His right hand was extended fully, groping inside for the handle of the casement window, a twentieth-century improvement in the historic castle. The moon glowed at the corner of his eye, spinning a webbed and haunting light around the sky.

Anneliese screamed.

The sound of it carried so clearly the hundred feet from the center tower that she seemed to be just below him. For several minutes he had shut out all the vague night sounds, hearing only the accelerated beating of his own heart. The scream was hideous and despairing, and it shocked him loose from his perch. His left foot slipped out of the embrasure as he instinctively looked back; the fingers of his right hand raked for purchase on the steeply slanted sill, but he couldn't catch himself.

In falling, David managed to twist a half-turn to get his hands under him, but he had forgotten about the big pistol that he'd tied to his belt. He hit sideways on the angled roof of the wall-walk. The butt of the pistol broke three of his ribs; the impact, even with the deep thatch of the roof yielding beneath him, knocked him cold.

But his weight cracked a roof beam and, instead of glancing off and tumbling to the stones of the courtyard twenty feet below, he was let down more gently as an entire section of roof buckled and collapsed. He fell to the walk as if from a hayloft, surrounded by hunks of thatch and flimsy lath.

In the Renaissance chamber, Franziska sprang off the bed and struck Anneliese in the jaw with her fist.

Anneliese collapsed. Franziska ran from the room without looking back.

74 Traudl Hecker had entered the *palas,* the great hall of the castle, when she heard Anneliese scream. She stopped dead in front of a tall tapestry depicting the temptation of Adam and Eve, and tried to decide what the scream meant.

Possibly it didn't mean anything. It might have been a diversion, meant to throw them off guard.

The room which she had entered was on two levels, with a curved Roman ceiling over all, constructed of gilt-trimmed wood and huge crossbeams. The walls were salt-glazed tiles in checkerboard shades of green, the floors marble. The gallery of the *palas,* raised about six feet above the main floor, had been built over a kitchen and was backed by a fireplace with a copper chimney-breast ten feet high and a mantel, covered in tiles, like a Greek porch. The windows of the *palas* were high and small. Moonlight slanted in, illuminating suits of armor along the walls, wicked clumps of pikestaffs, battle-axes, shelves of pewter tankards, a long trestle table on the gallery at which mannequins sat eerily feasting from long-empty plates. There were metal bowls of plastic flowers on the table.

When she was satisfied that she was alone, Traudl went quickly across the floor to the gallery steps. There was a door in the wall by the steps that didn't look tightly closed. With her shotgun braced against her side, Traudl nudged the door open with one foot, looked at a dim gray passageway filled with portraits. She closed the door again and went up the steps, studying the mannequins.

On one side of the fireplace there was a stairwell to the kitchen below. Iron pots hung in the interior of the fireplace. The hearth extended a good five feet into the room. In the fireplace a hanging kettle seemed to be swaying slightly on a hinged black arm, but she couldn't be sure. Traudl knew that if she stared too long at any object she could deceive herself into thinking it had moved.

She walked slowly by the fireplace, eyes again on the dozen mannequins lined up at the narrow table.

The head of one of them—she was sure of it—had moved.

She swore to herself and brought the shotgun high, approached grimly. She nudged the mannequin, a stout female, and it fell easily off the bench. A rat as plump as her fist popped out of the hollow broken head and trudged away.

Traudl sighed, her skin coldly electric. Her bad tooth gave her another wicked jolt. She leaned the shotgun against the table and took the oil of cloves from her vest pocket. It hurt to open her mouth, even a little. She tilted her head morosely toward the ceiling, inserted the finger with the dollop of oil.

She saw a momentary glitter before her eyes, like a swarm of golden motes in the air. Then Franziska's necklace of strong gold links was around Traudl's throat, choking her. Traudl nearly bit her own finger off.

Instinctively she tried to claw the links from her throat, but they had snuggled deep. She was dragged backwards. She did the next best thing, kicking high with both feet and throwing herself down on the floor in an attempt to unbalance her assailant and shake loose the hands that were knotting the golden garrote. She succeeded in pulling Franziska between her and the trestle table. Traudl stiff-armed her blindly, followed with a nimble kick to Franziska's exposed back. Some vital bone cracked audibly; Franziska screamed. Traudl backed away from her, strangling, again trying to dig the embedded chain from her throat. Blood gushed internally, and she began to feel faint and drifting.

Franziska began desperately to flip-flop along the floor, trying to reach the shotgun. Traudl gathered herself wearily and got there first, collapsing to her knees as her hands closed on the precious weapon. She turned, fumbling to find the trigger, and they were face to face in the dim light: Traudl, dark as a thundercloud from the neck up, her eyes bulging, Franziska on her broken back, hands slapping the stone floor like a playful corpse.

Traudl moved in closer with the shotgun, gagging, so woozy she could scarcely see.

A pot of the artificial flowers had spilled; Franziska was littered with them. The flowers had long stems, stiff wire covered with tough plastic. The tip of each stem was exposed, bitten off at an angle by sharp cutters.

As Traudl tried to bring the muzzle of the shotgun up under her chin, Franziska turned it aside and sat up awkwardly. She had one of the flowers in her hand. She thrust it, with all her remaining strength, point-first into Traudl's right eye.

Traudl went over backwards, but slowly, still clutching the shotgun, the huge waxy bloom of the flower protruding inches from the violent pupil of her eye. The stem had penetrated deep into her brain. Some fatal disturbance there caused her finger to tighten on the trigger of the shotgun, which discharged, illuminating, in its gusty orange light, a floor washed in blood.

75   Ernst, coming slowly up the circular stairs inside the northwest tower, heard the scream and then the dumping of the roof on the wall-walk as David crashed into it. He didn't think it was Traudl screaming, but the source and direction were unidentifiable through walls. He hurried up the final spiral of the wide worn steps, illuminated by slits of moonlight through the cruciform embrasures, to a drafty passage with opposing ironbound doors some thirty feet apart.

At the door that led to the center tower he explored the box lock and latch with one hand, then raised the latch spur that had prevented David from entering the tower. He opened the door an inch at a time, using the stout oak planks as a shield in case he was fired upon; they would stop anything but the highest-velocity bullet.

He found a chink to one side of the square iron lock plate of the door and put his eye to it, looking out at the walk and the considerable pile of debris a few feet from the side of the tower. He saw a bare foot sticking out of the pile.

Ernst jumped out to the walk aiming his shotgun at David, but David didn't move. Ernst heard only a vague groan. He looked up at the breached roof, trying to figure out what had happened. Apparently the damned fool had tried to climb the outside of the tower to reach a window. He moved closer to David and, centering the shotgun on the pile of thatch, kicked at a bare foot. There was no response. He decided to move on, and heard the report of Traudl's shotgun in the *palas*.

The gunshot claimed all of his attention. He looked down toward the courtyard and *palas,* knowing it was Traudl who had fired; he hoped for a glimpse of Jürgen, who was supposed to be in the chapel. Jürgen failed to appear.

Behind him, Ernst heard a dry rustle of thatch; he whirled, bringing the gun to bear. But he fired too quickly and too high, the load of shot kicking off the outside parapet, and there was an answering muzzle-flash, like a lantern thrown into a haymow.

The .60 caliber ball fired from the officer's pistol struck Ernst massively under the breastbone and tore the heart out of him. He was jarred loose from his shotgun and flung back against the railing.

The tinder-dry thatch blazed quickly from sparks thrown off by the ignited gunpowder; David had loaded a pinch more than he needed. He crawled out of the pile before he could catch fire himself, nearly fainting from the pain of broken ribs. His left wrist was badly sprained or broken as well, he couldn't use it. His head ached ferociously. He picked up the shotgun in his good hand and tried to stand, but settled for a hunchback crouch. He stared dumbly at the man he had killed, unable to recall what he was doing out here on the wall, or what had happened to make him hurt so bad.

The terrorists were inside the castle walls, probably all over the place. How many of them could there be? He'd had a plan, a clever plan. Get help quickly. But what *was* it? He'd told Anneliese...The fire crackling behind him, a boil of dense smoke, he saw his shadow flickering on the tower wall. Sure. *Fireworks.* If he could set them off, the whole town would come running. But where was Anneliese now? Was she safe? He'd left one of the pistols with her. Good. But she'd probably be too afraid to use it. Get to the outer wall, then, set off the fireworks, get back to her. But it was killing him to move. He clenched the shotgun under one arm, held his stove-in side with the other hand. He had a taste of fresh blood on his tongue. The pistol with which he'd killed Ernst still dangled from his belt, of no use now. He left it there and pried open the door to the tower.

This slight effort brought tears to David's eyes; his wind was cut severely by the inward press of broken ribs. He knew then he'd never make it to the outer wall.

Instead of continuing to the opposite door of the passageway, he went down inside the tower, leaning heavily against the wall of the spiral stairway.

76 In the *palas,* Jürgen found Traudl on her back with her face bloated and a flower in her eye, Franziska partly blown away.

As he looked incredulously at the dead women and tried to visualize their struggle together, Ernst's shotgun went off outside, followed by a second shot. Jürgen leaped down from the gallery and ran across the floor to the heavily studded courtyard doors and opened one cautiously; the door yawned out into the moonlight. He smelled smoke and noticed a flicker of fire. He peered around the shield of the door and saw a body sagged over the railing of the wall-walk, but he was too far away to see just who it was. There were hedges in the courtyard in front of the *palas,* and he darted between two of them, keeping low. When he looked up again the fire was blazing hotter and he saw that it was Ernst who was dead. He felt a dismal heavy blow in the pit of his stomach.

Jürgen couldn't help himself, he began to sob, from astonishment and rage. Ernst, and Traudl was dead too—their motivating force—the Tribunal scarcely existed without her. It had gone badly and no one was left, there was no one and nothing to fight for. On the wall-walk the fire had spread to the underside of the roof and, with a roar, was rapidly eating it away, sending bushels of sparks into the air, casting a yellow light over the courtyard. Everywhere people would look up and see that the castle was burning. The body of Ernst had caught fire too; his ball of frizzy hair turned momentarily incandescent, like a paper lantern, then was reduced to sparky char.

Jürgen gagged on bile and considered his difficult circumstances. The castle had become a great rat-trap. They'd been blindly overconfident, bursting with ego, convinced that they could outwit any man's defenses. They thought they had proved their cunning and superiority the night they invaded the banker's home and caught Anneliese with her pants off. Now he understood that it was a matter of luck and the phase of the moon as much as confidence in their moral position. Tonight their luck was all bad.

He knew he was no coward. He could stay and die, perhaps futilely, submit himself to execution; he could be shot in the back from any one of a hundred embrasures or machicolations. But to die now was contemptible, a cheap victory for the pigs he had eluded so easily for so long. It would be better to save himself and eventually coax the Tribunal back to life, recruiting others in Traudl's name and memory. A great task was unfinished: to shape the class struggle, reorganize the proletariat. There was always a way to fight on, to gain revenge. Jürgen smelled the burning flesh of his comrade on the wall and choked back a scream. He picked himself up and fled across the courtyard to the drawbridge tower. The shotgun was a hindrance to him; he threw it away and ran faster.

77   David, coming out of a door at the base of the northwest tower, missed Jürgen by a few moments.

To get back to Anneliese, he had to cut on a diagonal across the courtyard to a sunken passage and then mount a stairway that jogged steeply upward around a wall of the *palas*. It took him a long time. He tried to be alert, to remind himself of the danger, but the thought of having to kill another man was almost enough to turn him to stone. He was half-smothered in torrents of pain, terrorized by the necessity to keep moving, fearful that he could never hope to protect Anneliese in his condition. He was breaking up inside, churning through chest-deep pulverized glass with each step. Behind him what was left of the wall-walk erupted in hot drafty clouds that soared above the castle. As good as fireworks, he thought. Someone had to come soon and help them.

He climbed and climbed the endless stairs, the shotgun sagging in his good hand. Darkness. A door; he pushed through it. The cold and forbidding tower. He would have given his soul for a candle. More stairs. Up. He wanted to call to Anneliese, but was afraid to make a sound. Dragging step by step up the circular stairway. Pausing. Listening. A glimpse of his half-lowered, sullen head, like a faded decal, in a window.

David located the chamber in which he thought he had left Franziska and Anneliese, stood blinking in the doorway. No one was there.

But he had to be in the right place: the mannequins were the same, the canopy bed was there on the left, beside the fireplace. The velvet drapes had been pulled all around, creating space within a space, a child's pretend-hideaway.

He angled the shotgun over one shoulder and crossed the chamber, parted the drapes.

Anneliese was sitting inside, crosslegged, her back against the headboard. He could just make her out. Her head was down; she held the large pistol he had given her in both hands in her lap, as if she had fallen asleep that way.

"Thank God," David said, flooding with tears.

Anneliese looked up slowly, raising the pistol at the same time. She stared at David. He twitched uneasily and started to speak, to reach inside and take the pistol. But she fired at him, from a distance of five feet.

It was like being struck by a train; the shot cut him down.

78 "Mrs. McNair?"

The door between the anteroom and the office of the hospital's administrator had opened again; belatedly Reba was conscious of the efficient enginelike hum of voices from the other room, which was crowded with policemen on the Federal level, and the subdued jingling of telephones. The BKA official who had looked in on her was one of her principal interrogators. He had pretended to be unsure of his English while re-addressing numerous questions to her, listening all the while, with a quiet cynical infallibility, for nuances of error.

Reba sighed; they were just not going to leave her alone for even two minutes.

"Yes; have you heard anything more about Joby Ben?"

"He's still undergoing emergency surgery. I've sent someone for a report on his condition. The Minister of Defense has arrived this minute from Bonn, and he would like very much to meet you."

Before she could reply, the door opened wider and the room became chockablock with cordial princely men built into wonderful suits. They carried themselves as if their heads were crowned with impressive racks, like staghorns in spring, which only they could discern on each other. The minister's name was Spengler. He had beautiful cheekbones and eyes like sunken treasure, the great politician's knack of relating instantly on a level more intimate than blood kinship. She didn't feel at all uncomfortable sitting in the palm of his hand.

He was deeply sorry, he said, about the ordeal she'd suffered, and gratified she had come through so splendidly. He had, moments ago, assured the President that she was all right.

"Of the United States?" Reba said blankly.

"Yes. Your families are very close, I believe."

"Well—" They had met on two widely separated social occasions. It was just Burton Bowdrie at work, responding to her phone call. Her opinion of the senior senator from Georgia needed revising, Reba thought, and she smiled at Spengler.

"Have you caught them yet?"

"No. Because their car was wrecked, it's likely they've split up. But we have a good chance—better than good, I think—to apprehend them all. You've given us accurate descriptions. That's the best break we've had in several months. It's fortunate they kept you alive."

Reba squirmed. "They didn't seem all that bad to me...they tried to be nice."

The minister's eyebrows came together, forbiddingly.

"They are not nice at all. Between them they may have killed a dozen men."

Someone else had slipped into the room, a doctor in a white coat. He spoke to the BKA chief. Reba caught sight of him. Was it about Joby Ben? She couldn't concentrate on what the minister was saying. He saw how uneasy she had become, turned and looked at the doctor.

Then they were all looking at him. He came slowly toward Reba. She felt a flutter of dismay in her breast. No one spoke. It seemed to Reba that the distinguished company of men had turned into a group of pallbearers. She looked into the doctor's eyes. Now she knew what it was about. The flutter became more solid, slamming against her heart like a broken door in a high wind. She wanted to hold her ears and cower, back away from them all and into a lonely corner. *Don't tell me. Don't tell me! I don't want to hear it.*

Reba smiled, raising her chin a little. Her voice was husky, but it didn't break.

"Is it David?" she asked.

79 On a bright afternoon coded in small clouds, Anneliese sat in a fourth-floor conference room of a wing of the hospital in Bad Kulmbach, facing the windows and the cheerful blink of the sun through wide-open blinds, listening without emotion to her voice as it came from a tape recorder. It was the oral statement that she had made, in hour-long sessions for the past two days, and it concluded:

Until last Sunday afternoon in Lüttring—that was Sunday, the twenty-eighth of April—it had been more than five years since I last saw Traudl Hecker. Other than the phone calls which I described, I have not had any contact with a member of a terrorist organization during the past five years. Nor do I have information now regarding the activities of, or the whereabouts of, any known terrorist.

The tape stopped, finally. It was rewound.

In the room with her was her own counsel, two elite Frankfurt lawyers whose services Otto Kolner had engaged, and four officials of the BKA. They conversed, behind her back, in low tones, their voices measured, solemn, in counterpoint to the squeaky high-velocity jabber on the reversing tape. Anneliese looked around slowly, the sun encircling her neck and shoulders, and stared at the men who were huddled, smoking, ignoring her. The older counselor, Geibel, made points by counting them off on his spread fingers. His associate, a younger man with a meek jaw and brutal eyebrows, frowned at a transcript of the tape.

Anneliese reached out and picked up a crushed package of cigarettes from the oval conference table, then changed her mind about smoking. She'd begun to shudder. She got up from the wheelchair, which she had no real need of, and slowly walked around the unoccupied end of the room. There were medical-school posters on one wall, full-color drawings of human plumbing. She felt skinless herself, undignified by flesh. Her nerves were rustling again and another headache was coming on. Franziska's punch to the jaw had dislocated it; her subsequent fall to paving stone only thinly padded with a Turkish rug had resulted in a hairline fracture of the skull and a memorable goose-egg. But that had been nearly a week ago, no surgery was required, she was almost fully recovered.

And prepared to go to jail until her hair turned stringy with silver.

Anneliese approached a set of windows and raised the blinds, immersing herself in light. For a few moments she was transfused with a mild energy. She leaned on the sill and looked down and saw someone who resembled Reba McNair cutting through the Japanese garden in a hollow of land between the hospital and the *kurpark* of Bad Kulmbach. Anneliese's mood abruptly changed for the worst. She felt tears about to let go—a flood to wash away the supporting light and all of her shaky courage.

The conference ended; the BKA men, to her surprise, filed out with only a glance or two at her. Giebel came over, looking pleased.

"How long do you think it will be b-before I'm brought to trial?"

"You're not under arrest, Anneliese."

It seemed cruel of him. He had not quite answered her question.

Giebel, who was an egg-shaped man about her height, touched her arm in a placating manner.

"There is always that possibility, but for now the government is taking a lenient view."

She felt as if a carapace of iron had cracked. Her lungs lifted, filled, a luxury she hadn't known she was missing.

"I don't understand."

"The Tribunal has been cut to pieces. All but Jürgen Sollmann are in confinement or dead. For the past week your photo has been in every newspaper in Germany—"

"All of Europe," Giebel's associate amended, with a sudden bold grin to acknowledge her celebrity.

"I know, but—"

"The people are excited about you; they tend to forget about Traudl Hecker and her boyfriend. The government has reasoned that should they prosecute you, it might be interpreted as an outrage, a miscarriage of justice. The publicity wouldn't stop. The Tribunal would be resurrected. Traudl Hecker might well take on the luster of Joan of Arc."

"Then I can—just go?"

"As soon as you're released from the hospital. I understand you have tests to complete."

"Dr. Schulte said I'd be finished this afternoon." She shook Giebel's hand and kissed him at the same time. "What you've done for me—I never expected—I thought my life was over."

"Well—a word of caution, fräulein. All known members of the Tribunal have been accounted for."

Giebel's young associate made a gun of thumb and forefinger. He looked at her over it, raising his bulky eyebrows.

"But there may be one or two no one knows about."

"You shouldn't run into difficulty," Giebel said. "But if you do, don't hesitate to call the police."

"Yes," Anneliese said, pulling back, growing subdued. "I've heard that before."

80 By one o'clock Anneliese had finished packing; she arranged for the flowers that had piled up on every surface in her room to be redistributed, and was checked out of the hospital. The car and driver Otto Kolner had given her for as long as she might want them were waiting at a side entrance, near the ambulance bay. The car was a dark blue Mercedes 450SL. The chauffeur had stout shoulders and skeptical, restless eyes; he looked as if he probably carried a gun beneath his double-breasted blazer.

Anneliese told him where she wanted to go and settled back uneasily for the short ride, putting on glasses with sun-sensitive lenses. She had taken unusual pains with her appearance, but she was still self-conscious about the smudge of bruise on her jaw that might show, despite makeup. She had lost weight, ordinarily a pleasing discovery, but her subtly frosted, putty-colored dress, which she had chosen to give her that touch of exuberance and high-style flash she was missing at the heart, felt wrong in the waist and under her arms. For ornament she was wearing a small jade pendant that was seven hundred years old.

Reba was waiting for her on the side terrace of the Davenstedlerhof, not the top hotel in the spa but one of the best. She sat sideways to Anneliese's long approach. She had chosen a table at the far end of the terrace, in a setting of cherry trees in full bloom—outrageously lush, pink fantasy clouds emphasizing the pulled-back deep sable of her hair, which seemed deftly calligraphic against the pink and green of this still, warm May afternoon: a dark statement Anneliese felt challenged to interpret.

"Hello," Anneliese said, and Reba looked around and up at her with the quick unfelt smile of someone who has been lost in thought. The chairs at the table were small, low-backed, and she was too lanky for her seat; she sat on one hip with her legs thrust out as if she had tried to make herself comfortable at a child's birthday party. Rather than looking awkward and put-upon, as might be expected, she had adapted to the accommodations with a slack insouciance.

Looking down at her with a little nod of envy, Anneliese thought again, *She isn't so pretty.* Reba had a good tan with some red at the high points where she had peeled and peeled; long arched eyebrows like the unopened wings of an interesting bird; wide-awake eyes that were startlingly similar in lightness to David's; an infestation of freckles beneath those eyes, like the shadows of unshed tears. Her teeth jutted, just a little, and were very white. But her face was long and Anneliese felt that it would someday malform into a kind of jawbony horsiness.

"Hello," Reba said, frank enough to stare at Anneliese, not hostilely but with a definite pique, as if her reverie had been ended too soon. She shifted in the chair, bringing her knees toward her, folded her hands in her lap.

Anneliese sat down. "How is the hotel?"

"Dusty. It must have been closed all winter." She did have a slight stuffiness, a nasal intonation Anneliese hadn't noticed before. Perhaps it was an allergy.

"You've had some good news. Or so I hear." The last spoken with a slight bitter emphasis.

"I'm not going to jail, if that's what you mean." Reba didn't seem overjoyed by this turn of events. Anneliese sighed. "Look, I know what I promised. Not to get in touch with David until...but I had to call him and tell him—that much, at least."

Reba's lips pressed together until they made a single livid line; then she shrugged and glanced up at the elderly waiter who had appeared, slumped to one side as if he carried an anvil in his pocket.

"Have a drink?" Reba invited. She reordered Johnny Walker Red. Anneliese asked for white wine. With this formality out of the way, they faced each other again, occupied with the task of breaking the bones of the dilemma before them.

"You've had—a great deal of time to talk to David," Anneliese said tentatively. "I had a minute or two today. But that was long enough to know that he—loves me, and wants to stay with me."

Some blossoms had fallen, through no apparent impulse, to the table. Reba picked up each of them delicately, studied them in the palm of her hand. Though her hand was steady, the flowers trembled there, as if forecasting an upheaval.

"That's what you want?"

"I love David."

Reba blew the petals away with one shocking exhalation.

"Is that why you look so happy, you came dancing in here?"

"No, I—"

"It's all horseshit—Anneliese. You think I don't know it? That bullet barely missed putting David's lights out, by the grace of God I suppose, but it must have hit the crazybone in his brain. I mean, he is beyond *reason*." Reba laughed, but it was more like a scalded cry. "I was the first one Frank told about the tumor, and the day I saw him in the bathroom shaking at the knees and wailing like he'd seen a ghost, I knew we were in for it, but good Lord, I never expected the ghost to look like *you*." Her mouth twisted in a grudging expression of admiration. "How can you sit there and look so calm? Aren't you shaking inside too? You have to be. Because it's wrong. Oh, let's forget that there's an obvious physical infatuation involved; you went off with him, I understand all that—if he didn't have enough trouble, David was overdue anyway, we've been married ten years. Forget about it and try to see the reality of the situation."

"Reba, believe me, I know what's real—"

"You don't! You're not thinking. David's obsessed by what his father did. God, when he told me about that, I thought, there it is, that's the end of the world. I couldn't understand how Frank could just go about his business for the next twenty-five years after committing such a horrible...Sorry, that wasn't kind of me to bring it up. The point is, David's so confused, chewed up by guilt, he thinks the only way to make things right, so the sun'll still come up in the morning I guess, is to pay you off with the rest of his life—*all* of our lives."

Reba's nose was leaking, she used the crisp napkin to stop it. Anneliese felt a twist in her heart, a loss of blood to the head.

"It isn't that way. I told him—he owes me nothing. David and I would have fallen in love, no matter what the circumstances were. I'm very sorry for you, I don't want to hurt you."

They were served their drinks; and Anneliese noticed something, a fleeting but crucial shift of Reba's full attention to the shot glass even before it was lifted down from the waiter's tray, an attitude of absorbed expectancy as she picked up, with scarcely a pause, the unwatered whiskey and began to sip. How many had she had while waiting?

"Try to see it my way," Reba said. The sun had vanished behind a cloud and her face, robbed of light, lost eloquence, the passion that had carried her through a difficult week. "I've been sitting up there in the hospital room, day after day, as close to David as I am to you right now. His head hurts a lot, and he's been groggy off and on from painkillers. My heart goes out to him, but sometimes I'm not even sure it's my husband I'm talking to. He apologizes, all the time. Can't help himself, he says. It was a good marriage, no complaints. But it's over. I'm expected just to take it and like it. Well, how do I fight back? You're way above the standard for homebreakers. You're exalted, some kind of irresistible force, when your name is mentioned I'm supposed to think of cathedrals. What the hell would *you* do?"

Anneliese resisted being suddenly recast as a confidante.

"So much has happened to David in the past three weeks. You must understand that the shock of his father's death, and the confession he made before he died, has changed David's life forever. Changed the way he looks at everything: his home, his work, his family. I don't think you can appreciate as well as I do what David is suffering, because his father nearly succeeded in destroying both our lives."

"Frank killed your mother with his bare hands. You never forgot what you saw that night, and you never will. It almost drove you crazy. Having David around from now on won't help."

"I think it will."

"What kind of relationship can you hope to have?

It's goddam masochistic. Oh, pardon me, for a second there I forgot where I was."

Anneliese smiled thinly. "You seemed to be too intelligent for slurs and stereotypes. And this conversation isn't getting us anywhere."

Reba, looking harrassed, finished her whiskey. The sun came out and struck her a glancing blow; she turned her face aside.

"I sincerely hope it is. What I really wanted to say, he's come groveling with this load of guilt on his back, and it's too much power for a woman to have over a man. I know you're incredibly turned on by David. I'm married to him and God, I still think he's gorgeous too. But aside from sex, you probably resent him. Or maybe it's even worse than that."

"What do you mean, Reba?"

Reba leaned on the table and shielded her eyes with both hands, narrowing her focus to Anneliese alone.

"Tell me how you felt when your sister, what was her name—"

"Franziska."

"—told you about Frank."

"I didn't believe her."

"Franziska made you believe it, though, I mean you finally accepted that the story was true. Then what happened?"

Anneliese touched her jaw, which had begun to ache again. She'd been gritting her teeth.

"Franziska was angry with me, for some reason. She'd worked herself up into a rage t-talking about Mother, and naturally she t-took it out on me."

"But you were shocked. You had to be. David hadn't told you. You'd been to *bed* with him. It was as if he was using you. Didn't that go through your mind?"

"No. I don't—"

"Okay. Your sister hit you and nearly broke your jaw, you went out like a light. Then you woke up. And?"

"It was dark. And I was alone in the room. I heard a—s-shotgun."

"Scared you?"

"Of course. My jaw hurt, I couldn't get my teeth together, and sa-saliva was running out of my mouth. There was a knot on the back of my head where I'd banged it on the floor."

"I guess you were in a panic, being all alone, not knowing what was happening outside. And you must have been furious with David, weren't you? In a way he'd lied to you, and then when you needed him he wasn't there."

"That's not it at all."

"Tell me what happened then."

"Why? What do you want? What are you t-trying to prove?"

"Just tell me what happened next," Reba said urgently, "and *listen* to yourself. Really listen to what you have to say."

Anneliese's mouth was dry; she sipped a little of the wine.

"I don't remember very clearly—"

"You were alone in the dark. There was something wrong with your jaw, you'd lost your bite—that's happened to me, a dislocated jaw, and it's an awful feeling. You needed help. Where was the pistol David left you—on the bed?"

"I suppose it was."

"You got up on the bed and pulled the curtains all around and sat there holding the pistol. Yesterday morning I went out there, Anneliese. To the castle. I was in the chamber where you shot David. Trying to imagine what it was like for you, what you were thinking while you waited. I couldn't take it for very long. I was trembling when I left, sick to my stomach."

Suddenly there were tears in Reba's eyes; she sobbed and held her head, sorrowing luxuriously, trying not to fall apart. Anneliese reached across the table and took one of her hands. Reba stared at her, partly annoyed, baffled and shy. But she didn't pull her hand away.

"Reba, someone came into the room. He took his time, he seemed to be l-looking around. Then he came to the bed and pulled the drapes aside. A man, I didn't know who he was. I raised the pistol and shot without thinking."

"Without thinking?" Reba's nails bit into the palm of Anneliese's hand. "Without really seeing him?"

"Yes. That's exactly how it was. The bullet hit the barrel of the shotgun on his shoulder and disintegrated, a big piece of it tore away part of his scalp and nicked his skull, and thank G-God that's all that happened. Please stop crying now. There's nothing more any of us can say or do. It's over, it's begun."

Anneliese let go of her hand; Reba twisted sideways in her chair with one elbow on the table, chin in hand, sniffing.

"You don't know what you're saying; *he* won't listen. Maybe you deserve each other, then. I was going to be dignified about this. But I don't know how to act. I don't know how to feel. I don't know what I'm going to tell Sharon. When I think about you screwing him, I just want to crawl under a rock. I feel like such a loser, the lowest piece of shit there ever was. I wish I didn't let you get to me that way, but I can't help it. Would you leave me alone? I think I'd like to have another drink all by myself. Then I think... I'll just go home. There ought to be some kind of flight out of here tonight."

Anneliese, staring at her, felt both pity and relief.

Could it be as easy as that? A mighty cloud had blocked the sun, there was a patter of wind in the awnings, a change in the weather seemed likely. Relief turned to elation, as if she were about to be lifted into the gliding air. Above them in the hotel a chambermaid sang unemotionally near an open window. Anneliese rose to go, feeling herself turning already toward David.

Reba looked up sharply as if, sensing her rival's eagerness, she regretted dismissing her. She swallowed something hard to take—remorse, pride—and grinned.

"You still don't look very happy to me."

"I think...I'm a bit out of practice. It will come."

"There's just one thing, Anneliese."

"About David?" She paused, one hand on the table, knotted, half expecting another tirade or at least a threnody she felt would demean them all.

"About David. We didn't quite get to it before." Reba's expression had changed; she seemed quenched, colder, difficult. "One thing you'd better ask yourself. Are you absolutely sure you didn't recognize David— before you pulled the trigger of that pistol? I told you that I went to the castle. I couldn't stay in the room for very long. Because what I felt in the pit of my stomach was murder. You wanted to kill David. You tried. And if you lie to yourself about that, then I guarantee the two of you are going to live in hell together."

Anneliese, with a half-smile meant to be tolerant, was suddenly visited by a Fury of proportions she couldn't deal with. She felt a shock of red in her cheeks.

"Did you dare say that—to David?"

"No." Reba looked down. "Anneliese. You're the only one who can make any kind of rational decision now. I only want you to *think,* for God's sake."

"Think? No. You want me to feed on it." With that,

the red mounting to her eyes, panic causing her to jerk instead of turning smoothly, Anneliese left the table and walked around the few people who remained on the terrace, old men and women flashing sunpert winter faces as they looked up, new leases on life written there in disappearing ink.

She looked back before going down the steps to the drive and the waiting limousine, saw Reba's head, even more youthful amid crones, lowered solidly, her dark hair whipping across one cheek as the wind freshened. Reba had a grip on the edge of the table with one hand; her arm, bare almost to the shoulder, seemed long and open and vulnerable, as if offered for a bloodletting. The light was moistly radiant behind her, deepening her isolation. Anneliese felt a grave sense of loss, of violation, that made her teeth chatter. They had, like soothsayers, broken the bones of their dilemma, and discovered an enigma inside.

"Where may I take you, fräulein?"

"I don't know," she said to the chauffeur. "It doesn't matter. Just drive for a while."

81   After a while he began to get a little cold waiting in the Japanese garden, which, with its delicate anomalies and quaint artifacts, seemed jarringly incongruous next to the massive intersecting slabs of the Bad Kulmbach hospital. The sun had been shunted behind moving mountains of cloud and its light was seen only in deflection, never quite touching the earth.

It was past three in the afternoon, and Anneliese was late.

David was still a patient but confinement was driving him crazy, so two nurses had helped him put his clothes on over the tightly taped ribs and allowed him to go down into the garden. The right side of his head above the ear was shaved; a bandage covered the sixty stitches and a scab the size of a tarantula where the chopped ball from the officer's pistol had hit and removed a bloody hank of hair, semi-peeling him like a hasty Apache. His worst problems had been shock, a flattened lung, and loss of blood. They'd needed to pump nearly a full quart of blood into him on arrival at the hospital. For two days he suffered from double vision, and his head had hurt so bad all he could do was lie there and weep involuntarily. Medication controlled the ache now, he only hurt when he turned his head too sharply. His cracked wrist was in a cast. He had been watched closely for indications of trauma in the abused brain, but so far nothing terrible had happened there. Probably nothing would.

Restless, David took another turn around the shallow levels of the garden, past cedar, quince, and flowering crab, pagodas and quiet pools. The oddity of the light, like a slowly revolving waterwheel in the sky, the sensation of having grown fabulously amid the waist-high but perfect trees, the lilt of strange architecture, and the gentle crinkly bells hung from crossbars combined to give him a feeling of moving from peril and close quarters into a spacious if unimaginable new life. All that was lacking was Anneliese. He tried to hold her image firm in his mind, but it was printed on water, flooding away alarmingly at the first treacherous thought that she could not be, after all, as real as he desired, the extraordinary companion with whom he must explore, as long as he lived, this unproven territory.

"David?"

He turned and saw her, levels away and above him, at the corner of a miniature teahouse. She came down slowly, frowning at first, as if an apparition moved to join her. Then she ran, down the short wide wooden steps, eyes squeezing shut at the last heartfelt lunge into his arms. David, mindful of his cracked ribs, maneuvered her gently, shying from too exuberant an embrace. He buried his face in her hair, quietly rejoicing. He no longer needed to feel dispossessed by an image on water.

"Oh, David, I'm so happy to see you!"

Anneliese stepped back to recover her balance and her breath, glanced up at the unseemly side of his head, the long healing scratch on his forehead from another fragment of the calving bullet. She reached up as if to touch the bandage, thought better of it.

"Does it hurt?"

"Yes," he said. "And you're a lousy shot."

Her reaction was extreme; she wheeled around, fists clenched, face gone grim.

"Don't joke about it!"

"Hey. It wasn't your fault." David reached for her too abruptly, the movement foreshortened; he grimaced at the strain on his rib cage. Anneliese had walked a little distance away. He came up behind her.

"Don't be mad. I've been waiting a long time for you. All week."

"You know why," she said, giving him a troubled glance.

"Yes. Reba."

"I've seen her, off and on, this week. I felt I should. I was with her earlier this afternoon. Where does this path go?"

"Around and around." They took the path, walking slowly, just touching, her hand against his.

"How is she?" David asked.

"Well, it's so very hard for her. I try to put myself in her place. David, I like her very much. She has a good character."

"Sure." David couldn't think of anything else to say, a gallant compliment for the fading woman in his life. But he felt, at that moment, the absence of Reba, with a keenness that surprised him.

"Do you know anything more about your uncle?"

"They took Joby Ben out of here this morning, transferred him under guard to the 97th General Hospital in Frankfurt. He'll be a cripple when he leaves there. And an old man when he gets out of Leavenworth. The family has really gone to hell."

"I bought a plot for Franziska. Buried her on Wednesday. No one came, of course. Except the press. I don't know how they found out. They would have been all over me, but for Otto's people. So it's finished...No. There's the money. If you don't mind, I'll give it to charity."

"Yes. Do. I don't even want to think about it." He turned and put an arm awkwardly across her body. "Anneliese, I wanted to tell you about my father. I'm ashamed that I couldn't."

She stared at him; her eyes seemed to have a pulse in them, like those of an animal dreaming of panic. Anneliese smiled and started to speak and to her horror strangled on a monstrous stutter. Her mouth turned down, grief-stricken. She felt his fingers digging into her shoulder.

"You t-t-tried," she got out. "And it t-truly doesn't matter."

"Oh, God. It matters."

"David, no, stop it!" But her face was ashen. "Your

father and my m-m-mother...they shouldn't concern us any more. Let them rest in peace. Let us have peace too, David." She kissed him bruisingly. They'd both been holding back, wanting, feeling slightly awkward about their passion for each other in this serene and pebble-perfect garden; now they were like thirsty children, jostling at a crystal fountain, faint with expectation.

When they parted, Anneliese sank a little into the crook of his wounded arm, fingers like a light half-manacle gripping the plaster cast. He looked down at her partly hidden, smiling face, her eyes wide open in a stare of solitude.

"Oh, sure," she said. "This will always work. You know I love you, David."

"And I love you."

"I don't think I'll ever feel such a fullness, David. I'll never be so genuinely full of a man." Anneliese straightened and hooked a hand inside his elbow. "Take me somewhere," she said gaily.

"Anywhere."

"Well, let's just walk down this path and out the back way of the garden. And then...we'll see."

They went slowly, because she wouldn't be hurried despite a rapidly cooling wind that was giving her goosebumps. Anneliese couldn't have enough of touching him, of tracing, with an artist's precise eye, the familiar lines of his head. An immense cloud like a fractured bell let loose a crack of sun that warmed David's forehead; she brushed it wistfully, for luck, and was kissed again.

At the rear of the garden the blue Mercedes was waiting, the chauffeur at the wheel with a folded newspaper.

"I love you," David said again.

"Yes," she said. And smiled. And stepped away, holding up her hands, asking him not to follow. It was a warning, a farewell.

"Anneliese..."

"But it's pity too, David, pity and remorse. And that isn't what I need from you. It could have been so wonderful for us—but not this way. I love you but I'm weak, and I'm afraid of your father. I want to bury him and be done with it, but I know I can't."

"Anneliese, don't."

Her voice rose. "I'm telling you the *truth*, David! As much as I love you now, I know it'll be spoiled. Not right away, but gradually, and some night in bed I'll look at you and you'll be him, trying to drag me down into the grave. Oh, David, don't let that happen to me!"

"My God, what are you—"

She raised a stiffened hand, pointing at his head.

"Reba's right. That night in the castle, I knew it was you. I wanted you to k-kiss me and hold me, and while I was wanting that I raised the pistol and tried my best to k-k-kill you. How can I love you and want you dead at the same time? It just tears my heart out." She took a deep gulping breath and sobbed. "I'll *never* understand. That's why I want you to leave me, and just go home. You're free now, David; you've done more than you were ever asked to do. Don't k-keep on, until there's nothing good for either of us to remember."

Slowly Anneliese lowered her hands, falling into a more helpless, unaggressive stance. She found herself tugging psychically at David, willing him to make some sort of drastic change happen, to carry them leaping into another dimension of time where her pain could be cast away like a worn-out enchantment. A cloud shadow was flung over them and she thought barrenly of the afternoon on the hillside in the Lahn Valley, the shadows of gliders, the rub of satiny grass against her bare skin; and David's sleeping, basking face, sweet as a melon in that field. She saw in his face, now vaguely congested by the gathering darkness of mid-afternoon, that in fact he could do nothing. A pang like a stab of ragged iron caught her beneath the heart. Smiling fiercely, she looked at David for the last time. Then she turned and walked down the last of the path toward the car.

"Anneliese!"

She wouldn't turn.

"I'm going to Otto, David. And we're going away together. To South America, I think. I don't know. I didn't ask. It doesn't matter."

"Anneliese!"

"Reba's leaving tonight. Don't let her go without you, or you'll always regret it."

"Anneliese!"

She got into the car and closed the door, shutting him out.

"Frankfurt," she said, and doubled over as the Mercedes pulled away.

Oh, David. Dear David. Do you hear me now? Do you feel me as I feel you, a cramp, an ache, a creature that whirls and twists into a fury to suck my breath away? We are trapped in each other, the wrong magic has struck, and we must suffer: but only for as long as we lament the chances we never had. I think because it was so improbable and ill-fated, our time together was that much more absorbing: My love, my love, it came so close to being perfect! It happened, it never happened, it will live for us as long as the light that shines from our particular stars. Rejoice, David; you must know that when the storm ends I will still hold you in me, not as a prisoner of everlasting melancholy but as something more precious than my own blood. Now, wherever you look, I will not be. But we're not lost, we've just misplaced each other. My vision of you is whole; it's what I wanted, more than the fatal reality. Trust that I was right. Have hope for me, David. Love me, just a moment more: love me forever. And I will love you.

THRILLS * CHILLS * MYSTERY
from FAWCETT BOOKS

NEW FROM FAWCETT CREST